MUSIC IN AMERICAN LIFE

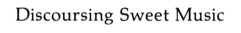

Discoursing Sweet Music

DISCOURSING
══ SWEET MUSIC ══

Town Bands and Community Life
in Turn-of-the-Century
Pennsylvania

KENNETH KREITNER

UNIVERSITY OF ILLINOIS PRESS
Urbana and Chicago

Publication of this work was supported in part by a grant from the Wayne County, Pennsylvania, Historical Society.

This book is printed on acid-free paper.

Library of Congress Cataloging-in-Publication Data

Kreitner, Kenneth.
    Discoursing sweet music:town bands and community life in turn-of-the-century Pennsylvania / Kenneth Kreitner.
        p.   cm.
    Bibliography: p.
    Includes index.
    ISBN 0-252-01661-0 (alk. paper)
    1. Bands (Music)—Pennsylvania—Wayne County—19th Century.
    2. Bands (Music)—Pennsylvania—Wayne County—20th Century.
    I. Title.
    ML1311.7.P4K73 1989
    785'.06'70974823—dc19
                                                        89-4766
                                                          CIP
                                                          MN

to R.L.K.
Musician, historian, and mayor of Honesdale

Contents

Tables

Figures

Preface

According to the family legend, in the summer of 1957, when I was less than a year old, my mother became ambitious to introduce her firstborn to Culture. So she bundled me up and took me to a concert of the Maple City band, the community band of my hometown of Honesdale, Pennsylvania, which was playing in the park of a village a few miles north. The concert started late for some reason, but I was, typically, the perfect infant, lying patient and quiet through the long delay, as the more mature members of the audience became increasingly restive—until, that is, the first cymbal crash of "The Star-Spangled Banner," when I started to scream my head off and would not be comforted. Home I went.

This is a legend, and I strongly suspect it of being apocryphal. But the point is, it doesn't matter how the twig is bent. Despite the un-Mozartlike beginning, I ended up learning the cornet, playing in the Maple City band myself, even directing it for awhile, and finally pursuing a career as a music historian. Percussion instruments hardly scare me at all any more, and bands have turned out to be a big part of my life as a musician.

So—more than two dozen summers later, when I had enrolled in graduate school in musicology and was spending my break working a day job at home, and wanted to find some musicological way of spending my free time, I suppose it was only natural and necessary that I return to the tradition in which I had grown up. I decided to read a few newspapers from the turn of the century, take some notes on the bands of that time, and produce a quick little term paper when I got back. It seemed like a good plan, but I had to abandon it after about two evenings by the microfilm reader.

The world that emerged from those old papers astonished me. I had known that Honesdale had a town band in 1900, but I suppose I had imagined it as a loosely organized ensemble trotted out for holidays and for the occasional summer concert, something like the Maple City band of my own time. I found instead a musical culture of great sophistication and vitality—two town bands competing and then merging, dozens of band performances a year, a tradition spreading beyond Honesdale and into half a dozen tiny villages out in the country. All these bands (and their short-lived sister, the Honesdale Philharmonic) were described in vivid and enthusiastic detail by the press and were clearly a very central part of the cultural life of their communities. It was a world where the presence of a band in town was apt to inspire the inhabitants to poetry. This was, in short, a much bigger and better story than I had planned on, and a story that had been told for the whole nation only in vague and undocumented outline.

My summer project has lasted for some four years now, and after all this time researching and writing about these musicians, I come away above all with a tremendous respect for what they did. From my own experience running amateur bands, I know how close to the edge of disaster the conductor always has to walk; to do it in an age of so much less leisure time, and an age when wind instruments were not taught in school, is hard for me to imagine. That these young men somehow learned to play their instruments at all, that they put together a band that could play as an ensemble, that they could keep such bands alive and performing for years and in some cases decades, is a remarkable tribute to the gumption and hard work of the musicians and to the strength of the moral and financial support given by the communities around them.

And what's even more amazing is that there is no reason at all to suspect that Wayne County was in any way unusual. The same story could be told of thousands of towns and villages all over the country. It is, all in all, quite an inspiring chapter of American history; and by coming a little closer to these bands and the people who played in them, I hope readers can come a little closer to what is good and beautiful in themselves.

The research for this book was made possible through the aid of two institutions, different perhaps in scope and resources, but comparable in intent and wisdom and generosity: the Wayne County

Historical Society in Honesdale, and the Smithsonian Institution in Washington, D.C.

In 1984, when I was conducting my first local researches, the Wayne County Historical Society was kind enough to give me a key and allow me the run of their extensive collections and library after hours—an inestimable privilege and an enormous practical advantage. In the years since, their continued eagerness to cooperate has been a great honor and comfort; and as if all that were not enough, they have also assisted financially with the publication of this book. Among the members and leaders of the society who have particularly helped along the way are Vernon Leslie, Kurt Reed, Charles and Alma Hames, Richard Eldred, and perhaps above all Phyllis Barth, who drove all the way into town and rescued me from the police on The Night The Burglar Alarm Went Off.

In 1986, the Smithsonian Institution awarded me a Summer Graduate Fellowship to do some broader research at the National Museum of American History in Washington. And the Smithsonian too was most generous and helpful in allowing me access to its library, its collections (including the Hazen collection of band ephemera, which had just been acquired), and the splendid staff of the Division of Musical Instruments—of whom I must particularly thank Robert Sheldon, Horace Boyer, and Margaret and Robert Hazen for sharing so much knowledge and so many hours of stimulating and memorable conversation. The Smithsonian grant also gave me an opportunity to do further work at the Library of Congress and the National Archives.

I would also like to extend public thanks to the Equinunk Historical Society (particularly Robert Kramer and Wellington Lester); to the Susquehanna County Historical Society (particularly Betty Smith); to *Highlights for Children* (particularly Kent Brown), for their assistance in printing the book; and to the various businesses and organizations around Wayne County whose names appear in the bibliography as publishers and sponsors of the works of Vernon Leslie and of the reprinting of three invaluable original sources— *Illustrated Wayne*, Beers's *Atlas*, and Mathews's *History*. I was very lucky to be able to work in an area where so many people were interested in local history and where so much of the general historical work had already been done.

Besides these institutional thanks, I must express my gratitude to a number of friends, scholars, teachers, and acquaintances who have helped me individually along the way:

- to Kristen Ammerman-Scofield and J.W. Johnson of the *Wayne Independent* for allowing me to make copies of their microfilms;
- to Mrs. Margaret Murray and Dr. Edward Murray of Honesdale, for lending me the photograph of Lawyer's band;
- to Mrs. Hazel Peake of Equinunk, aged ninety-five when I met her, for sharing her photograph of the Equinunk band and her recollections of the band when she was little and her brothers played in it;
- to Joe Silberlicht and Sandra Fenske, gracious hosts and intrepid pilot, for their help while I was in Washington;
- to Elizabeth Bartlet, Paul Bryan, and especially Tilman Seebass, of Duke University, for their continuous supply of goodwill, support, and wise counsel;
- to a loyal group of friends in Honesdale who have joined me for years in apparently pointless pursuits of music and local history without a hint of where I was going: Stephen Cook, David Erk, Florence Gammerdinger, Harry Gammerdinger, Kent Kester, Edward King, David Mill, Catherine Rosenkrans, and James Willow.

And finally, to my family—my parents, my sister Kitty, and Liane Curtis—who have betrayed no sign of impatience with this project over all these years and all these ever-lengthening, never-satisfying drafts, I extend all gratitude and sympathy.

1

Discoursing Sweet Music

Close your eyes and you can almost see them—the blue uniforms, the brass buttons, the silver cornets, the bandstand in the court-house square, the still summer evenings under the maple trees. To most Americans, the Victorian town band has become a kind of icon—an enduring, eloquent symbol of the tranquility and self-sufficiency of the American small town. The tiny world, warm and fragrant, in the pool of light around the bandstand is somehow more real, more quintessentially us than the real world of exit ramps and universal product codes that we inhabit every day. How far out of reach the older America is, we would rather not speculate: as long as the icon is in place, maybe everything that goes with it is still there too.

But as with most such icons, we tend to pay more mind to the virtues the image represents than to the historical reality it reflects. And the more clearly we try to focus on the picture itself, the blurrier it gets. How many people played in these town bands? Were they working-class people, or were they the more cultivated, educated, artistic members of the community? Were these all-brass bands, or were they more like today's concert bands, with brass and woodwinds together? Did they play mostly marches and patriotic music, or did they have a large and varied repertory? What did they sound like—if we heard them today, would we be pleased or pained? Indeed, was there really a substantial tradition of amateur bands in nineteenth-century America at all, or is the icon just a pleasant fiction, fashioned by our imagination from a few unusual examples?

The answer to the last question, at least, is reasonably clear: the development of the piston valve in the 1830s and 1840s, and its application to all sizes of brass instruments, from the little E-flat cornet to the tuba, suddenly created a new and wonderful instrumentation—inexpensive, relatively easy for amateurs to play, loud and spectacular, beautiful to hear and see. Brass bands spread rapidly through America in the decades before the Civil War, and even more so afterward, as a large industry developed to mass-produce their instruments and music. Professional band directors and virtuosi like Allen Dodworth, Patrick Gilmore, and of course John Philip Sousa were among the greatest celebrities of their day. By the nineties, town bands were "discoursing sweet music," as the journalists of the time seemed unable to avoid saying, in thousands of cities, towns, and even tiny villages all over the country.

From the Mexican War to World War I, the amateur band was arguably the most conspicuous and influential musical institution in the United States. It dominated the musical experiences and tastes of millions of our grandparents and great-grandparents. It is well worth a closer look—a look that will go beyond the general outlines and explore the day-to-day workings of the bands, the musical details of their repertory and performances, and their position in the lives of their players and their communities.

My approach here will be a kind of case study. Rather than trying to do justice to the whole tradition, over many decades and a large geographic area, I have chosen to concentrate on one specific area for one short stretch of time. By taking as small a slice of the pie as is practical, and examining it as minutely as possible, I believe we can come closer to understanding them in the intimate way we need to understand music.

For this purpose I have selected Honesdale and Wayne County, Pennsylvania, during five years at the turn of the century, 1897 through 1901. The place was chosen for personal and practical reasons: Honesdale is my home town, its bands in the 1960s were the beginning of my own musical career, and its historical records have been convenient and accessible to me. I chose this particular half-decade because it was near the peak of the American town-band tradition, because the late nineties were a time of intense and still poorly understood musical activity nationwide, and because these five years were a period of particular change in the area.

Whether these reasons are sufficient or not, the choice turns out to have been very lucky: the bands of Wayne County were documented in exceptional detail and with exceptional enthusiasm in the contemporary press, and these years showed a sudden (and, to me, unexpected) surge in band activity in the remote country villages around the county. At any rate, I believe Wayne County will stand as entirely typical of the rural northeast at the turn of the century: it was an area with a thriving musical tradition, but not an especially noteworthy or distinguished one, and it happens to provide a useful contrast between these village bands and the bands of larger industrial towns. It is as good a place as any to begin.

By far the most abundant resource for any study of this kind is contemporary local newspapers; at the turn of the century, Honesdale, the county seat and principal town, had three: the *Wayne County Herald*, the *Honesdale Citizen*, and the *Wayne Independent*.[1] The first two were long-established weeklies representing the Democratic and Republican interests respectively; both usually ran to four pages, focusing on local news but giving some limited coverage to world, national, and state news—as well as fictional stories, household hints, recipes, and interesting facts. The *Independent*, founded in 1878, was a considerably larger paper than either of its older rivals: it was published twice a week, usually alternating eight-page and four-page editions, and gave more space to world and national news.

All three newspapers devoted a page of each edition to the news of Honesdale, but the *Citizen* and *Independent* each added a page or two on news from the smaller towns around the county. The outlying villages were represented in these papers not by reporters from the regular staff, but by correspondents who would send periodic letters telling about recent events. These letters are uneven in usefulness: sometimes they are thorough and reliable, sometimes maddeningly brief and vague, sometimes colorful and even bizarre. They provide, one senses, only part of the picture of life in these country villages, but that part is very interesting indeed.

Of the three papers, the *Independent*, with its greater size and more balanced coverage of the world outside the county, comes the closest to twentieth-century journalism — which may explain its survival (in remarkably similar form) to the present. On the whole I have relied on the *Independent* for thorough coverage of the facts, on the *Herald* for lyrical prose and memorable descriptions, and on the *Citizen* to fill in the gaps. A fourth paper, the *Hawley Times*, published in the second-largest town in the county, has apparently not survived from the turn of the century.

In 1900, the *Independent* published a hardcover book entitled *Centennial and Illustrated Wayne County*, intended to present a more or less comprehensive view of Wayne County past and present. As a history, *Illustrated Wayne* often proves unreliable and superfluous: an article on the Honesdale Electric Light, Heat, and Power Company, for example, begins with an account of Thales of Miletus and his experiments with amber.[2] But as a view of its time, the book is invaluable. Its biographies of prominent citizens, its discussion of local industries and businesses, and particularly its hundreds of photographs, offer a deep and broad understanding of what Honesdale and Wayne County were like at the turn of the century. *Illustrated Wayne* does give specific and unique information about bands, but its great contribution is to our intimacy with the culture in which they played.

Although the town bands will be my primary focus, the sources have led me to give some attention to town orchestras as well—not only because these ensembles are interesting in their own right, but also because they provide a particularly instructive contrast to the bands. Once made, however, this decision has sometimes proven awkward to implement.

The word *band* is used quite precisely by the newspapers of the time: it almost always refers to a relatively large group (say, more than ten) of wind and percussion players. The word *orchestra*, on the other hand, can mean just about anything—from the Honesdale Philharmonic of some two dozen performers, down to small dance groups of four or five. In identifying town orchestras I have tried to limit myself to large, organized ensembles that include at least some strings, that make at least some pretense of specializing in more cultivated music, and that are in some sense community organizations rather than private, closed groups. All of these criteria, however, are sometimes hard to apply from the information that has survived.

"There is no more pleasure-giving feature in a town than a good band." This sentence appeared in the *Wayne County Herald* on March 23, 1899, and doubtless the same sentiment has been expressed countless times in countless other places. The editor of the *Herald* writes with obvious conviction and public spirit. But what is the truth behind his words? This is the question that I propose to explore—the place of the town band in one small group of towns at the end of the nineteenth century.

It is a relationship that must be examined from both sides—we must find out not only what this music was like, but what the people thought of it. The first part is easy: we stick close to the facts, looking at the descriptions of the performances and at whatever pieces of music we can find. But for the second part, we must listen not only to what the newspapers say, but also, as it were, to their tone of voice. So I have tried whenever convenient to quote the papers directly rather than simply summarizing them. The ponderous prose of the Victorian small-town journalists makes for rather cumbersome reading at times, but it is worth the effort if it gets us closer to the audience and closer to the music.

NOTES

1. For a good summary of the history of journalism in Wayne County, see Kristen Ammerman, Centennial Edition of the *Wayne Independent*, February 4, 1978, A1-A4.

2. *Centennial and Illustrated Wayne County*, 2d ed. (Honesdale: The Wayne Independent, 1902; rept. Honesdale: Wayne County Historical Society, 1975), 37.

2

Wayne County and Honesdale

> From the New York state line on the north to the
> border of Monroe county on the south, the eye will
> meet but few barren spots. Where the fields are not
> undulating in green or golden waves, or the pasture
> lands not white and yellow with daisies and butter-
> cups, the rich foliage of the woodland clothes the
> hill-sides and crowns the mountain tops . . . . And
> scarcely a valley in all the borders of the county but
> that has its crystal lake reflecting all the glory of the
> hills and sky . . . . The broad, well shaded streets of
> [Honesdale], its spacious lawns and handsome parks,
> public and private, its attractive business places,
> handsome churches and good schools, combined as
> they are with the hum of industry that vibrates
> through the air on every week-day, and the peaceful
> quiet that settles down upon its streets on every
> Sunday, make it a charming town to reside in and
> form the keynote of every town and village in the
> county.[1]

Illustrated Wayne County may not have been the most impartial or
restrained voice on the subject, but factually its description of
Wayne County was quite accurate. At the turn of the century the
county, in the very northeastern corner of Pennsylvania, was for
the most part agricultural and forested land, with rolling hills and
abundant lakes and streams. Most of its thirty thousand people
lived on isolated farms or in small villages out in the country; but a
few towns, like the county seat, had attained a fairly substantial size
and some urban development. The area was, in short, fairly rep-

resentative of much of the northeastern United States.

Although the first settlers had arrived in the area in the mid-eighteenth century, farming in the hills and trading on the Delaware and Susquehanna rivers, Wayne County as we know it began to take shape in the 1820s, with the building of the Delaware and Hudson Canal.[2] When huge deposits of anthracite coal were discovered in the Lackawanna valley to the west, means were sought to transport the coal to market in New York. At the time, a canal was the only sensible choice—except that the Moosic Mountains just east of the mines made an all-water route impractical. Instead, the canal was dug from the Hudson River near Kingston, New York, a distance of 108 miles to the base of the Moosics, and from there a gravity railroad extended over the mountains to the mines at Carbondale. This point at the foot of the mountains, where the coal cars were unloaded and the canal boats filled, was to become Honesdale.[3] The canal and the gravity railroad were completed in 1828 and 1829, and were an immediate success. Both were repeatedly enlarged and improved over the next seventy years. And as the canal grew and prospered, so did Honesdale. Almost from the start it came to dominate the affairs of the entire county; it was incorporated as a borough in 1831, and ten years later the county government was moved there from Bethany.[4]

During the nineteenth century, the progress of the canal led to the development of two distinct spheres within the county's life. Honesdale and Hawley, along the canal, grew to have about five thousand and two thousand inhabitants[5] and maintained a small-town economy based on transportation and light industry; but the rest of the area remained rural, with small villages of a few hundred souls. In addition to Honesdale and Hawley, the county in 1900 had four other incorporated boroughs—Waymart (population 432), Starrucca (404), Prompton (258), and Bethany (130)—and dozens of little hamlets in the country.

The abandonment of the canal in 1898 was plainly an epoch in Honesdale's history, and thus the target period 1897 to 1901 is a particularly interesting time, standing as a turning point between the canal years and the post-canal era. Fortunately for the people of Honesdale, a number of industries had moved into town in the past few decades; and as a result, the transition from transportation center to industrial center was accomplished without economic catastrophe.

This shift may be seen in Table 1, which is abstracted from the census returns of 1880 and 1900. The table shows an obvious decrease in the number of boatmen and other canal-related trades (carpenters, draymen, blacksmiths), and an equally dramatic increase in the number and variety of jobs in light industry. Note also the drop in the number of dressmakers as a further sign of the dominance of manufactured goods over homemade. The greater number of professional people and the falling-off of day labor are still more evidence of the economic health of the community at the end of the century.

Table 1.
Occupations of the Citizens of Honesdale

	Percent of population employed	
	1880	1900
Industries		
Shoes	——	3.8
Clothing	——	2.1
Glass	——	1.0
Flour milling	——	.7
Cigars	1.5	——
Transportation		
Canal	1.5	——
Railroad	1.2	3.5
Horse workers (liverymen, porters, coachmen, etc.)	2.0	1.0
Crafts and Building Trades		
Carpenters	2.3	.7
Dressmakers	2.7	1.4
Metalwork (blacksmiths, tinsmiths, molders)	1.5	.3
Miscellaneous (masons, shoemakers, printers, etc.)	2.3	2.4
Retail Sales (merchants, salesmen, butchers, etc.)	4.6	5.2
Professions (doctors, teachers, clergy, editors, etc.)	2.7	4.9

Table 1. (Continued)
Occupations of the Citizens of Honesdale

	Percent of population employed	
	1880	1900
Local Government (including police)	.4	1.0
Day Labor	5.0	3.1
Servants	4.6	5.6
Miscellaneous (clerical, machinist, army, etc.)	.8	3.8
No Occupation		
Adult men	.8	2.1
Adult women	25.6	29.7
At school	22.6	17.1
Children (under 18) at home	17.6	10.1

Data represent every tenth name in the 1880 and 1900 census returns for Honesdale borough.

The most quintessentially Victorian of these new industries was decorative cut glass. Honesdale's own cut glass factories were perhaps overshadowed by the famous Dorflinger works at White Mills, five miles to the east, but *Illustrated Wayne* lists three cut glass factories within the borough. Honesdale also had two large shoe factories and five factories connected with the clothing industry, making silk, woolen goods, underwear, and gloves. Other local factories, most of them small, made axes, lumber, elevators, umbrella sticks, stone monuments, doors, wagons, paper boxes, machinery, barrels, flour, iron goods, books, beer, soft drinks, harnesses, and cigars.[6] Hawley was similar, although of course on a smaller scale, with two cut glass works, a silk mill, a knitting mill, and a flouring mill.[7]

The rest of the county, however, remained more or less unaffected by this industrial revolution. Table 2 compares occupations in Honesdale with those in Manchester and Buckingham townships, which contain the village of Equinunk, in the northeastern part of the county. Farming and farm-related work, such as day labor,

Table 2.
Occupations in Town and Country, 1900

	Percent of population employed	
	Honesdale Borough (see Table 1)	Manchester & Buckingham Townships
Agriculture		
Farmers	—	13.7
Farm labor	—	4.3
Industries		
Manufactured goods	7.6	.4
Quarrying	—	1.7
Creamery	—	.4
Transportation		
Railroad	3.5	—
Horse workers	1.0	.9
Crafts and Building Trades		
Carpenters	.7	.9
Dressmakers & milliners	1.4	1.7
Metalwork	.3	.4
Miscellaneous	2.4	1.3
Retail Sales	5.2	1.3
Professions	4.9	.9
Local Government	1.0	—
Day Labor	3.1	7.3
Servants	5.6	2.6
Miscellaneous	3.8	—
No Occupation		
Adult men	2.1	1.7
Adult women	29.7	22.7
At school	17.1	21.7
Children (under 18) at home	10.1	15.9

Data represent every tenth name in the 1900 census returns for Honesdale borough and Manchester and Buckingham townships.

which probably meant largely farm labor, dominated the rural economy.

In 1890, there were 3,659 farms in Wayne County—about one for every nine inhabitants.[8] Poultry, fruit, and sheep accounted for some of these farms; but most were small, family-owned dairies of less than two hundred acres. And the farms in turn supported a number of small agricultural businesses—milk routes, creameries, feed stores, grist mills, implement dealers, and the like—throughout the area.

Lumbering was the first industry in Wayne County, and it remained a potent economic force throughout the nineteenth century. And like agriculture, lumber, too, spawned a number of smaller industries to prepare and use the forest products: sawmills, excelsior factories, acid factories, and tanneries.[9] Indeed, lumbering, farming, and small business seem to have been compatible; the more prosperous citizens of the rural areas frequently combined their pursuits. Here, for example, is a more or less typical biography from *Illustrated Wayne:*

Jacob I. Bates, one of the most enterprising residents of Dyberry township, was born October 10, 1843. He assisted his father on the farm and attended the public school until he was 21 years of age when he enlisted in the construction corps of the Union army and served until the war closed when he was honorably discharged. He returned to his native township, purchased a farm in the eastern part thereof and shortly afterward, in partnership with his brother, a saw mill was purchased and later a feed mill added to the plant. In 1870 he erected the grist mill which has since been successfully operated by him at Dyberry post office. The excellent product of his mill has given him a wide patronage. . . . Mr. Bates is one of Wayne county's best citizens. He has made his success in his milling business by giving the people what they want—good service and honest tolling.[10]

A third rural industry, rapidly growing at the turn of the century, was summer tourism. The great resort areas of the northeast, the Catskills and Shawangunks of New York State and the Poconos of Pennsylvania, bordered Wayne County to the east and south, but still there wasn't enough room for all the people escaping the heat of the city. By 1901, the New York, Ontario and Western Railway (the O&W) was publishing a twelve-page pamphlet extolling the great virtues of Wayne and Delaware counties, "where one's first thoughts upon visiting is [sic] to forget the busy turmoil of constant city life which he has been subjected to and turn his attention to the beautiful lakes, green fields, shady streams, and invigorating air, thus dreaming away a short vacation close to nature's heart, and returning home once again with renewed energy and hope, to resume duties for another year."[11] The pamphlet lists about fifty places in northern Wayne where summer boarders would be taken in—many of them just farmhouses with a few extra rooms. As the century progressed, there would be many more resorts in all parts of the area.

Isolated rural areas like nineteenth-century Wayne County were especially dependent on transportation routes for every aspect of their development. Railroads, of course, were by far the dominant mode of transport at the time, the web that connected the whole continent. And as a result, towns along the railroad had a way of prospering not only economically, but culturally as well. It is no coincidence that of the ten bands and orchestras I have been able to document between 1897 and 1901, only one, the Beach Lake band, came from a community more than two miles from a train station.

As the story of the canal suggests, transportation in Wayne County was in transition during the 1890s; this, combined with the sheer number of railroads built to haul the anthracite out of the Lackawanna Valley, makes for rather a confusing picture. The various lines may, however, be conveniently sorted out into four systems: the Delaware and Hudson (D&H); the Erie; the New York, Ontario and Western; and the Delaware, Lackawanna and Western.

The Delaware and Hudson Canal Company's gravity railroad, which brought the coal in for the canal, was one of the oldest railroads in the country.[12] The principle of the Gravity is suggested by its name: the line was operated by gravity instead of by locomotives. The cars were pulled on cables up a steep incline (called a plane) by a stationary steam engine at the top of the hill; when they reached the summit they were unhooked and allowed to drift down a gentler slope to the next plane, where the process was repeated. The system seems odd today, familiar as we are with locomotive railroads; but in 1827-29, when the Gravity was built, locomotives were still a novelty. In fact, the first commercial steam locomotive in America, the *Stourbridge Lion,* was bought in England by the canal company and shipped to Honesdale in 1829 for a trial run on the Gravity.[13] The test was a failure, and the railway continued its anachronistic (and successful) operation long after locomotives were in use all over the country.

Apart from its unusual workings, the Gravity played the same role as other railroads of the time, carrying general freight and passengers as well as the coal that was its raison d'être. In 1898, the ride from Honesdale to Carbondale took about eighty-five minutes; twelve passenger trains traversed the line every weekday.[14] Carbondale was the nearest bigger town (population 13,536), and there passengers could change trains for Scranton (population 102,026), the largest city and cultural center of the region. In 1899, when the canal had been abandoned, the Gravity was changed from two lines (separate tracks for eastbound and westbound trains), sixteen and twenty-three miles long, to one twenty-eight-mile route; from narrow to standard gauge; and from a gravity to a conventional locomotive operation.[15] In 1901 there were eight passenger trains on the line each weekday, and the trip to Carbondale took about seventy-two minutes.[16]

On a typical day in Honesdale in 1897, three passenger trains arrived and three departed on the Erie Railroad.[17] Because central Honesdale was clogged with canal activity, the Erie station was actually located at Tracyville, about a mile south. This remoteness of the station was taken by arriving bands as a fine excuse for a parade through town; for most passengers, though, it was merely an inconvenience.

The Honesdale branch of the Erie connected in Hawley, nine miles away, with the Erie and Wyoming Valley Railroad.[18] The E&WV was a coal line from the Scranton area to Hawley to Lackawaxen, where it met the Erie mainline along the Delaware River. There passengers could change trains for New York to the east, or Buffalo or Chicago to the west. The Erie and E&WV, although operated as separate railroads, were closely allied and shared trackage rights from Hawley to Lackawaxen. In January of 1901, the Erie and Wyoming Valley was officially consolidated into the Erie.[19]

In the fall of 1899, a year after the abandonment of the canal, the D&H demolished the canal works in Honesdale and built a railroad yard in the old basin. The following February, the new Delaware and Hudson station was opened at the foot of Ninth Street. After some wrangling, the tracks of the Erie were extended uptown to meet the D&H, and on October 1, 1900, the first Erie passenger train left central Honesdale—accompanied, as befitted the occasion, by the Maple City band.[20]

A third railroad, the Scranton branch of the New York, Ontario and Western, had been completed across northern Wayne County in 1890.[21] Although the O&W did not actually pass through any of the towns that had bands at the turn of the century, it was only a few miles from Lake Como and Pleasant Mount, and it was surely used by many of the bands in the northern part of the county.

And finally, the main line of the Delaware, Lackawanna and Western cut through the very southwestern corner of the county for a distance of a little over a mile—seemingly a trivial incursion, except that this mile contained the village of Gouldsboro and the Gouldsboro band.

All the railroads encouraged excursion travel, and each road owned or otherwise supported picnic grounds to lure the public out for a good time and a train ride. On the Gravity Railroad, the place to go was Farview, eleven miles from Honesdale, near Waymart; after the steam line superseded the Gravity, Farview gave way to nearby Lake Lodore. Shohola Glen, on the Erie mainline, was twenty-nine miles from Honesdale, and Lake Ariel was twenty-five miles from town on the Erie and Wyoming Valley. All of these spots attracted large and small parties from many miles around throughout the summer, and all were popular places for band concerts—yet another example of the intertwining of the railroads and the culture of the area.[22]

It was a lucky accident of geography that gave Wayne County more than its fair share of rail lines, and thus more mobility and more access to the outside world than it might otherwise have had. But railroads serve both to develop an area and to channel that development in their own directions. And the peculiar circumstance that all four of these railroads were essentially east-west routes led the county to develop as a series of horizontal bands. Both Honesdale and Hawley—indeed, five of the county's six incorporated boroughs—were in the central band, around the D&H and Erie; travel east and west within this band was easy, but travel north and south was much more difficult and infrequent, and thus Honesdale had relatively little contact with the people (and bands) of northern towns like Equinunk and Lake Como or southern towns like Newfoundland and Gouldsboro.

The spirit, or character, of turn-of-the-century Honesdale is a difficult matter to pin down from this distance. In most respects, Honesdale was probably a fairly typical small town of its time, a working-class community with a strong local economy supported by various small factories. The abandonment of the canal did not lead to mass unemployment; most of the former canal employees either got new jobs or moved away. Thus the town was spared the social problems, such as a high crime rate, that are usually associated with poverty. Indeed, to judge from the sometimes hair-raising tales of violence and arson in Vernon Leslie's histories of Honesdale from 1825 to 1875, the post-canal years were a decided improvement.[23]

One can easily point to everyday signs of the quality of life—for example, that Honesdale had a central gas supply since the 1850s, central water and at least some sewers since the sixties, and electric lights since the eighties, but did not pave its streets until 1914.[24] But these statistics tell only part of the story; for the rest, we must look behind the accounts of the contemporary events, trying to see the attitude that people brought to their life in Honesdale.

One important sign, surely, is the attention paid to the town's appearance. The newspapers were constantly exhorting their readers not to litter or to dump trash on the streets or in the canal. Indeed, in this respect the abandonment of the canal must have been a very concrete blessing: the disappearance of the huge, unsightly coal piles that had dominated the town for decades, and the draining of the polluted canal basin, must have done much for the general appearance of the borough. And the Honesdale Improvement Association was formed in 1891 by a group of prominent local women, with the intent to "promote public convenience and health, and render the town more attractive as a place of residence."[25] The most conspicuous activities of the association involved the design and maintenance of the town's parks; but the names of the committees reveal other spheres of concern as well: Sanitary and Street Vigilance, Humane, Entertainments, Children's Auxiliary, Flowers, Parks and Trees, and Collecting.[26] The Honesdale Improvement Association seems to have been much appreciated by the citizens and much copied by other towns around the area,[27] and contemporary photographs show that their labors were well spent. In the pictures, Honesdale's streets, although unpaved, are mostly tree-lined and always tidy, and its parks are very beautiful indeed.

The publication of *Illustrated Wayne* was in itself an unusual and auspicious event: such a book, polishing up the past and celebrating the present, could only have appeared in a town that was prosperous and pleased with itself. And the fact that the book sold many copies shows that the citizens themselves were also interested in local history. Editors T. J. Ham of the *Herald* and B. F. Haines of the *Independent* were both students of local history, and their enthusiasm shows in the numerous historical articles appearing in their papers.

1. Engraving of Honesdale, looking east, in the late 1880s. The large Victorian building on the cliff (#7) is the Irving Cliff Hotel, which burned just before it was to open in 1889. The Delaware and Hudson Canal is visible between Main Street and the base of the foreground hill, with the first plane of the light track

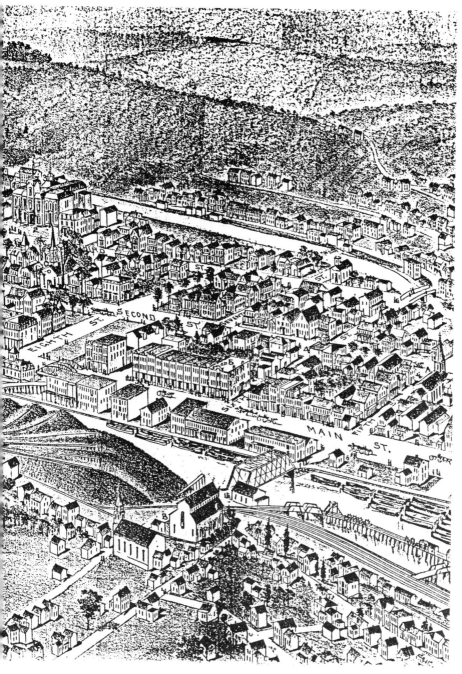

of the Gravity Railroad ascending the hill to the lower left. The Wayne County Courthouse (#2) is visible on Third Street between Tenth and Ninth, and Central Park is in front of it (engraving published by the A. E. Downs Co., Boston, 1890; Wayne County Historical Society).

Above all, no newspaper wanted to miss a chance to mention the *Stourbridge Lion* and its significance as the first steam locomotive in America. This proud preoccupation with local history, including the veneration for the *Stourbridge Lion*, has persisted in the citizens of Honesdale, and today is one of the town's most distinctive features.

In short, the citizens of turn-of-the-century Honesdale were proud of the town's past, confident in its future, and above all conscious that it was a good place to live. The closing of the canal must have been a little frightening; after all, the town had been built around the canal and had never tried to live without it. But from the newspapers, from *Illustrated Wayne*, and even from the pictures, one senses a calm sort of faith in the spirit and the abilities of the citizens—faith that has been amply justified by later events.

NOTES

1. *Centennial and Illustrated Wayne County*, 2d ed. (Honesdale: The Wayne Independent, 1902; rept. Honesdale: Wayne County Historical Society, 1975), p. viii.

2. See Vernon Leslie, *Honesdale: The Early Years* (Honesdale: Honesdale 150 Committee, 1981), pp. 1-15; and Alfred Mathews, *History of Wayne, Pike and Monroe Counties, Pennsylvania* (Philadelphia: R. T. Peck, 1886; rept. Honesdale Citizens for the Preservation of Our Local Heritage, n.d.), pp. 336-51.

3. On the history and workings of the Delaware and Hudson Canal, see Manville B. Wakefield. *Coal Boats to Tidewater* (Grahamsville, N.Y.: Wakefair Press, 1971); E. D. LeRoy, *The Delaware and Hudson Canal* (Honesdale: Wayne County Historical Society, 1980); Dorothy Hurlbut Sanderson, *The Delaware and Hudson Canalway: Carrying Coals to Rondout* (Ellenville, N.Y.: Rondout Valley Publishing, 1974); and Leslie, *Early Years*, pp. 20-27.

4. Leslie, *Early Years*, pp. 69, 78-81; Mathews, *History*, pp. 125-26.

5. The 1900 census listed the population of Honesdale as 2,864, but this figure is misleadingly small, as the settled area of the town far exceeded it official boundaries at the time. The boundaries were extended to their present size in 1926. See Kristen Ammerman, Centennial Edition of the *Wayne Independent*, February 4, 1978, pp. A13-A14.

6. Honesdale's industries are discussed throughout *Illustrated Wayne*; see especially pp. xi-xii, 24-33. See also Mathews, *History*, pp. 365-74.

7. *Illustrated Wayne*, p. 102.

8. Ammerman, "Centennial Edition," p. A46; see also pp. A42-A43.

9. Ibid., pp. A22, A45, C16.

10. *Illustrated Wayne*, p. 152.

11. *A Summer's Vacation in the Highlands of Wayne and Delaware Counties* (New York: New York, Ontario and Western Ry., 1901), p. 2.

12. See especially Wakefield, *Coal Boats*, pp. 13-31; and Leslie, *Early Years*, pp. 28-34.

13. The *Stourbridge Lion* is discussed in many of the works cited here; the most comprehensive discussion by far is Vernon Leslie, *Honesdale and the Stourbridge Lion* (Honesdale: Stourbridge Lion Sesquicentennial Corporation, 1979).

14. From a public timetable of the Delaware and Hudson, dated September 5, 1898, in the author's collection.

15. *Illustrated Wayne*, p. 94; Jim Shaughnessy, *Delaware and Hudson* (Berkeley, Calif.: Howell-North Books, 1967), pp. 192-95, 313.

16. Timetable in the *Honesdale Citizen*, July 4, 1901.

17. Timetable in the *Wayne Independent*, July 7, 1897.

18. See *Illustrated Wayne*, p. 94.

19. Gerald M. Best, *The Ulster and Delaware* (San Marino, Calif.: Golden West Books, 1972), pp. 111-13.

20. *Illustrated Wayne*, pp. 94, 140-41. For more details, see pp. 61-63 of this volume.

21. *Illustrated Wayne*, p. 95.

22. On Farview, see Wakefield, *Coal Boats*, pp. 22-23; on Lodore, see *Illustrated Wayne*, p. 143; on Shohola Glen, see George J. A. Fluhr, *Shohola Glen* (Shohola: Edward S. Jarosz, 1970); on Lake Ariel, see *Illustrated Wayne*, p. 99.

23. Leslie, *Early Years*, especially pp. 82-84; idem, *Canal Town; Honesdale 1850-1875* (Honesdale: Wayne County Historical Society, 1983), especially pp. 1-21, 67-91, 137-56; idem, *A Profile of Service: Protection Engine Company No. 3, 1853-1916* (Honesdale: Protection Engine Co. No. 3, 1986), especially pp. 1-12, 21-44.

24. Leslie, *Canal Town*, pp. 33-35 (gas), 169-70 (sewer), 104-7 (water); *Illustrated Wayne*, 37 (lights); Ammerman, "Centennial Edition," p. A28 (paving).

25. From the Constitution of the Honesdale Improvement Association, quoted in *Illustrated Wayne*, p. 21.

26. Ibid.

27. The claim that the Honesdale Improvement Association was a pioneer among such organizations in Pennsylvania is made periodically throughout the local newspapers of the time as well as in *Illustrated Wayne*. This may, however, have been a case of revisionist history in the act; Richard Lingeman, in *Small Town American* (Boston: Houghton Mifflin, 1980), pp. 296-97, says that Improvement Societies became popular all over the country after the Civil War.

3

The Bands of Honesdale

Honesdale between 1897 and 1901 was the home for three brass bands and one orchestra. The Honesdale band, founded around 1880, and Lawyer's band, founded in 1898, were consolidated to form the Maple City band in 1900;[1] the Honesdale Philharmonic Society, an authentic, if diminutive, classical orchestra, was formed in 1898. The histories of these organizations overlap.

EARLY BANDS OF HONESDALE

By the end of the nineteenth century, Honesdale had had a more or less continuous history of town bands for many decades. Although they fall outside the bounds of this study, these bands are interesting and important if only by way of establishing the tradition that the turn-of-the-century bands inherited and the musical past within which they were understood. The activities of some of the early bands were later described in vivid detail by their members—in particular, Thomas J. Ham, editor of the *Wayne County Herald*, and his brother, William H. Ham.[2]

The history of bands in Honesdale may have begun almost as early as that of the community itself, in the late 1820s. According to W. H. Ham, the very first band in town was organized by a keyed-bugle player named Bissel, "out of the odds and ends of the musicians who were found in the place at the time," for the trial run of the *Stourbridge Lion* in August 1829.[3] Ham admitted, however, that this band proved difficult to document, and it may be a myth. The various eyewitness accounts of the event do describe huge crowds, cannon salutes, and so forth, and one might expect them to mention a brass band if one had been there; thus the absence of music from these descriptions, combined with Ham's uncertainty, raises suspicion.[4] At any rate, it seems clear that there were no bands in Honesdale before 1829; bands were present at a number of ceremonies surrounding the building of the Delaware and Hudson Canal, but only at the more populous New York end of the waterway.[5]

Perhaps a more reliable candidate for Honesdale's first band is the ensemble organized by Allen Plum in the early 1840s. W. H. Ham discusses this band in some detail.

> The next [band] was under the tuition of Allen G. Plum, who had been away in the army playing the bassoon and had acquired some knowledge of harmony. Zara Arnold, a favorite of the boys, with more willingness to spend his money for the band than musical ability, was appointed leader and given in charge of the first clarionet. He successively failed on every new instrument brought in until he graduated in disgust on the bass orphcleide, a comical instrument with one key and a lot of holes. . . . I am unable to ascertain the names of all the players, but besides Mr. Arnold there was A. J. Bowers, clarionet; Carley Wallace and our friend J. C. Delezenne, French horns, the trombones being managed by the late Ezra M. Genung and our well-preserved townsman J. H. Sutton. This band was in existence several years, their first public performance being on the occasion of the funeral of President Harrison in April, 1841, which was generally observed throughout the country, and their last notes being wasted upon the unappreciating Washingtonians, a lively temperance society of those days.

Ham goes on to describe this final appearance of Plum's band, at a Fourth of July picnic in an unspecified year:

> It seems that the band was in a rather dilapidated condition at the time, but in order to please the committee and do their employers and themselves justice, they sent, at a cost to the band of one hundred dollars, to Chenango Forks for Lot Crosby, a celebrated teacher and player of the day, to come down and drill them for a month. Mr. Sutton says he was obliged to learn a new instrument for the occasion, the plain [i.e., natural?] trumpet. Mr. Crosby having completed his contract three or four days before the Fourth, was induced to

remain and help them on that day, and perhaps many Honesdalers may remember his clarionet solo in the Presbyterian church before the oration.

Well, after the boys had marched and countermarched through every street of the dusty town, they were glad enough when they were permitted to clear their throats with the cold water dinner provided them in the square. While the meal was progressing some one went through about the tables, hat in hand, and collected eight dollars in sixpences and shillings, and emptied the heap in front of the band as payment for their services. Imagine their disgust. The leader blew a blast on his bugle, the boys assembled, held an indignation meeting, expressed their opinion of the whole business, and then and there disbanded. They never played another note.[6]

As the 1840s progressed, the situation in Honesdale became much more fluid and changeable. Musicians moved from band to band, and in and out of the community; new bands were born, and old ones died or merged; bands changed leadership and thus, often, names. The historians mention Vancuren's (or Van Keuren's), Bowen's, and Knapp's bands, as well as describing a number of events with bands unnamed.[7] But the decade did produce two relatively long-lived and influential ensembles, each of which went under a number of names, but which were best remembered as the Silver Cornet band and Broad's band.

The Silver Cornet band began in the early to mid-1840s, and both Ham brothers were members. William tells the story of its earliest form:

I well remember when a young lad, the start of pleasure I experienced when I was invited to become a member of a new band about to be started, composed chiefly of men working in the boat yards in the place. Dr. Hawley Olmsted, a fair clarionet player, was employed as teacher at five dollars per night, and we were to close our course with a grand concert. The doctor worked hard with us, but as our instruments were chiefly the old *debris* of former bands and none of us knew at the beginning one note from another, our pieces and parts were necessarily very simple. If I remember rightly our chief reliance was placed upon "Kinloch O'Kinloch," "Pleyel's Hymn" and "Araby's Daughter." We made demonstrations on "Wood-Up" and "Wrecker's Daughter," but with very little satisfaction to ourselves and still less to our listeners.[8]

In another article, published in 1900, Ham went into some detail about the instrumentation and repertory of this band, and his comments are worth quoting at length:

Band instruments are generally expensive affairs and consequently the fit out of the impecunious youth with unsympathizing fathers generally consisted, at first at least, of the wreckage of defunct bands of the vicinity. We believe that the first instruments in use here, came from Montrose and Dundaff, much older towns. And a motley lot they were. The old copper key bugle led the list. It had the true horn shape but it was covered all over with keys, looking like so many huge warts. The keys were moved by long levers convenient for manipulation and in the hands of an artist were capable of giving forth pretty good music—at all events the best of its day. The bugle idea extended down to the extreme end of the band. The base orpheclide, was a collection of pot curves small or great, fastened along the sides of brass cylinders as big as a sewer pipe. . . . The melodies of the bands were generally played by clarionetts E flat and B flat, and flutes and bugles also in the same keys. The bases were the Eb and Bb orpheclides and the filling up between these ends was accomplished by the following: French horns with a bell like a morning glory and an infinitude of twists and curls and loose crooks for change of keys, which were generally carried upon the arm of the player when not in use. There were no keys upon the instrument, but the tones between its harmonic sounds, the first, third, fifth and octave, were produced by the aid of the performer's fist which was thrust as was required more or less deeply into its yawning mouth. It was a good "mellow horn" and is used to-day in all of the best orchestras without change. Then there were the slide trombones in different keys. Having no valves or keys, every sound was a rich "open note" and consequently good. It is still the main reliance of most military bands and an orchestra without would be impossible. The clarionet, the flute, the horn and the trombone survive, but the rest are only to be found in museums.

We must not forget the trumpet, which was also made in Eb and Bb. The trumpet was the bane of all bandsmen. No self-respecting man with a spark of music in his soul, or who otherwise stood well in the community would touch it. But when a band is organized. there are always a lot hanging around who will do anything to get into the "band." They will carry with pride and pound all day, a great fat drum, or they seem to see no disgrace in monkeying with the triangle or banging the cymbals. Such men, after the other instruments are assigned will accept with thanks the trumpet. Where the trumpet secures its tremendous and overpowering sound no one knows. It is a quiet, peaceable, rather pretty instrument, but every one who has once heard it gives it plenty of room. The band masters know it and dread it, and consequently fill its music up pretty well with rests. But it would not do to have the part all rests, so in the more noisy and triumphant passages the trumpet is sometimes given a chance. Whether the player wishes to make up for long time or is animated by a spirit of vengeance, no one but a trumpeter knows, but certain it is that when he begins the rest may as well stop. Its inventor, however, knew his business. It is well adapted to move frenzied soldiers on to desperate deeds. We cannot even recall the names of the trumpeters of our bands, which is another proof that they were not worth remembering. . . .

The arrangement of music in those days differed considerably from that of the present. Now the custom is to have such an elaborate scoring as to confuse the listener, to have half a dozen at once playing different solos, so that no one can tell who is leading. In the old scores, after a noisy introduction, which gave every one a chance, the music simmered down to a solo—a popular song, or what not, with a simple accompaniment by the band. Generally the solo would include a duet with another of the small horns, and during the piece somewhere would be a solo for the bases. We must confess to a partiality for the old music.[9]

Ham's account is not only detailed and colorful but also authoritative: the descriptions of the instruments, allowing for some confusion on the more arcane spellings and a bit of musical prejudice here and there, are perfectly accurate, and the instrumentation seems quite typical for an amateur band before the dominance of the saxhorn and the rise of the cornet band.[10]

In 1847, the instructor's duties were taken over by John Littlewood, probably an itinerant music teacher, who also started another band of the community's youth. In 1849, it and the Silver Cornet band merged into the Juvenile Brass band, with a more modern instrumentation of valved brasses: two cornets, three E-flat tenors, two baritones, and bass.[11]

The Juvenile Brass band continued to play throughout the 1850s, adding members, changing instructors, and generally emerging as a first-class amateur band.[12] They purchased their silver instruments in 1860, probably changing their name at that point (indeed, most of the members could hardly be called "juvenile" any more), and the following year had two E-flat cornets, two B-flat cornets, three E-flat tenors, two baritones, an E-flat tuba, and two drummers.[13] And in 1898, one of the Ham brothers, presumably Thomas, provided a glimpse of the band's everyday life: "Years ago, when we used to blow our own horn, the Silver Cornet band would climb out upon the little balcony of the old court house, and took great delight in playing for an hour or so of an evening to the multitude that thronged the walks of the park. The generous applause that met our efforts showed that our people enjoyed the music. We weren't paid for it to be sure, and often some over-officious janitor of the old building locked us out, but we always managed to find a weak spot to burglarize, and then to give the people what they wanted— good music."[14]

In 1861 and 1862, as more and more of Honesdale's young men went off to fight in the Civil War, the Silver Cornet band was on hand to lend moral support and martial spirit, sometimes accompanying the soldiers on the trains as far as Wilkes-Barre. By some accounts this was their finest hour—but it was also their last. Four of its members joined the army, two never returned, and the band dissolved.[15]

The chief local competition of the Silver Cornet band during almost this entire period was an ensemble, or series of ensembles, centered on John Broad. Again, W. H. Ham tells the story:

> Our old organization [i.e., the Juvenile Brass band] lorded it around to all the parades, picnics and parties, the pride of the girls and the envy of the boys, until 1849. One afternoon of that year old Johnny Smith, the down-town barber, who could scrape the fiddle a little, heard John Broad, his near neighbor, playing upon his cornopean. Johnny Smith called upon Johnny Broad, complimented his musical abilities, and proposed that they should organize a band, to which proposition John Broad assented, and that was the origin and nucleus of all the bands that have existed in this town since that day, excepting what we claimed and without much dispute, as the Honesdale Band.
>
> The new, or opposition band, as we called it—for we were at outs on many an occasion—bore in its time many titles, such as

"Johnny Smith's Band," "Beck's Band," "Bierman's Band,"
"Diller's Band," "Karslake's Band," "Sehl's Band," according to
the names of the various leaders; yet through it all the individuality of John Broad was so plainly discernible, that it was
generally known all the time as "Broad's Band," and it was
about him that the disorganized musicians crystallized after
the "break-ups," which were of frequent occurence. And right
here, perhaps, it is no more than fair to say that, to the
unappreciated, unrequited, painstaking of John Broad, the
people of Honesdale are much indebted. Such excellent musicians as the five Hawes boys, John Broad, Jr., Geo. Hill,
William Reif, and many others, received their early training at
his hands. He was always unfortunate in his bands in one
respect. In the main they were composed of transient people,
and as the places of leaving members had to be filled with new
players, there were generally one or two who could not play
their parts properly. All old musicians know what a drag they
are. . . .

Some time in '55 or '56 the band was much improved by the
addition of Mr. Henry Diller, a thorough musician from New
York, who had come here to live. He at once took the lead,
playing the solo alto, his favorite instrument. The Karslake
boys, Will and Harry, also joined them about this time and
were a great help. . . .

In 1860 Broad's band, then under the lead of Wm. Karslake,
bought their new silver horns of Allen & Co., of Boston, mates
to ours. In the matter of instruments I question if any band
within one hundred miles of us was so well supplied, before or
since, as was [sic] our two. They were all of the same pattern,
bells over the shoulder, large calibre, splendid finish and
beautiful tone.

Ham goes on to give their instrumentation at that time: one E-flat
cornet, two B-flat cornets, two E-flat tenors, one baritone, bass, and
drums—a much smaller band than the Silver Cornet. And he
concludes: "The rebellion, however, that interfered with everything,
broke up their band as well as ours. The two Karslakes, Nihart,
Richmond and Broad went off to the wars. Nihart was killed in
battle, Nash died of consumption, and that was the last of that
band.[16]"

Despite Ham's doom-laden pronouncement, some incarnation of
Broad's band does seem to have survived the war. Various refer-

ences from the late 1860s and early 1870s refer not only to Broad's band but to "Sehl's band" (or "Sehl's German band") and "Hawes' band," both evidently named after members of the old organization, possibly among others.[17] And W. H. Ham reports that a band of six local young men, including four of John Broad's protégés, had contracted to provide music for a travelling circus.[18]

By the late seventies, however, there was more sporadic evidence of bands in Honesdale. For its enormous celebration of the national centennial in 1876, Honesdale supplemented two of its own bands with the Plymouth band, probably from Luzerne County, and the Erie band of Port Jervis, New York.[19] Broad's band appeared once again the following year,[20] but by 1879, it appears that Honesdale again had no town band of its own; at any rate, as Vernon Leslie has shown in a meticulous and elegant discussion of a photograph taken on October 16 of that year, a firemen's parade had to rely on a band from Scranton.[21]

THE HONESDALE BAND

According to *Illustrated Wayne*, the Honesdale band was formed around 1880.[22] The early history of the band is therefore not within the scope of this study. But 1897 does seem to have been a time of rebirth, or at least rejuvenation, for the Honesdale band: on April 22, the *Herald* reported:

> Our Honesdale Band, under the leadership of Daniel Storms, has always furnished us good music, but not enough of it. The boys have resolved to try and give us better than ever this season and have already commenced their rehearsals. They need new uniforms very much and in order to secure them they will give a series of hops with full orchestra at the opera house once a week. . . . The boys say that if the Court House stoop or other suitable place is provided with seats or lights they will give free out door concerts once or twice a week during the summer. We hope our public spirited citizens will encourage them in every way. There is nothing that adds more pleasure to residence in a town than a good, well equipped band, not too chary of its music. Help our boys.

The *Independent* added a list of personnel: "The members of the band are Daniel Storms, John Metzgar, Henry Wagner, George Conzleman, Fred. Gill, Andrew Cowles, Henry Rehbein, Charles McElroy, R. M. Dorin, John Bussa, Prof. Wagner, Geo. Richards,

Charles Brown, John Broad [presumably John Broad, Jr., son of the leader of Broad's band], Charles Marsh, Henry Miller, Wm. W. Ham."[23]

Table 3 shows all of the engagements I have been able to identify for the Honesdale band from 1897 to 1901, a list representative of the kinds of functions that would feature a band: parades, outdoor concerts, picnics, and dances. These events normally followed a more or less stereotyped pattern.

Table 3.
Performances of the Honesdale Band

Date	Location	Event (Sponsor)
	1897	
April 24	Opera House	Benefit dance (Honesdale band)
April 28	Opera House	Benefit dance (Honesdale band)
May 5	Opera House	Benefit dance (Honesdale band)
May 29	Honesdale	Memorial Day parade, cemetery exercises
c.May 30	Bapt. church?	Concert (Baptist church)
June 16	Farview	Excursion (Lutheran church)
June 17	Honesdale	Procession and dinner (Hsdl. Liederkranz, for Forest City Maennerchor)
July 7	Maennerchor Park, Hawley	Excursion (Maennerchor)
July 19	Central Park	Concert (Red Men)
July 20	Shohola Glen	Picnic (Red Men)
July 30	Honesdale	7-County Veteran Reunion: parade, concert
c.August 4	Lake Ariel	Reunion (IOOF)
August 12	Shohola Glen	Picnic (M.E. Sunday School)
August 18	Honesdale	Parade and picnic (St. Joseph's Society)
October 15	Honesdale	Parade (Protection Engine Co. #3)
November 3 (&ff.)	Pioneer Hall	3 dances
November 18	Liederkranz Hall	Concert (Liederkranz)
December 25	Armory	Social (Honesdale band)
	1898	
March 17	Honesdale	St. Patrick's Day parade
April 27	Honesdale	Parade to depot with Co. E
May 17	Upper station	Meeting visitors (Red Men)

Table 3. (Continued)
Performances of the Honesdale Band

Date	Location	Event (Sponsor)
	1898	
May 18	Court House	Public reception (Red Men)
May 19	Honesdale	Parade (Red Men)
May 30	Honesdale	Memorial Day parade, concert in park, cemetery exercises
May ??	Scranton	Parade (German Catholic Societies of Pa.)
June 7	Scranton	Parade (AOH)
July 4	Honesdale	4th of July parade, ceremonies in Riverside Park
August 2	Central Park	Concert (IOOF)
August 3	Lake Ariel	Excursion: parade, picnic (IOOF of N.E. Pa.)
August 16	Central Park; Scranton	Excursion: parade, picnic (Honesdale Liederkranz); also parade in Honesdale?
September 15	Court House	Speech by gubernatorial candidate S.C. Swallow
September 16	Allen? Hotel	Supper for J. Wanamaker etal before political rally
October 13	Honesdale	Parade (Protection Engine Co. #3)
	1899	
May 30	Honesdale	Memorial Day parade, cemetery exercises
June 24	Florence Thtr., White Mills	Concert and ball (Honesdale band)
July 3	G.W. Searles's house	Social (Ladies of the Maccabees)
July 4	Narrowsburg	4th of July celebration
July 31	Russell Park	Concert (Red Men)
August 1	Lake Ariel	Excursion (Red Men)
September 7	Irving Cliff	Concert (Liederkranz)
September 27	Liederkranz Hall?	Entertainment (Liederkranz)

All locations Honesdale except Farview, Hawley, Shohola Glen, Scranton, Lake Ariel, White Mills, Narrowsburg.

Parades were probably the most conspicuous situation in which bands played. Some parades were held irregularly, even spontaneously, for special occasions; but the biggest processions of the year were the Memorial Day parade in the spring and the Firemen's parade in the autumn.

The Memorial Day festivities, a patriotic spectacle arranged by the Honesdale post of the G.A.R., usually consisted of two parts, a parade through town and a ceremony by the soldiers' graves in Glen Dyberry Cemetery. The celebration of 1899 was unusual in that it featured two bands, but otherwise it will serve as a typical example.

Memorial day was bright and clear. The showers of the night before left muddy roads, but that made it seem more real to the veterans of the two wars. The town was well decorated with flags in honor of the occasion. Lawyer's band escorted Companies E and L from the armory and the Honesdale band brought the Pioneer Corps to the place of formation at the corner of Main and Eighth streets. The line was thus formed by Major Whitney, in uniform, the marshall of the day:

> Police on foot.
> Mayor and Council in carriages.
> Lawyers' Band.
> Co. L, N.G.P., Capt. Osborne.
> Pioneer Corps.
> Honesdale Council, J.O.U.A.M.
> Clergy and choir in carriages.
> Honesdale Band.
> Co. E, 13th Reg., P.V.I. Lieut. Dodge.
> G.A.R. Post, H. Wilson, Com.
> Disabled Veterans in carriages.

At the high school building the pupils in charge of Prof. March, W. W. Baker, Misses Gillen and Lee fell in line.

The line of march was down Main to Fourth, to Second, to Twelfth, to Main, to Fourteenth, to Glen Dyberry, where details were dispatched to decorate the graves. Minute guns were fired from Beers' Hill by the Post artillery squad during the moving of the procession. The program at the cemetery was as follows: Dirge by Lawyers' band; reading list of deceased comrades by Adj. Kesler; vocal quartet, "Silent Heroes," by A. J. Rehbein, J. J. Curtis, Mesdames I. J. Ball and C. E. Baker; patriotic address by H. Wilson, esq.; ritualistic memorial service; "Peacefully Rest" by the quartet; address by Rev. W. H. Swift; dirge by Honesdale band; volley by squad under command of Lieut. Lane, Co. L, 11th Reg., N.G.P.; benediction by Rev. J. P. Ware; taps by Bugler H. Parrish.[24]

The Firemen's parade, held usually in late October, was organized by the oldest of the fire companies in town, Protection Engine Company No. 3, as a prelude to the company's annual fund-raising ball. This parade was concerned less with patriotism and more with fun; it usually contained an element of the minstrel show, a tradition that continued in the Protection Engine Company's entertainments until the 1960s.

The 45th annual parade of Protection Engine Co. took place last Thursday evening; was most successfully carried out, and far surpassed any previous efforts. The following was the order and line of march.

LINE OF MARCH.

Down Main to 4th; 4th to 2d; 2d to 9th; 9th to 3d; 3d to 10th; 10th to 2d; 2d to 12th; 12th to Main; Main to North Park; countermarch to Engine House.

ORDER OF MARCH.

Form in front of the Engine House, in the following order:

Mounted Police.
Carriages with Burgess and Town Council.
American Flag.
Honesdale Band.
Alert Fire Company, of Texas.
Hook and Ladder Truck.
Torch Boy—Banner—Torch Boy.
Hawley Band.
R.W. Ham Steamer.
Protection Engine Co. No. 3.
A.M. Atkinson Steamer.
Horse Hose Truck.

Darktown Fire Brigade:
Mounted Police.
Drum Major.
Band.
Mayor of Darktown.
Honorary Members.

Darktown Fire Brigade.
Hose Truck.
Engine Drawn by Horses.

Many dwellings and stores were brilliantly illuminated and there was a generous display of Old Glory all through town. Twenty-eight of the marching men of No. 3 carried lanterns with red, white and blue globes, which presented a very pleasing and attractive appearance, and elicited frequent and hearty applause. They executed a number of manoeuvres during the parade, including the formation of a Greek cross. The company never appeared to better advantage. The sidewalks were lined with dense masses of humanity. The firemen were liberally supplied with Roman candles and red fire, 40 pounds of the latter being burned along the line of march.

The Alert Hook and Ladder Co., of Texas [Township], 40 men, were attired in a uniform comprising black pants, blue shirts with the initial "A" prominently displayed, and blue caps. Their truck is a beauty, and is fully supplied with every requisite. The men carried lanterns with red globes. One would have to travel a long distance to find a better organized company or a more thoroughly equipped truck.

The Darktown Fire Brigade, under Foreman Robert M. Dorin [a member of the Honesdale band], secured an unlimited amount of applause, with their gorgeously arrayed Drum Major and fourteen musicians. It would be almost an impossibility to fully describe their uniforms and instruments, and the firemen were a good second in every respect. Such music was never before heard in our borough. The whole contingent, honorary members included, numbered about 40. Their steamer comprised a hogshead mounted on a buckboard wagon, with a stove pipe smoke stack, a boat pump, and everything else in keeping. The motive power of the engine was unique, consisting of a diminutive white pony and a large, raw-boned dark horse. The driver was Capt. Stephen F. Wells.

The Darktown police and foreman were mounted on hobbyhorses, and fully sustained their parts.

One Darktowner had a bottle some four feet high, and a tin dipper strapped to his back. One was fully attired as a woman and trundled a baby carriage with a large doll for an occupant, and led a little pickaninny by the hand. Another was fitted with stilts, mounted on a little pony, and kept step with the animal.

At the conclusion of the parade all participants repaired to the firemen's headquarters, and were liberally supplied with coffee, sandwiches, cigars, etc.

The armory was packed on Friday evening for the concert and reception of the firemen. "The Yachting Glee" and "The Night Alarm" were evidently the favorite numbers with the audience.[25]

Traditionally, outdoor band concerts are supposed to take place under a bandstand in the town square. But Honesdale has never had a permanent bandstand—possibly because of an old borough ordinance restricting the erection of permanent structures in Central Park, the most logical place. But whatever the reason, the bands and the citizens felt the need for such a bandstand very keenly. Throughout 1897 and 1898, the papers periodically reported that the band would play weekly concerts in the summer if a suitable structure were erected, and that various institutions would help to build one if a suitable place were found, and that this or that place would be perfect—Central Park, Riverside Park, the courthouse lawn. When a substantial temporary bandstand was erected in a vacant lot in the spring of 1899, however, it was immediately taken over by Lawyer's band; the Honesdale band played there only once—on a double bill with Lawyer's.

As a result, the band played its outdoor concerts from the ground, from someone's porch, or, on especially important occasions, from a temporary stand erected by the concert's sponsors. Perhaps the most gala of these band spectacles was a double concert of the Honesdale band and the Mozart band of Carbondale, held in Central Park, under the auspices of a local fraternal organization, on the evening of July 19, 1897. The *Herald's* report is eloquent and nostalgic.

The Park concert given on Monday evening by our Carbondale and Honesdale bands was greatly enjoyed by our people. The Mozarts, of Carbondale, were engaged by the Red Men to accompany their society to a picnic in Shohola on Tuesday, and as they were to be here over night, and were to play in Central Park, the ladies of the Improvement Society thought to turn an honest penny by furnishing refreshments to the listeners. Platforms, with arc lights had been arranged at both end[s] of the park for the musicians, and south of the fountain a large number of daintily dressed tables had been placed for the cream and other ices. Over them, on wires strung from tree to tree, were a myriad of Chinese lamps, all of which gave a very gay and festive air to the scene. Three or four thousand men, women and children were in and about the park during the two hours of the concert, while the porches of surrounding residences were alive with people enjoying the spectacle and the music. Our prettiest girls attended the tables as waitresses, and the ices were of the best. Red fires on the outside lighted up the drooping foliage and threw a beautiful, rosy, misty light on the happy young folks—and older ones as well—that patiently marched from one end of the park to the other in order to better hear the really excellent music of the bands as they alternately played. The programmes of both bands were mainly made up of "concert pieces," and were listened to with the greatest pleasure. The Mozart is generally recognized as one of the best bands in this vicinity. They have been most carefully drilled, and play with much taste. They have an excellent set of instruments, which showed by their polish the loving care bestowed upon them by their owners. Our own band, which is seldom heard except while on the march, surprised every one by their really good music. Altogether it was a matter of common remark that there had never been a more enjoyable outdoor entertainment in every way than the Red Men's concert.[26]

As the story says, the concert in the park was given by the Red Men as a prelude to, and advertisement for, their picnic at Shohola Glen the next day. Both events received enthusiastic coverage in the newspaper, and the Red Men had published a special advertising supplement in the *Independent* of July 17 (Fig. 2).

The picnic was also a success, despite less-than-perfect weather. The *Independent's* report shows the function of the bands before and during events of this kind; although it mentions only the Mozart band at the picnic, other papers indicated that the Honesdale band was there as well.

Tuesday morning the bands discoursed sweet music through our streets bright and early and although the sky was not as clear as it might have been the people commenced to wend their way to the cars. Soon the 16 coaches were well filled with merry excursionists. At Hawley 6 more coaches were added which necessitated making two sections of the train which arrived at the Glen at 10 and 10:20 a.m. respectively. Metzgar's orchestra [a small dance orchestra from Honesdale] began

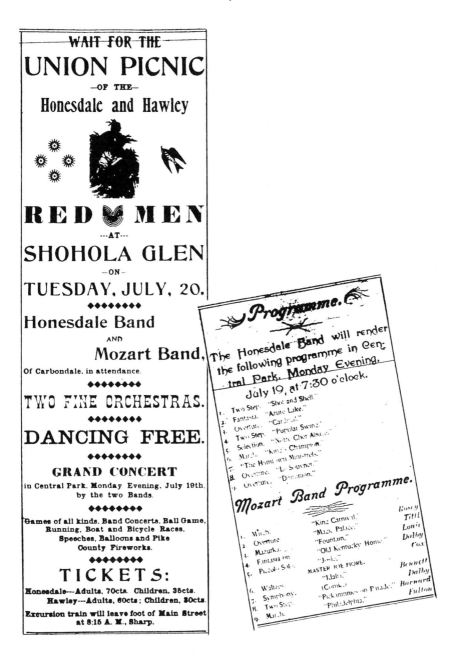

2. Advertisements for the Red Men's concert and picnic,
July 19-20, 1897 (*Wayne Independent*, July 17, 1897).

playing dance music as soon as they arrived and everything connected with the doings of the day was in full swing. The Mozart band furnished concert music and they did their share of the work to the satisfaction of all. There was a short shower about noon to dampen things but the spirits of the crowd were not effected [sic] by it. After a most pleasant day the excursion left on its return home at 6 p.m. first section, and 6:30 second section. . . . The total receipts were nearly $1,400 and the Red Men will clear about $375.[27]

In the winter, the band was less active, but by no means dormant. Outdoor concerts, obviously, were impossible, but in their place the band occasionally held dances, usually in the Armory, to raise money for instruments, uniforms, and music for the next summer. The dances were less newsworthy than the summertime concerts, receiving an announcement a few days before and, rarely, a little report afterward. But we find out very little about these dances from the newspapers when all we read is, for instance, "The dance given by the Honesdale band, in the Armory, on Christmas afternoon, was largely attended."[28]

Such events were the usual fare of the Honesdale band and its successors, Lawyer's band and the Maple City band. But sometimes extraordinary occurrences in town required the use of the band as well, and two of these included the Honesdale band.

On April 27, 1898, Company E of the Thirteenth Regiment, National Guards of Pennsylvania, left Honesdale to answer President McKinley's call for volunteers to fight in the Spanish-American War.[29] Their departure was a huge patriotic occasion, as described in the *Independent* on April 30.

The people of Honesdale and vicinity demonstrated on Wednesday afternoon that Co. E is not composed of "tin soldiers." Nobody can say that the enthusiasm and patriotism shown was not genuine. For weeks the boys have been ready for the call, "To arms," and when it came on Tuesday morning not a soldier faltered. . . .

The buildings from which "old glory" did not float all day were very few indeed. It was said that so many flags were never before unfurled in Honesdale town. "The streets were rife with people passing restlessly up and down" all the afternoon and at four o'clock they began congregating at the armory. The company were soon in marching order. The Honesdale band marched up Main street, picked up Capt. James Ham post, G.A.R. at the INDEPENDENT building, and joined the company at the armory. Captain Smith [of Co. E] gave a short, spicy talk which aroused enthusiasm to its highest pitch. At 5:15 amid repeated cheers, the firing of cannon just south of Irving Cliff, the company marched out of their armory. The line was formed thus:

Honesdale Band,
Capt. James Ham Post,
Ex members Co. E,
D.T. & Co. Shoemakers,
Major Whitney, Adjt. Wood,
Company E, N.G.P.,
Citizens.

Next to the Post flag was borne a banner on which was the motto, "Remember the Maine, Boys." B.C. Bryant carried the Durland Thompson & Co. flag. The line moved up Eleventh street to Third; Third to Ninth; Ninth to Main; Main to Fourth; over covered bridge to the Erie depot. It was a triumphal march. Cheers resounded and handkerchiefs fluttered the whole distance. It is estimated that from 3,000 to 5,000 people gathered about the station to give the boys a parting demonstration. Men, women and children were packed from the train back to the opposite side of the bridge. Every inch of space on top of the freight cars in the yard was occupied by men and boys.

At the depot, Capt. Smith spoke a few words, good-byes were said and the company boarded the cars. After a few minutes wait the train pulled out as a mighty cheer went up and the band played "Tenting To night."

Many of the faces of the gentler sex were tear moistened as they turned homeward from watching the train disappear around the bend and the smoke dissolve in air. Such partings must necessarily bring sadness in many homes yet there is hope that the boys will not become the targets of Spanish lead. It is believed that most of the service will be used to man the coast defenses.

The *Independent's* story, which ran to two full columns, went on to report that "The Honesdale band made no charge for escorting the company from the armory to the train. A subscription was taken by G. H. Seaman to pay the band but it was used for another purpose." The boys of Company E were also serenaded by the Hawley band as their train passed through Hawley, and they were met by Lawyer's band when they returned—as predicted, unscathed by Spanish fire—on March 13, 1899.

On September 15, 1898, Dr. S. C. Swallow, candidate for governor of Pennsylvania on the tickets of the Prohibition, People's, and Liberty parties, visited Wayne County on a campaign tour. After giving a speech at Farview in the afternoon, Swallow took a train to Honesdale and spoke in the evening at the courthouse. The Honesdale band was in attendance.[30] Not to show partisanship, however, the band played the very next day at a supper for the famous Philadelphia merchant John Wanamaker, who was in town to speak at a rally for the Democratic party.[31]

What was the music of the Honesdale band like? Were they any good? The questions are not easy to answer, because the newspapers tended to describe the band in polite terms that cannot be taken literally. But a close critical look at the sources does not give much cause for enthusiasm. Evidence is that the Honesdale band was good enough to entertain people who had not heard better, but that when Lawyer's band came to prominence in 1899 and provided music at a much higher level, the old Honesdale band was eclipsed in the public's mind, robbed of some of its members, and finally snuffed out.

Before the formation of Lawyer's band, the newspapers frequently referred to the Honesdale band in terms of jovial affection and local pride, as two separate entries from the *Citizen* of June 2, 1898 illustrate:

> The Honesdale band that made music for the parade in Scranton, heading the Honesdale societies in attendance, was the recipient of many happy compliments from press and public.

> The reason why the graceful bass drummer of the Honesdale band labors under the disadvantage of pounding a badly painted drum, is because the head of the best end of the regular old one in use since Washington crossed the Delaware, is *busted*.

On December 3, 1898, however, the *Independent* reported tersely that "A new cornet band is being organized in Honesdale." And a month later, the *Citizen* went into more detail: "The old Honesdale band has about been absorbed by the new Ideal band, which numbers close on to sixteen pieces. Many of the members of the old band have joined the new organization, which promises to be an up to-date band. This is just what our borough needs now. Bring out the band when the thousands of New York city excursionists shall visit us in the spring."[32]

Presumably both of these items refer to Lawyer's band, which was to be described in February as having seventeen pieces, and which was to have its debut in March. The use of the name "Ideal band" may be accurate (the band may have changed its name thereafter), or it might be a confusion with the Ideal orchestra, a five-piece dance ensemble in which the band's leader had already been playing the cornet. In any case, the article in the *Citizen* suggests that the new band was touting itself as a vast improvement over the old band and that it managed to lure away some of its members—a claim and a practice unlikely to foster good relations.

The rivalry between the two bands was confirmed at the first concert of Lawyer's band on March 17, 1899. Although both the Honesdale and Hawley bands were invited to participate and assist with the festivity, only the latter appeared.

The Honesdale band and Lawyer's band first appeared together in the Memorial Day parade of 1899. The *Independent's* article on that celebration (above, pp. 30-33) describes how the two bands divided the duties formerly taken by the Honesdale band alone. In a separate item in the same issue, the paper tactfully declined to choose between them. "Honesdale's two bands rendered good service on Memorial Day. It would take an expert bandman to say which played the better. The Honesdale band has been in existence for a long time. For a new organization, Lawyer's band do exceedingly well. They looked very neat in their new uniforms. In the afternoon they played at the ball grounds."[33]

The enthusiasm that greeted Lawyer's band in the summer of 1899, and the great success of their concert series in the new bandstand in Russell Park, will be chronicled later. Still, the Honesdale band hung on: at the end of June there was even talk of building a separate bandstand for them:"A movement is on foot looking to the erection of a band stand on the bank of Park Lake, at the head of 2d street. The services of the Honesdale band will probably be secured for weekly concerts."[34]

This stand was never built, and the Honesdale band continued to use whatever it could find. On July 31-August 1, 1899, the Red Men had another concert and picnic, this time featuring both of the bands of Honesdale. The advertisement and program are shown in Figure 3—note that the new band's name is in slightly larger type than the old.[35] The *Herald* reported on the concert with enthusiasm:

The band concert at Russell Park on Monday evening was a hummer. An extra platform was erected upon the south end of the park for the use of the Honesdale Band, Lawyer's Band

3. Advertisements for the Red Men's concert and picnic,
July 31 and August 1, 1899 (*Wayne Independent*, July 29, 1899).

occupying the stand at the north end. The whole affair was in charge of the Red Men, who used it to the best advantage in advertising their picnic of the next day. The grounds were early filled with people, as were the adjoining streets and windows and roofs of onlooking buildings. Roman candles filled the air with shooting balls, and red fires cast a beautiful, if lurid, color over all. A balloon rose among the stars, which at the last it so much resembled. The bands did their best, and were cheered to the echo. Their repertoire was extensive so there was little wait between the numbers. Such a contest must stimulate the members of both organizations to great efforts and the whole affair seemed to give so much pleasure to our citizens present as to promise a liberal support to the performers in a pecuniary way. We now have a good start for two bands that may in time give Honesdale a widely known additional attraction.[36]

The *Herald* suggests that having two bands in town might be a good idea, but in fact the handwriting was already on the wall. In the summer of 1899, the newspapers reported fourteen performances by Lawyer's band and only five by the Honesdale band. And on the same day as the *Herald* article above, the *Citizen* opined, "What delightful music Honesdale's two bands would make if united into one organization." The last known performance of the Honesdale band took place on September 27, 1899:

The Honesdale Liederkranz assisted by Gustave Hilmer, of the Olympia theatre, St. Louis, Mo., and the Honesdale cornet band, held their first entertainment for the season of 1899-1900, on Wednesday evening. A social dance followed the splendid musical program:

Overture	Honesdale Band
Wander March	Liederkranz
How Fair Thou Art	William Schloss
The Gold Diggers	Gustave Hilmer
Selection	Honesdale Band
Malen Abend	Liederkranz
Bell Song	Gustave Hilmer
A Funny Tragedy	Fritz Breidenstein
Selection	Honesdale Band
The Sorrowing Widower, song	G. Hilmer
Two Little Fools From the Circus,	Phil and Bob
March	Honesdale Band[37]

When the Maple City band was formed the following spring, the Honesdale band was evidently much depleted: the new organization contained fourteen musicians from Lawyer's band and only seven from the Honesdale band.[38]

LAWYER'S BAND

From the news items quoted previously, we know that Lawyer's band was organized sometime around the beginning of December 1898,[39] and that by early January it numbered about sixteen members, some of them evidently defectors from the Honesdale band.[40] And at the beginning of February 1899, all three newspapers began heralding the arrival and progress of the new band:

> Lawyer's band of 17 pieces, a new musical organization, is rapidly improving. They meet twice a week for practice, and propose next summer to give a series of free concerts in our parks. Give the boys encouragement.[41]

> Edwin Lawyer is the leader of a band of seventeen persons who play upon portable musical instruments. They meet frequently for practice and the people of our place may expect to hear pleasant things from them ere long.[42]

> Lawyer's new band is now fully organized, and promises to be a fine addition to the list of local musical associations here. Capt. Jas Ham Post has generously loaned the band its base drum.[43]

The leader of the band, Edwin Lawyer, was a cutter in a shoe factory and a cornetist, although apparently not a member of the Honesdale band; at any rate, his name does not appear in the roster given by the *Independent* of April 21, 1897 (pp. 27-28). Lawyer may, however, have moved to Honesdale only shortly thereafter: he, his wife, and their two children are all listed in the 1900 census returns as having been born out of state,[44] and no reference to him appears in the newspapers of early 1897. His entrance into the local musical scene apparently took place at a banquet for the Honesdale Masonic Lodge on December 2, 1897—note that the ensemble is newly formed: "The Ideal orchestra made its debut under the leadership of John Stopford and rendered several excellent selections. The orchestra is composed of the following young men: John Stopford, 1st violin; M. J. Hanlan, 2d violin; Charles Brown, flute; Edward Lawyer, cornet; Fred List, piano."[45]

Throughout the winter and spring of 1899, Lawyer's new band planned a gala debut for St. Patrick's Day.

> The Armory will be occupied on the evening of St. Patrick's Day, Friday, March 17th, by Lawyer's full band, who will give a promenade concert and ball. The new cornet band of about twenty-five pieces, promises to be a credit to Honesdale, and second to no band in this part of the State, and as they promise to furnish summer evening concerts, during the coming season, should be encouraged by our citizens. On the occasion of this concert and ball, they expect to be assisted by the regular Honesdale band, so well and favorably known, and also by the Hawley cornet band, both organizations having been invited to assist.[46]

But on March 13, Company E returned from the war, and the band was unveiled four days ahead of schedule.

> Standing room at the Gravity station, on the adjacent streets and sidewalks, was at a premium on Monday evening, long before the arrival of the late train, the occasion being the return of some thirty members of Co. E, 13th Penn'a Volunteers, from Augusta, Ga. It seemed as though the whole town had turned out. They were all a self-appointed committee of reception, the most enthusiastic among them being the omnipresent small boy. Lawyer's band patriotically volunteered their services for the occasion, and delighted hundreds by their music, it being their first appearance in public. . . . That [Co. E] did not see active service and participate in numerous conflicts, was no fault of theirs. They enlisted from the most patriotic motives, and are justly entitled to a full measure of praise.[47]

The St. Patrick's Day dance was a great success nonetheless, but the Honesdale band was conspicuously absent.

> The first promenade concert and ball given by Lawyer's band, took place last Friday evening at the armory. The new band was assisted in its concert and dance program by the Hawley band and by Freeman's well known orchestra [possibly a later incarnation of the Ideal orchestra]. The Lawyer band met the guests from Hawley, who came in private conveyances, at the down town covered bridge, and together the two bands marched up Front street to inspiring music, followed by a large crowd of enthusiastic music lovers, all bent on closing up St. Patrick's Day in a lively manner. The program at the armory

opened with some fine selections by both the Lawyer and
Hawley bands. The former organization was greatly aided in
its renditions by Fred. C. Gill, popular trombonist, late of the
band of the 13th Penn'a Volunteers. Mr. Gill is a finished and
talented performer on this difficult instrument, and his advice
and instructions are greatly appreciated by the members of the
new Honesdale band. After the short concert of the two brass
bands, Freeman's orchestra of ten pieces appeared on the
platform, and their music was simply entrancing, the big
auditorium, with its hundreds of similing faces and nimble
feet, all keeping time to the beautiful strains. The floor, though
large, was entirely filled with dancers, who one and all enjoyed
the happy occasion. Supper was served behind attractive
screens put up in one of the front corners of the room.[48]

Lawyer's Band, composed of eighteen members, held its first
benefit ball at the armory last Friday evening and it was a
great success both in music and proceeds. Before going to the
armory the bands discoursed some fine music in the streets,
the Hawley band having accepted an invitation to participate in
the exercises of the evening. Lawyer's band, taking into consid-
eration the short time it has been in existence, has made
splendid progress. The concert and ball were largely attended
and the boys feel greatly encouraged by the liberal patronage
their first effort received, the net proceeds having amounted
to about $75. They have secured the services of Fred. Gill of
the Thirteenth Regiment Band as director. The money taken
in by the sale of tickets is to be used to purchase uniforms.[49]

Fred Gill, mentioned in both articles, was a member of a musical
family from Seelyville, a village just west of Honesdale. Several of
his brothers also played instruments in various bands, and he
himself had been a member of the Honesdale band in 1897.[50] As the
news stories indicate, he had just returned from the Thirteenth
Regiment band of Scranton;[51] in early April he opened a machine
and bicycle shop in Honesdale.[52] He acted as musical director of the
new band and was frequently featured as soloist on their programs.
  On April 20, 1899, the *Citizen* and *Herald* both reported that Jacob
Freeman and Son, a firm of local clothiers, were busy making
eighteen uniforms, and in a few weeks they were completed: "The
new uniforms for Lawyer's band have arrived. They were furnished
by J. Freeman & Son, and are very neat in appearance. The cloth is
fine and of good quality, color—green, with black trimmings, caps

4. Lawyer's band, by the Wayne County Courthouse, summer 1899 (collection of Margaret Murray).

the same color, with bullion chin straps. The cut is that of the fatigue style of the regular United States army."[53]

A splendid photograph survives showing Lawyer's band in the summer of 1899 (Fig. 4). The new uniforms are just as described in the papers, with one added detail—the name "Lawyer's" embroidered on the caps. This sort of uniform, with the short, unadorned jacket and soft, visored cap, was gradually replacing the more ornate uniforms of earlier decades; it shows the influence of the professional bands of the day.[54] Its use by Lawyer's band, in contrast to the elaborate braids and epaulettes so popular among earlier bands, shows that Lawyer's band was trying to be au courant sartorially as well as musically.

In the picture are seventeen musicians, with instruments (plus a man with neither instrument nor uniform): a piccolo or fife, a B-flat clarinet, four B-flat cornets, three altos, two valve trombones, a slide trombone (probably Fred Gill), a tenor or baritone, a tuba, a snare drum, a bass drum, and cymbals. This instrumentation, an exceptionally balanced one, will be discussed in more detail in chapter 7.

The functions of Lawyer's band were similar to those already outlined for the Honesdale band: Table 4 shows the usual run of concerts, picnics, and parades. Perhaps the most noticeable departure from the Honesdale band's tradition was a regular concert series in Russell Park, a park apparently created specifically with this band in mind, although it was used by the Maple City band in later years.

The Honesdale band never had a bandstand of its own, despite many requests and suggestions by various voices in the community. For some reason, however, Lawyer's band managed to get results within a few months of its founding. In mid-April 1899, the Honesdale Improvement Association, in publishing a report of its annual meeting, remarked regretfully that "the Band Pagoda is still to be built, and band concerts inaugurated."[55] But within a few weeks, the *Independent* was reporting that Lawyer's band had succeeded where the Improvement Association, and years of importuning by the Honesdale band and doubtless its predecessors, had failed:

How delightful! We are to have music during some of the coming summer evenings. On our shady streets we can loiter or sit on our piazzas and let the sounds of the band's sweet notes creep into our ears. Of the many arts, good music is the one to raise the soul above all earthly storms. Lawyer's fine

Table 4.
Performances of Lawyer's Band

Date	Location	Event (Sponsor)
		1899
March 13	D&H station	Return of Co. E from war
March 17	Armory	Concert and dance (Lawyer's band)
April 3	Upper Main St.	Playing in street?
April 3	Armory	Ball (Red Men)
May 5	J.W. Kesler's lawn	Concert
May 16	Russell Park	Concert
May 23	Russell Park	Concert
May 30	Honesdale	Memorial Day parade, cemetery exercises
May 30	Athletic park	Baseball game (Honesdale vs. Wyoming Seminary)
June 7	J.W. Seamans's lawn	Lawn festival (Ladies of Maccabees)
June 16	Russell Park	Concert
June 23	Russell Park	Concert
June 30	Russell Park	Concert
July 4	Bellevue Park	Picnic (Texas #4 Fire Co.)
July 14	Russell Park	Concert
July 21	Russell Park	Concert (IOOF)
July 22	Farview	IOOF reunion (also in streets of Honesdale before, IOOF Hall after)
July 31	Russell Park	Concert (Red Men)
August 1	Lake Ariel	Excursion (Red Men)
August 11	Russell Park	Concert
August 18	Russell Park	Concert
August 25	Russell Park	Concert
September 1	Russell Park	Concert
September 7	Russell Park	Concert
September 14	Russell Park	Concert
September 26	Armory	Concert and ball (Lawyer's band)
October 5	Scranton	Fire Parade (with Forest City F.D.)
October 12	Honesdale	Parade (Protection Engine Co. #3)
October 20	Baptist church	Musical festival (Baptist church)
		1900
February 17	Opera House, White Mills	Concert and dance (W. Mills Pastime Club)

All locations Honesdale except Farview, Lake Ariel, Scranton, and White Mills.

band offered to play one evening each week, weather permitting, for the entertainment of the townspeople, if Mr. Russell would erect a suitable platform on his lot at the rear of the National Bank. This he has kindly consented to do. Surely our community owe to Mr. Russell a hearty vote of thanks.[56]

Russell Park was to become an important part of Honesdale's musical life for the next several years; unfortunately, however, we know little about it. The lot, on the west side of Second Street (now Church Street) between Seventh and Eighth, had been the site of a small side basin of the canal, although this had apparently been filled in even before the canal's abandonment: an 1897 insurance map shows the whole eastern half of the block as vacant.[57] In 1898, when the idea to put a bandstand there was first brought up, the area was described as a lumber yard,[58] further evidence that this was a little piece of industrial land, recently vacated, in a prime location, whose use after the canal had yet to be decided (Fig. 5).

In any case, it seems clear that Mr. Russell's improvements were regarded as temporary, and that the new park (only a block away from Central Park) would within a few years be sold off for building. Unfortunately, no picture of the park as such survives, but the bandstand is barely visible in two photographs of other nearby buildings. In these tantalizing little glimpses, the bandstand appears to have been on the northern edge of the lot, along Eighth Street, and to have been a small, simple wooden platform, hexagonal or perhaps octagonal, with a railing but no roof.

The bandstand in Russell Park was used by a number of visiting organizations over the next several summers in addition to Lawyer's band. Its continued existence was always somewhat doubtful; in June of 1900, the *Herald* reported that the land was being eyed by "a prominent department store,"[59] and a few months later the *Independent* said, "That nice band pagoda at the rear of the National bank has not been occupied this year."[60] But the bandstand was used sporadically at least through 1901, and indeed was still in existence as late as 1903, when it appears in a photograph of the Lutheran Church under construction.

The career of Lawyer's band at the new bandstand in the new park was inaugurated with a concert on May 16, 1899:

We all enjoy listening to music because it pleases us and does not tell us of any unpleasant things. In spite of the chilly air of Tuesday night a throng gathered within hearing of the fine selections rendered by Lawyer's Band. It was the organization's first appearance in the new pagoda erected for them by

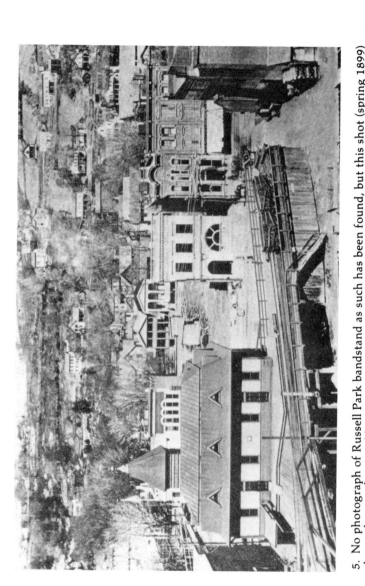

5. No photograph of Russell Park bandstand as such has been found, but this shot (spring 1899) shows the site that would soon become the park—the vacant lot and board piles behind and to the left of the Wayne County Savings Bank under construction (Wayne County Historical Society).

Mr. Russell. The listeners made favorable comments on the concert and Mr. Gill's trombone solo, "Love's Old Sweet Song." At the close Mr. Russell refreshed the band boys with lemonade and Mr. Hoover treated them to light refreshments. On Memorial Day the members of the band will appear in their new uniforms.[61]

The Russell Park series continued, at more or less weekly intervals, through mid-September. Most performances were not so newsworthy as the double bill with the Honesdale band for the Red Men on July 31 (pp. 39-41), and the papers describe few of them in detail.

Fortunately, however, Lawyer's band had a good public relations manager, and occasionally their concerts were announced in the paper with a program. Six such programs have survived.

[Kesler's lawn, May 5, 1899]
PART I.

March—Salute to Trenton...................... Albert Winkler
Overture—Little Beauty ....Ben J. Dale
Loving Hearts Gavotte........................ Theo. M. Tobani
March—Princeton Cadets .... W. Durand

PART II.

Selection—Waiting for You, Sweetheart .... M.D. Pelmer
Galop—Volante Galop .... A. Catozzi
Heap Big Injin War Dance...................... Geo. Southwell
  Dedicated to Buffalo Bill's Wild West
March—Valley Forge .... J.H. Wadworth[62]

[Russell Park, June 16, 1899]

March, Masked Battery ....W. Buckley
Song, Banner of the Sea .... arr. by Sousa
Overture, The Cracker Jack .... Mackie
March, The Silver Jubilee .... A. Winkler
Selection, In Old Madrid .... Laurendeau
Overture, Little Beauty .... Benj. Dale
March, Jasper Jenkins Cake Walk ....H. Vogel
Galop, The Club .... Laurendeau[63]

[Farview, July 21, 1899]

March, "Champion"............................Rockwell
Overture, "Little Beauty". .... Dule [Dale]
Trombone solo, "Love's Old Sweet Song"
              Fred C. Gill
March, "Silver Jubilee". .... Winkler
Waltz, Dannie Murphy's Daughter...................... Engle
Medley, "Yankee Hash". .... Miller

Waltz, "Just One Girl". .... Mackee [Mackie]
March, "Lehigh Valley". .... Scholl[64]

[Russell Park, July 31, 1899]
March—Silver Jubilee .... Winkler
War Dance—Heap Big Injun .... Southwell
Trombone Solo—"In Old Madrid". .... Troterrer
Cake Walk—Dance of the Dofunnys .... Walker
Schottisch—Comique .... Miller
March—Salute to Trenton. .... Winkler
Cake Walk—"Marfy and Lize". .... Miller
Medley—Yankee Hash .... Miller[65]

[Armory, September 26, 1899]
The Crackerjack Medley Overture .... Mackie
The James Park March. .... Miller
Intermezzo Sinfonico .... Mascagni
          Cavalleria Rusticana
Masked Battery Q S. .... Buckley
Love's Old Sweet Song, tromb'e solo. .... Malloy
Jasper Jenkins' De Cake Walk Coon .... Vogel
          Character Two-Step.
Just One Girl, waltz. .... Mackie
Serenade, the Old Church Organ. .... Chambers[66]

[Opera House, White Mills, February 17, 1900]
Overture—Cracker Jacks .... Mackie
March—James Park .... Miller
Cornet Solo—Love's Old Sweet Song .... Molloy
          Edward Lawyer.
March—Silver Jubilee .... Winkler
Overture—"Waiting for You, Sweetheart" ....
Trombone Solo—Romance. .... Bennett
          F.C. Gill.
March—True to the Flag .... F.V. Blon
Overture—Yankee Harp .... Miller[67]

One unusual performance by Lawyer's band was a concert given on October 20, 1899 for the Baptist church. Here, instead of playing with another band or by themselves, the band shared the bill with a variety of local talent.

The music festival under the auspices of the P.A.S, of the Baptist church, on Friday night last, was a grand success. The excellent program was rendered to a large and appreciative audience. The programs were in the form of an invitation which stated that the object of the entertainment was to procure the wherewithal to purchase the winter's fuel and each person was requested to bring the price of 100 pounds of coal in a silken bag which was enclosed. The Society received $66.01 in the little sacks and $14 from the sale of homemade candy.

The program opened with two selections by Lawyer's band, the celebrated "Silver Jubilee March," and "Waiting, Sweetheart, for You." The band was stationed in the gallery and the applause they received demonstrated that the best people of Honesdale appreciate good band music. Mrs. Wm. Clark sang "Out On the Deep." Mrs. Clark has a good contralto voice and her selection was well rendered. Her accompanist was Miss Carrie A. Kalisch. Isabel C. Harroun, accompanied by Mrs. Jessie Dolmetsch, captured the audience by singing "A Simple Little String" in such a pleasing manner that she was encored. Mrs. H. J. Whalen recited "Skip's Ride" in a manner that disclosed the fact that singing is not her only accomplishment. She has a full, clear, round tone of voice and in both singing and speaking every word is heard and understood. "Io Vivo, E T'amo," was the title of the duet so well rendered by Mr. and Mrs. A. K. Harroun. They would not respond to an encore. F. C. Gill's trombone solo was well executed and heartily applauded, as was also Mrs. Dolmetsch's piano solo.

The second part opened with "Intermezzo Sinfonico" by the band. Mesdames A. C. Tolley and T. A. Crossley maintained their popularity with Honesdale music lovers in their duet "Good Bye, Ye Flow'rets Fair." Miss Grace Whitney was their pianist. A German legend was told in poetry by Miss Eleanor S. Kimble. The story was well interpreted, clearly enunciated and gave ample scope to her elocutionary ability. "A Haydn Trio" was sweetly executed by Dr. E. W. Burns, violin, A. M. Leine, 'cello, and Mrs. Dolmetsch, piano. The harmony and blending of the tones of the three instruments were perfect. The baritone solo "Just as of Old," showed the great compass of A. K. Harroun's voice. As a soloist Mr. Harroun has few equals in this section. The last number on the program was the serenade, "The Old Church Organ" by the band.

After the entertainment the band was given an oyster supper in the parsonage. Post prandial addresses were made by Rev. H. J. Whalen, F. P. Kimble, Edward Lawyer, F. C. Gill, R. M. Doran and Dr. E. W. Burns. Just before leaving the band played a serenade in front of the parsonage.[68]

Lawyer's band also participated in parades, both official and private. We have already seen examples of both: the former in the Memorial Day parade of 1899 (pp. 30-33), and the latter in the procession through town before their St. Patrick's Day debut (pp. 43-44). Whatever the size of the parade itself, its audience was always large. But one of the smaller parades, a part of the Red Men's picnic of July 31, 1899, achieved fame of another kind.

As Lawyer's band was parading down Second street, Monday night, Edwin Bidwell and George Vandermark were standing near the street opposite the M. E. church, when a horse became frightened by a red light [presumably carried by someone in the procession] and sprang on the curbing. Edwin was struck by the breast of the horse and thrown to the ground where he was tramped upon, receiving a cut and several bruises about his head and face. The wheel of the wagon ran over his arm. His companion received only slight injuries though the wheels of the same vehicle passed over his chest and lower limbs.[69]

All the evidence—the number of concerts, the proportion of members in the succeeding Maple City band, the tone of the newspaper articles—suggests that Lawyer's band was the dominant band in Honesdale almost as soon as it was formed. Note also that they were invited to a parade in Scranton by the Forest City Fire Department on October 5, 1899; there is no record of the Honesdale band's being engaged by an out-of-town organization, except for their attendance at one Fourth of July celebration in Narrowsburg, a village without a band of its own. It is, of course, still impossible to judge the band by any external standard, but clearly the rise of Lawyer's band was a step ahead for music in Honesdale. For their part, the newspapers were enthusiastic in their praise of the new band.

The opening outdoor concert at Russell Park on Tuesday night was attended by hundreds of people, who by their quiet attention showed their pleasure in the music. Many of the selections were liberally applauded. The band was under the excellent direction of Mr. Fred. Gill. The organization is young yet, but we prophesy that in a short time it will not only be a pride and pleasure to this community, but to this section of the State as well. We hope next to hear from our older and well known "Honesdale Band." Competition is the life of music as well as of trade.[70]

Many encomiums were bestowed upon Lawyer's band while in Scranton last week attending the state firemen's convention. The band accompanied the Forest City firemen and the latter organization was well pleased with the music rendered. Bands that were not engaged early in the season obtained large sums of money for their service. Lawyer's was among the latter and consequently received more money for their service than any other Honesdale band that ever left town. Mr. Lawyer has received several letters from city people inquiring the name of one of the popular marches played by the band while in the Electric City. This is certainly a high compliment and shows that our boys were noticed.[71]

Lawyer's band has certainly made a commendable record. It was organized about nine months ago and at this time it is well uniformed, has a good set of instruments, and is out of debt. But what must be most pleasing of all to Messrs. Lawyer and Gill is the popular favor the band is receiving. This fact shows that a band loses nothing by being accommodating to the people who patronize good music.[72]

But despite all these nice words, Lawyer's band didn't last very long: its first concert and its last were less than a year apart. The reasons for the early demise of the band are perhaps not all clear; one problem may have been a sudden lack of leadership. Lawyer's band became part of the Maple City band in April of 1900; and it is surely no coincidence that Fred Gill, their instructor and trombone soloist, had moved out of town late in March: "Mr. Fred. Gill left Honesdale on Friday last to join a circus band at Columbus, Ohio. Every one will greatly regret his departure, as his absence will be such a decided loss to our band and orchestra. We hope, however, that our bandsmen will arrange in some way to give us just as good, if not better, open air concerts than we were favored with last summer."[73]

Edwin Lawyer's name is also notably absent from the roster of the Maple City band given in *Illustrated Wayne*. It disappears from the Honesdale Philharmonic about this time, too: Lawyer played in a concert on March 15, but not in the next one, on November 13. Evidently he stayed in Honesdale—he was counted in the 1900 census that June[74]—but he wasn't playing his cornet in public any more. One is tempted to imagine some sort of power struggle or a falling-out between the band and its founder, but a host of other reasons, personal, medical, or mundane, may have contributed to his decision. In any case, the departure of Lawyer and Gill seems to be associated with the merger of their band with the old Honesdale band in the spring of 1900.

THE MAPLE CITY BAND

The formation of the Maple City band was announced in the *Citizen* of April 26, 1900: "Fourteen members of Lawyer's band and seven of the old Honesdale band, have been consolidated into one organization, the Maple City band. They are perfecting arrangements for a home talent minstrel performance, to be given some time next month, under the direction of J. H. Carroll and R. M. Dorin."

The *Independent* of May 2 announced that this performance would be held on May 14 in the Opera House, but no mention is made about the minstrel show after that, and probably it never actually took place. Even if it did, it would not have been a real band performance in the usual sense, and it should surely not be regarded as the debut of the Maple City band.

The proportion of members from Lawyer's band and the Honesdale band suggests that the former was the dominant force in the new organization, an impression confirmed by the phrasing of an appeal for funds in the *Independent* a few weeks later—note that Lawyer's band and the Maple City band are not really distinguished:

> Last year people enjoyed the open air concerts given by Lawyer's band. Those concerts were free to all but the band boys themselves who were obliged to purchase new music frequently and spend time in rehearsals. Now how much are the efforts made by the band appreciated? Last year F. C. Gill was the instructor. He is not here this year and the band must be at the expense of hiring an instructor. Are those concerts appreciated to the extent that people will contribute a purse toward meeting the necessary expense? If this is not done nobody can pass any criticism if there are no open air concerts. . . . The band was generous last year, and it is not fair to ask them to do all this again for nothing.[75]

On Memorial Day in 1900, the ceremonies in Honesdale were held without music, allegedly for the first time ever. The *Independent* explained: "The absence of the band was the cause of many remarks about town. The truth of the matter as stated by some of the members of the [G.A.R.] post is that it is not sufficiently strong in membership or financially to pay $40 for a band. The expenses of the day were about $65 and that drained the treasury. Had this fact been known the citizens of Honesdale would doubtless have contributed the amount necessary to have kept our band at home. We hope this will be done next year. Let our people have the matter in mind."[76]

As an ironic result, the first performance of the Maple City band was at the ceremonies in Waymart. The news story, unfortunately, is not very informative: "Memorial Day was celebrated in a proper manner at Waymart. Beside the usual ceremonies incident to the day the Patriotic Sons of America had a flag raising. A fine pole was erected on the corner of the school grounds with appropriate exercises. The introductory was conducted by Rev. William Rawling's, followed by Rev. L. W. Karschner. W. H. Lee, esq., of Honesdale, was orator of the day and we are informed that his address was a most excellent one. Mr. Lee is a logical and eloquent speaker. The Maple City band furnished music for the occasion."[77]

Illustrated Wayne, whose first edition was published later that same year, provides a brief factual account of the band's origins and membership.

> The Maple City Band was organized in April, 1900, by the consolidation of the Honesdale and Lawyer bands. The former had been in existence about twenty years. The members of this band are Andrew Cowles, Wm. Geltner, Judson Keen, John Bussa, H. W. Rehbein, August Lobbs, Michael Fannen, John W. Broad, Wm. Quick, R. M. Dorin, Henry Miller, Anthony Lenz, Robt. Murray, Geo. Schiessler, Rudolph Lobbs, Charles Marsh, J. Doetsch, Charles Guinder, R. Armbruster and D. Gill. The officers are R. M. Dorin, president; Robert Murray, corresponding secretary; A. Lenz, financial secretary; A. Cowles, treasurer; D. Gill, conductor.[78]

This roster, appearing as it does in a census year, is a valuable clue to more general questions of the personnel of these bands; it will be discussed in more detail in chapter 6. It is worth noting, however, that the band had a rather elaborate hierarchy of officers to take care of its business. David Gill, the musical director of the Maple City band, was the brother of Fred Gill of Lawyer's band. David had left town in June of 1898 to join another brother, John, in Walter Main's circus band,[79] but he seems to have been back shortly thereafter, as he played drums in the Honesdale Philharmonic the following March.[80] Whether he played the drums or another instrument in the Maple City band is unclear—he may have acted as conductor only.

6. The Maple City Band, by the Wayne County Courthouse, ca. 1900 (Wayne County Historical Society; also published in *Illustrated Wayne*, p. 139).

Illustrated Wayne also prints a photograph of the band standing just north of the courthouse in the summer of 1900 (Fig. 6). It shows seventeen men, most of them young, many of them familiar from the picture of Lawyer's band. Most of the musicians seem to be wearing the uniform from Lawyer's band, with the name removed from the cap; three have on another uniform with braid on the chest, probably the uniform of the Honesdale band; and one is wearing a frock coat and vest. Apparently, then, the new band did not at this point (it was only a few months old) have its own uniforms, but wore the uniforms of its predecessors. Whether this looked strange is hard to tell from the black-and-white prints: Lawyer's band had green uniforms, but the color of the Honesdale band's uniforms has not been recorded. In comparing the photograph with that of Lawyer's band, it is evident that the drum is the same; the word "Lawyer's" has simply been replaced with "Maple City."

Not all of the instruments show clearly, but an E-flat clarinet, a B-flat clarinet, three B-flat cornets, an alto horn, some sort of mellophone, a valve trombone, three tenor or baritone horns, a tuba, bass and snare drums, and cymbals are discernable.[81]

As Table 5 shows, the Maple City band continued to use the Russell Park bandstand throughout 1900 and 1901, although, for some reason, rather sparingly; the band seems to have been more mobile than its predecessors, playing in a wide variety of places rather than settling down in one. A good example of this imaginative use of the band is a lawn social held by the Honesdale Catering Company in late June 1900 for the Indian Famine Fund:

> The entertainment at Riverside Park in aid of the Indian Famine Fund was a great success. Hundreds of Chinese lanterns suspended over the trees bordering "Lover's Walk" and reflected in the water, gave the park a fairy-like appearance. Boats laden with merry-makers gliding up and down the lake, now disappearing beneath the bridge and now floating from under the dark arch, gave the scene a Venetian coloring. The park was filled with promenaders; the benches under the trees occupied by jolly groups. The excellent band—which by the way gave its services gratuitously—furnished charming music throughout the evening.[82]

Programs were printed in the newspapers for two concerts of the Maple City Band:

[Lake Lodore, August 5, 1900]

March, Teddy's Terrors .... Crosby

Table 5.
Performances of the Maple City Band

Date	Location	Event (Sponsor)
		1900
May 30	Waymart	Memorial Day exercises (Patriotic Sons of America)
June 9	Riverside Park	Lawn festival (Honesdale Catering Co.)
c. June 23	Riverside Park	Entertainment (Indian Famine Fund)
July 4	Honesdale	4th of July parade
July 21	Riverside Park	Excursion from Scranton (Hsdl. Catering Co.)
August 5	Lake Lodore	Concert
August 21	Russell Park	Concert (Knights of Columbus)
August 22	Lake Lodore	Picnic (Knights of Columbus)
August 29	Russell Park	Concert
August 30	Hsdl.; Lodore	Parade; excursion (Methodist Sunday School)
September 3	Lake Lodore	Labor Day picnic
c. September 10	J. Keen's house, Keene	Birthday serenade for Judson Keen
September 30	Binghamton	Excursion (Erie R.R.)
October 1	D&H station	Arrival of first Erie train
October 2	Armory	Social
October 10	Court House	Political rally (Democratic party)
October 27	Court House	Parade, rally (Democratic party)
November 14*	Armory	Hop (Maple City band)
		1901
May 30	Honesdale	Memorial Day parade, courthouse exercises
May 30	Armory	Dance (Maple City band)
June 30 (& ff.)	Lake Lodore	Sacred concerts
August 2	Lake Lodore	Sunday School picnic
August 4	J. Keen's house, Keene	Party (Maple City band)
August 5	Russell Park	Concert (Red Men)
August 6	Lake Lodore	Picnic (Red Men)
August 21	Lake Lodore	7-County Veteran Reunion
c. August 30	Street, Armory	Parade and dance (Maple City band)
September 4	Carbondale	Carbondale Semicentennial Parade (Protection Engine Co. #3)
September 10	City Hall	Smoker (Protection Engine Co. #3)
Sept. 24—Oct. 1	Fairgrounds	Concerts (Wayne County Fair)
September 25	Armory	Dance (Maple City band)
October 18	Honesdale	Parade (Protection Engine Co. No. 3)
November 12	Armory	Social (Maple City band)

*story says "Honesdale band."
All locations Honesdale except Waymart, Lake Lodore, Keene, Binghamton, and Carbondale.

Overture, The Crackerjack .... Mackie
Concert Waltz, Minerva............................... Miller
March, The Blue and Gray .... Chattaway
Serenade, The Old Church Organ ....Chambers
Overture, Olympia .... Miller
Cake Walk, Levi Jackson .... Winkler[83]

Program of the Knights of Columbus concert to be held on
Tuesday evening, Aug. 21, in Russell park: March, The Citizen
Soldier, Tayron; selection, The Irish Artist, Vernon; baritone
solo, Euphonious, Miller, by John Broad; march, Union Forever,
Scouton; serenade, Peaceful Slumbers, Miller; overture, Olym-
pia, Miller; march, The Nation's Pride, Scouton.[84]

Perhaps in compensation for its bandless Memorial Day in 1900,
Honesdale celebrated Independence Day that summer. The festivities were still not a great success, but at least the band was there.

Honesdale's celebration consisted of an all night's fire
cracker rattle and jubilee among "the boys" and a parade
during the following forenoon. Circulars had been printed and
scattered far and wide, telling of a grand celebration in Honesdale. It came off only in part, the general manager of the affair
claiming he was detained abroad by a sick horse (?) and did not
arrive in town until 3 p.m. on the day on which the great show
was advertised to come off. Messrs. J. S. Brown, C. G. Armbru-
ster and John Kuhbach took the matter in hand, secured
enough money to pay the band and arranged for the parade.
The horse show and athletic sports advertised did not take
place.
At nine o'clock the Honesdale band [i.e., Maple City band]
21 strong, appeared in their natty uniforms. The parade was
formed on Main street opposite Ninth, as follows:

Geo. H. Seaman, Mounted Marshall.
Honesdale Band.
St Francis Pioneer Corps.
Wm. Decker, Flag Bearer,
Alert Alert Hook and Ladder Co.
Alert Truck.
Glass Cutter's Union.

The parade marched through the principal streets of the
town. The Glass Cutters had 87 men in line.

There was quite a multitude of people in town and in the afternoon there was a large gathering at Athletic park but the crowd was disappointed so far as the horse show and athletic sports were concerned.[85]

The Maple City band, like its predecessors, also marched in smaller parades through town before picnics and concerts. And like Lawyer's band, it also caused a minor accident—also right before a Red Men's picnic:

On Tuesday morning, as Wm. Baird, a son of John J. Baird, of Tracyville, was driving down Main street, the horse, belonging to J.P. Dunn, took fright at a passing locomotive, near the D.&H. office. At the same time, the Maple City band was playing at the corner of Main and 8th streets, preparatory to the Red Men's picnic. This gave the animal further alarm, and it began to plunge and kick, breaking the harness and smashing the dash-board. Young Baird threw up his left arm to shield his face, when one of the horse's heels struck the forearm, badly bruising the limb and breaking one of the bones, and in the collision his forehead was slightly bruised. He sprang over the back of the seat to the ground, and in doing so, his right leg struck the end of a bolt, resulting in some laceration of the flesh. He was taken to the store of Dodge & Erk, and thence to his home. Dr. McConvill was called to attend him. The horse continued its struggles until it was thrown to the ground, breaking the shafts.[86]

The difficulties caused by the location of the Erie Railroad's station at Tracyville, about a mile south of central Honesdale, were finally eliminated on October 1, 1900, when, after long negotiations, the first Erie train came into the new Delaware and Hudson station at Main and Ninth Streets.

When the Erie Railway Co., in the contract which it took the "Jefferson Branch," between the coal pockets and Hawley, in 1868, stipulated to extend the road into our borough "within a reasonable time," no one supposed that we should be obliged to wait until the last year of the century before giving up the excursion to and from Tracyville, in order to take the train and return home. After many days, however, and many promises, this result has been reached, and a ticket to Honesdale, on the Erie, now means all that it expresses.

7. The arrival of the first Erie train uptown at the new railroad station, February 1, 1900; the Maple City band is playing (Wayne County Historical Society).

On Monday, October 1, 1900, at 8:20 A.M., the first Erie train left the D.&H. station at the head of 9th street, in our borough. . . . Close by the spot from which the train started, a little more than seventy one years earlier (Aug. 8, 1829) the "Stourbridge Lion" left on its historic run—the first made by a locomotive in the Western hemisphere.

Naturally, the occasion drew a large attendance of our citizens, men, women and children. Many of them boarded the train, to take part in the trip, as far as the former Honesdale station, now styled East Honesdale.

The first train to arrive at the Union station was the No. 117, at 10:37. . . . At this time the Maple City Band was present, and saluted the train with music.[87]

Illustrated Wayne gives a similar description of this event, with photographs of both trains.[88] Unfortunately the picture of the first arriving train is indistinct, but the band is seen very clearly in a snapshot in the collection of the Wayne County Historical Society (Fig 7). This picture shows four members of the band standing in a semicircle, playing from marching-size music, wearing probably the uniform from Lawyer's band, although this time with dark pants instead of white. Possibly the white pants were for summer and the dark for winter, or possibly the men are just wearing the trousers they had to wear to work that day. One has the impression that the ensemble is a small one of eight or ten players, that they are standing in a circle away from the center of things, providing music and festivity rather than playing a serious concert; the crowd, at any rate, is certainly more absorbed by the locomotive than by the musicians.

These bands played a great many concerts for others, but the Maple City band seems to have initiated a custom of throwing at least one party a year all for itself. This was the annual visit to the home of Judson Keen, a cornetist in the band who lived near Keen's pond, about four miles from Honesdale along the D&H.

Judson Keen, of Keene, was most agreeably surprised, the first part of the week. He was at home and upon hearing a familiar sound looked out of the window and saw the Maple City band of twenty pieces coming toward the house discoursing one of their popular marches. Mr. Keen is one of the cornetists of the band and the presence of the organiaztion [*sic*] and the elegant dinner served after the concert was in honor of his birthday.[89]

Eighteen members of the Maple City band were entertained at

the home of Mrs. Agnes Keen, of Keen's, on Sunday. Her son, Judson, is one of the excellent cornetists of this organization. The boys were served with a sumptuous turkey dinner on, and during the afternoon the band rendered some fine concert music. Benj. Dittrich was also present with his large grapha-phone and captured a catchy march entitled "Crack O' the Whip" played by the band.[90]

Unfortunately, no such recording has come to light.

In the summer of 1901, the band had a change of leadership: David Gill was replaced by John Neuser.

Honesdale has a right to boast that it has one of the best musical organizations in the Maple City band that can be found in this section of the country. As proof of that fact the Lake Lodore Improvement company alternate the Sunday concerts at the lake between our band and the famous Bauer's band, of Scranton. Much credit for this standard of excellency is due to Fred C. and David Gill. The former became musical instructor shortly after the [Lawyer's] band was organized and when he left town his younger brother was chosen to continue the work. While music is a special talent in the Gill family, yet modesty on his part has caused the able leader, David Gill, to resign his position and return to the ranks in favor of John Neuser, a musician of wide reputation. Mr. Neuser has a wide experience as a band man and the Maple City organization will undoubtedly be strengthened by his leadership.[91]

In another leap forward, when the band played at the Wayne County Fair in the fall of 1901, they unveiled an impressive new piece of hardware: "The Maple City band favored the fair visitors with many fine selections, and made a showy appearance in their handsome new chariot band wagon."[92]

In sum, the Maple City band should probably be thought of as essentially the successor to Lawyer's band. Such an attitude is betrayed in the article just quoted about John Neuser: note that even a year after the Maple City band's formation, the newspaper fails to distinguish it from its predecessor. In appointing Fred Gill's brother as director, the Maple City band was clearly trying to continue with the same sort of leadership as had worked so well for Lawyer's band. And the new band took a majority of its personnel and uniforms, and some of its repertory as well, from Lawyer's.

But the kinship to Lawyer's band goes even deeper. The Honesdale band was content, for the most part, to play at the invitation of others. But Lawyer's band marketed itself more aggressively, advertising its performances in the paper (sometimes with programs), seeking out new performing situations, and performing as frequently as possible. The Maple City band continued in these traditions. But most important, the band continued in the Lawyer band's tradition of high standards, and the effort seems to have been rewarded: "A Scrantonian said to the writer on Wednesday: 'That is the finest music I have danced to in many a day. Where does the Maple City band hail from? They are excellent.' Upon being told that they are a Honesdale organization and that they would furnish music there on Labor Day, Sept. 3, he said Honesdale ought to be proud of a musical aggregation as good as the Maple City band of 20 pieces. The stranger was a member of the noted Milton band for many years."[93]

THE HONESDALE PHILHARMONIC SOCIETY

The genesis of the Honesdale Philharmonic can be seen in the formation of the Musical History Club in the fall of 1897. This organization met about once a month, except during the summer, to listen to and discuss classical music.

The new musical organization (as yet without a name,) met for the first rehearsal on Thursday evening last, spending the evening with Bach. Mrs. L. B. Richtmyer had charge of the evening's study and entertainment, and read a brief account of Bach—his birth, musical career, etc., after which the following program was rendered:

Invention, No. 8 .... Bach
Miss Jennie Murran.
Vocal solo, Willst du dein Herz mir schenken? .... Bach
Mrs. Leisz.
Loure. (From 3d cello suite.) .... Bach
Miss Jeannette Freeman.
Vocal Solo. Pfingscantate: Mein Glaubiges Herz............. Bach
Mrs. Walter A. Wood.
Preamble. (From 6th Violin Sonate) .... Bach
Miss Florence Baker.
Ave Maria.. Bach-Gounod
Soprano, Mrs. Alice Tillon Rockwell,
Violin, Dr. Edward Ward Burns,
Flute, William Wallace Ham,
Piano, Mrs. L.B. Richtmyer.

The entertainment concluded with a chorus of 30 voices, "Unfold ye Portals," from the oratorio of "Redemption," being ably conducted by Mr. J. A. Bodie, Mrs. Dolmetsch presiding at the piano. The next meeting will be devoted to Handel; the evening's entertainment being in the hands of Mrs. Russell Whitney.[94]

This article shows the usual format for the meetings of the club. A meeting might be devoted to a single topic, such as one composer, or it might include various types of music. In 1898, for example, the club had seven meetings: three presented miscellaneous pieces; one each was devoted to Beethoven, Schumann, and Grieg; and one featured a local violin teacher, Professor Vanderveken, in a presentation on violin literature.

The Honesdale Philharmonic orchestra was evidently not affiliated with the Musical History Club in any official way, but clearly it was a spiritual relative and involved many of the same households; most club members were women, and most orchestra members were men. The Philharmonic was organized in October 1898, and its first concert was announced for the following March.

Oct. 26, 1898, a fine, music-loving people decided to make a venture in organizing an orchestra, which should be purely amateur. The opportunity of being able to secure such an efficient teacher and conductor as Ernst Thiele, of Scranton, gave the new society an impetus which has proven of great service. Rehearsals were held weekly, and the interest of the members grew, as progress was made in the studies undertaken. There is considerable expense attached to such an organization in the way of music, rental, instruments, etc., so it was decided to seek associate members whose donations would aid the society. So far, the society has met with great success. The society meets every Wednesday evening, in the Musical History Club Rooms, and all associate members are welcome at these rehearsals. At the last meeting the following officers were chosen: President, W. F. Suydam; Vice Presidents, J. A. Bodie, J. A. Brown; Concert Master, Dr. E. W. Burns; Secretary and Treasurer, A. M. Leine; Librarian, C. T. Bentley. The orchestra's first appearance in public will be in a concert, at the Opera House, Thursday evening, March 23, 1899, with from 25 to 30 performers, assisted by Mrs. Katherine Thiele, of Scranton, and others. The prime object of this society is to cultivate a love for a higher grade of orchestra music, there being no social lines, nor distinction drawn—it is strictly cosmopolitan.[95]

The debut of the Philharmonic went off on schedule on March 23, 1899, and was, in the *Independent's* words,

A GRAND SUCCESS.

A large, refined and appreciative audience attended the first orchestral concert of the Philharmonic society at the opera house on Thursday evening, under the conductorship of Ernest Thiele, of Scranton, and Mrs. Kathryn Thiele, soloist. It was a grand treat, and the classical music rendered very favorably displayed the recognized ability of our young people in that direction. Every number was enjoyed as evidenced by the applause given. The orchestra of 26 pieces was excellent; Mrs. Thiele, who has sung in Honesdale on several other occasions, delighted the audience with her solos and was encored. The violin duet by Mr. Thiele and Master Edmund Thiele, was well executed. Dr. E. W. Burns' violin solo was masterly, the violin trio, by Miss Nettie Campbell, Sigmund Katz and Mr. Thiele was very fine and the eighth number on the program met with hearty approval from the audience. Mrs. Thiele, C. T. Bentley and orchestra were obliged to respond to an encore. Mr. Thiele is to be congratulated for the excellent success in every particular of this entertainment and for the finished manner in which every number was executed, especially those of the large orchestra. Following was the program in full:

Thomas .... "Raymond." .... Overture
Nevin............. { (a) "'Twas April."
Schubert .... { (b) "Ungeduld."
.... Mrs. Kathryn Thiele
Alard..................... Concerto .... Op. 31
.... Mr. Thiele and Master Edmund Thiele
Haydn....... Andante from "Surprise" Symphony ...... Orchestra
Arditi .... "Se Saran Rose." .... Mrs. Kathryn Thiele
Handel } .... (a) Largo .... Dr. Burns, soloist
Delibes } .... (b) Pizzicato.
.... Orchestra
Hermann .... Burlesque .... (For three violins)
.... Miss Campbell, Mr. Katz and Mr. Thiele
Mascagni .... Intermezzo .... Cavalleria Rusticana
.... Mrs. Thiele, Mr. Bentley and orchestra
Meyerbeer........... "Coronation March." .... Orchestra

The active members of the society who so ably acquitted themselves are: Violins, E. W. Burns, Kevin O'Brien, W. L. Clark, Robert Murray, Miss Nettie Campbell, Sigmund Katz, M. J. Hanlan, Anthony Lenz; viola, Jeff. Freeman; 'cello, A. M. Leine; bass, Robert Dorin; flutes, C. T. Bentley, Michael Fannon; oboe, W. W. Ham; clarionets, Joseph Bondy, John Bussa; cornets, A. A. Cowles, Edwin Lawyer; trombone, John W. Broad; Drums, David Gill.[96]

The *Herald's* review shows still more enthusiasm and betrays even an element of pleasant surprise.

Our people, of course, were aware that an orchestra of twenty odd performers had been organized, and were being rehearsed under the tutelage of Prof. Ernst Thiele, of Scranton, but no one was prepared for the progress that had been made. When the twenty-five members took their seats upon the stage, many, no doubt, resigned themselves to an expected "bad quarter of an hour." But when Mr. Thiele had assumed the baton and signaled the opening of Thomas' overture, "Raymond," there came a burst of harmonious sounds that caused people to turn about and nudge their neighbors. By closing one's eyes one could almost fancy one's self seated at the "Metropolitan" waiting for the curtain to rise upon an opera. There was a vim, a shading, a delicacy in the performance that was most pleasing.[97]

Table 6.
Performances of the Honesdale Philharmonic Society

Date	Location	Event (Sponsor)
		1899
March 23	Opera House	Concert
October 7	Opera House	Concert (Wayne Co. Teachers' Institute)
		1900
March 15	Opera House	Concert
May 24	Opera House	Concert: Rossini's "Stabat Mater," with Musical History Club
September 20-21	Opera House	Juvenile production: "Princess Rosebud" (Honesdale Improvement Association)
November 13	Opera House	Concert (Wayne Co. Teachers' Institute)

All locations Honesdale.

Unlike the bands, the Honesdale Philharmonic prepared, for the most part, a new repertory for each performance, and as a result, its concerts were much bigger affairs and much less frequent. The organization performed only a handful of times in 1899 and 1900 (Table 6).

The orchestra's second performance was on October 7, 1899, during the annual convention of the Wayne County Teachers' Institute in Honesdale. For this concert, the Honesdale players were supplemented by musicians from Scranton and Carbondale, probably associates of the Thieles.

> The Philharmonic concert on Tuesday evening was a great success, the opera house being filled to overflowing with the teachers and their friends. After the overture, Mrs. Thiele sang Sicilian Vespers, with orchestra accompaniment; Serenade for flute and cello was rendered by Messrs. Bentley and Leine; Lion de Bal, by orchestra; piano solo, Cuban Dance, Miss Buchwald. In part second of the program Raymond, by orchestra, was given and Mrs. Thiele sang Marishka and Spring Flowers with violin obligato; Miss Buchwald, piano, and Mr. Thiele, violin, gave Fantaise, William Tell and Intermezzo— Cavalleria Rusticana, Mrs. Thiele Charles Bentley and orchestra. The program closed with Mendelssohn's wedding march by full orchestra. Instrumentation—Violins—Wm. Allen and Edwin Thiele, Scranton, Miss Nettie Campbell, E. W. Burns, Sigmund Katz, Kevin O'Brien, Lacey Brady, Paul Sohner. Viola—R. W. Bauer, Scranton, Jeff Freeman. Cello—Carl Koempel, Scranton, A. M. Leine. Basso—William Schiffer, Scranton, Fred. Gill. Flute—C. T. Bentley. Oboe—A. Rumsby, Carbondale. Clarinettes—Joseph Bondy, John Bussa. Cornets— Andrew Cowles, Edw. Lawyer. Trombone—John Broad. Drums—David Gill. Ernest Thiele, conductor. Soloists—Mrs. Thiele, Miss Buckwald, Ernest Thiele.[98]

The orchestra performed again on March 15, 1900. Both the *Herald* and the *Independent* referred to this as their second concert, although it was actually their third. Whether this was a mistake on the program, or whether a distinction was being made between concerts done under the society's own auspices and those sponsored by the Teachers' Institute, is not clear. In any case, this performance was also a success.

Philharmonic Concert.
The second orchestral concert of the Philharmonic Society

was held in the Opera House on Thursday evening, March 15. Owing to a prevailing storm the evening was one of the most unpleasant of the winter yet the hall was crowded with the music loving people of the Maple City. Ernest Thiele, of Scranton, is the musical conductor and has met with great success in his work. The overture, "Lustspiel" was rendered by full orchestra. J. T. Watkins, the popular baritone, of the Electric City [Scranton], sang "Vision Fair" and was heartily applauded. Master Edmund Thiele, the son of the conductor, gave three violin selections from Violin Concerto, No. 7 in A minor, and the orchestra an Andante from "Surprise Symphony"—Haydn, and march, "Alla Turka"—Mozart, Mr. Watkins sang "Bandalero" and for an encore sang "I'm Waiting in the Lane, Peggy Dear." The orchestra then rendered a selection from Bach and Gillet's beautiful "Lion du Bal." Mr. Watkins sang "But Who May Abide," from Handel's "Messiah," and the applause was so great that he sang "Love's Old Sweet Song" for an encore. "Orpheus," by Offenbach, orchestra, closed the program.

The instrumentation—violins—Miss Nettie Campbell, William Allen, Dr. E. W. Burns, Sigmund Katz, Leon Katz, John C. Metzgar, Thomas Moore, Edmund Thiele. Violas—R. W. Bauer, Jeffrey Freeman. Cellos—Mrs. H. T. Dolmetsch, Arthur Leine, Carl Koempel. Bassos—R. M. Dorin, William Schiffer. Flutes—Charles T. Bentley, J. Caufield. Oboe—A. Rumsby. Clarionets—A. Rehbein, G. Bridgeman. Trumpets— A. Cowles, Edward Lawyer, Horns—Joseph Ferby, Robert Murray. Trombones—Fred C. Gill. Drums—David Gill. Mrs. Dolmetsch, accompanist.[99]

As before, the *Herald* added a little critical commentary to its report, commentary reminiscent of its editor's own musical experience as a member of the Silver Cornet band: "It was evident that our orchestra made perceptible improvement, as they played with more precision, purer intonation, and a better blending of the instruments, which showed the result of constant rehearsing."[100]

On May 24, 1900, the orchestra, assisted by the Musical History Club, made its most spectacular offering so far: Rossini's "Stabat Mater." The performance was announced with some excitement in the press—"Don't fail to hear the greatest musical production ever attempted in Honesdale. The Philharmonic Society in conjunction with the Musical History Club will give Rossini's celebrated 'Stabat

Mater,' with full chorus and orchestra."[101] —and was no disappointment.

> The concert of the Philharmonic Society and Musical History Club, last Thursday evening, was without doubt the crowning event of the season. The concert was a grand musical success. The two numbers preceding "Stabat Mater," "La Dame Blanche" and "Mignon," were rendered by the orchestra in their usual good style. The great sacred work, "Stabat Mater," Rossini's master piece, was the principal attraction of the concert. The soloists were Mrs. Kathryn Thiele, first soprano, J. T. Watkins, basso, of Scranton, Richard Williams, tenor, of Wilkesbarre, and our own soprano, Mrs. W. A. Wood. Each of their solos was a gem and was most heartily and deservedly applauded, the climax being reached in the "Inflammatus." The chorus did exceptionally well, especially considering the few rehearsals they had, and the difficult accompaniment was well played by the orchestra. Those who were fortunate enough to be present could not help but take great pride in the way our townswoman, Mrs. W. A. Wood, sustained her part. The members of the Philharmonic Orchestra deserve great credit, for the concerts they have given for the past two years, and deserve the support of all our music loving people for the continuance of these excellent concerts. Thanks are due to the orchestra, Musical History Club and the subscribers for the rendition of this great work in its completeness. The untiring efforts of Ernest Thiele have made it possible for the orchestra to undertake these concerts and render them with such success under his direction.[102]

The "Stabat Mater" was attended with one slight dispute: an anonymous letter in the *Herald* of June 14 protested the use of English instead of Latin—still a perennial controversy among Honesdale's choir directors.

On November 13, 1900, the Philharmonic performed again for the Wayne County Teachers' Institute (Fig. 8). And again, the concert was well received.

> The entertainment of the evening was given by the Honesdale Philharmonic orchestra, assisted by Chester Bridgeman, W. H. Schiffer, W. Allen, Edmund Thiele, Charles Doersan, George Briegel, Mr. and Mrs. Ernst Thiele, of Scranton. The instrumentation of the orchestra was as follows: Dr. E. W.

TEACHERS' INSTITUTE ENTERTAINMENT

TUESDAY EVENING NOV. 13, 1900.

· · · The · · ·
Honesdale Philharmonic Orchestra.

ERNST THIELE, Conductor.

SOLOISTS—MRS. KATHRYN THIELE, Soprano,

AND THE TALENTED TEN YEAR OLD VIOLINIST,

MASTER GEORGE BRIEGEL.

. . . PROGRAM . . .

SELECTION—CARMEN, ...	BIZET
ORCHESTRA.	
WALTZ SONG—"SE SERAN ROSE," . .	ARDITI
Mrs. THIELE.	
With Orchestral Accompaniment.	
OVERTURE—ORPHEUS, . . .	OFFENBACH
ORCHESTRA.	
5th AIR VARIE, ...	DANCLA
Master GEORGE BRIEGEL.	
"ALLA TURKA,"	MOZART
ORCHESTRA.	
SONGS—(a) SUNSHINE SONG, . . .	GRIEG
(b) WHAT ROBIN FOT . .	REINECKE
(c) MIGNON, . .	GUY D'HARDELOT
Mrs. THIELE.	
WALTZ—"NEW VIENNA, . . .	STRAUSS
ORCHESTRA.	
INFLAMMATUS—STABAT MATER, . .	ROSSINI
Mrs. THIELE,	
With Orchestral Accompaniment.	
MARCH—THE ALLEGHANY, . .	THIELE
ORCHESTRA.	

8. Program for performance of the Honesdale Philharmonic Orchestra, November 13, 1900 (author's collection).

Burns, Miss Nettie Campbell, William Allen, Edmund Thiele, 1st violins; Sigmund Katz, Jeff. Freeman, Leon Katz, George Briegel, 2nd violins; Mrs. Jessie Dolmetsch, A. M. Leine, cellos; C. F. Bentley, flute; Chester Bridgeman, John Bussa, clarinets; Andrew Cowles, cornet; John Broad, alto horn; David Gill, drums; Charles Doersan, tympan; W. H. Schiffer, basso; Ernst Thiele, conductor. The music by this orchestra was soul inspiring. Mrs. Kathryn Thiele, solo soprano, had three numbers on the program. Her first selection was "Se Seran Rose," by Arditi, and her rendition was heartily encored. At her second appearance she sang "Sunshine Song," by Grieg, "What Robin To'd," by Reinecke, "Mignon" by Guy T. Hardelot, and her last was [the Inflammatus from] Rossini's "Stabat Mater." Mrs. Thiele has a clear and well cultivated voice and her singing is highly appreciated. George Briegel who is but ten years of age captured the audience. His violin solo "5th Air Varie" was encored and he played first violin in "Alla Turka", by Mozart, and "The Alleghany," by Thiele, two of the orchestra selections. Sigmund Katz played first violin in "New Vienna", by Strams [Strauss] and "The Alleghany", Dr. Burns taking the second.

Our Honesdale musicians deserve great credit for the labor and proficiency they exhibited on Tuesday evening. With them it is, no doubt, a labor of love. Such music as was rendered would soothe the most incorrigible pupil could the teacher transport the tones to her school room.

Every seat in the house was occupied, standing room was not to be had and a number went away.[103]

These five concerts are the only performances of the Honesdale Philharmonic Soceity that we know about in detail. A sixth was in September of 1900: the orchestra played for "Princess Rosebud," a "juvenile production" put on for the benefit of the Honesdale Improvement Association. The role of the orchestra is not described by the papers; most likely the performance involved only a few members.

Because the concerts of the Philharmonic are exceptionally well-documented in the newspapers, it is all the more puzzling to see nothing at all of them in 1901. And it seems unlikely, although not impossible, that the orchestra would have been revived after at least a year's hiatus. To all appearances, then, the Honesdale Philharmonic simply disappeared while at the height of its popularity and success, and without any reason visible from this distance. Perhaps, for example, the Thieles could no longer come over from Scranton, or perhaps the organizational hierarchy of the orchestra collapsed, but no evidence supports either of these hypotheses or any other.

The Honesdale Philharmonic is even harder to assess objectively than the bands have been, for its position in the community was more complex. A band was valued as a source of entertainment and local pride, but an orchestra adds to these an element of cultural fervor. The audience at a performance of the Philharmonic was there to have a good time, true—but they were also there because of a vague notion that classical music was good for them (a mixture of motives not, of course, unique to turn-of-the-century Honesdale). The formation of an orchestra was seen as a great leap forward for the culture of the town; there was no way that the newspapers were going to say anything bad about it. So it is hard to know just what to make of all these accounts.

It seems improbable that the Honesdale Philharmonic could have been very good, even by the amateur standards of today. Beyond that, however, three observations might be made:

1. that the musical community of Honesdale could not fill the orchestra by itself, but had to be supplemented by out-of-town musicians, some of whom may have been professionals;
2. that although the orchestra's repertory consisted mostly of popular light classics, they did essay a relatively ambitious work in the Rossini "Stabat Mater"; and
3. that the orchestra seems to have been enormously successful: the stories of people being turned away at the door should probably be taken at face value.

A detailed analysis of the Honesdale Philharmonic is not really a concern in this study of town bands. The orchestra's story is included here because its brief but brilliant career says much for, and against, the musical and cultural strength of Honesdale, and because its place in the life of the community provides an instructive contrast to that of the bands. My more general discussions of the bands, then, will use orchestras primarily as a kind of yardstick against which the bands can be compared.

NOTES

1. In recording the names of these ensembles, I have adopted the nineteenth-century convention of using a lower-case *b* in the word *band*, as a way of preserving a certain ambiguity in the sources, which sometimes do

not allow a clear distinction between titles in the usual sense (like "Maple City band") and more informal names based on the name of the town; for example, the band of Lake Como (see chapter 4) was officially named the "Keystone band" but the newspapers almost universally called it the "Lake Como band."

2. The reminiscences of the Ham brothers appeared as columns in local newspapers later in the century. The chief contribution of T. J. Ham (1837-1911) was a historical series entitled "The Old Cannon," published in the *Honesdale Citizen* between August 11, 1904 and August 3, 1905. W. H. Ham (1835-19??) published a three-part memoir entitled "The Bands of Honesdale—Personal Recollections of an Old Member" in the *Wayne County Herald* between May 12 and June 16, 1881, and a fourth entry on bands in another series called "Honesdale Fifty Years Ago" in the *Herald* of February 15, 1900.

3. Ham, "The Bands of Honesdale," May 12, 1881.

4. Vernon Leslie, *Honesdale and the Stourbridge Lion* (Honesdale: Stourbridge Lion Sesquicentennial Committee, 1979), pp. 76-93. See also Dorothy Hurlbut Sanderson, *The Delaware and Hudson Canalway: Carrying Coals to Rondout* (Ellenville, N.Y.: Rondout Valley Publishing, 1974), pp. 36-41.

5. Sanderson, *Carrying Coals to Rondout*, pp. 15, 20, 27.

6. Ham, "The Bands of Honesdale," May 12, 1881. Another account of this band is provided by R. M. Stocker in *History of the First Presbyterian Society of Honesdale* (Honesdale: Herald Press Association, 1906), pp. 312-13. Stocker's version of the story, taken from the recollections of another member of the band, agrees substantially with Ham's except for adding the name of a Mr. Maule to the personnel and citing the price of the instructor as $200, not $100. They do agree on the $8, however. Stocker asserts that this was the first band in town.

7. Ham, "The Bands of Honesdale," May 12,1881. For other references to events involving bands during this time, see Vernon Leslie, *Honesdale: The Early Years* (Honesdale: Honesdale 150 Committee, 1981), pp. 89-92, and Ham, "The Old Cannon," August 25, 1904.

8. Ham, "The Bands of Honesdale," May 12, 1881.

9. Ham, "Honesdale Fifty Years Ago."

10. For comparison, see the instruments described and illustrated in Allen Dodworth, *Dodworth's Brass Band School* (New York: H. B. Dodworth, 1853), pp. 11-12, 16-22, which include the same keyed bugles, ophicleides, trumpets, horns, and trombones, although not the clarinets and flutes. Dodworth, writing some ten years later than Ham's band, also includes saxhorns.

11. Ham, "The Bands of Honesdale," May 12, 1881. Where I say "bass," Ham actually says "tenor," which seems to be a misprint.

12. Ibid. For various accounts of events attended (or probably attended) by the band, see Vernon Leslie, *Canal Town: Honesdale 1850-1875* (Honesdale: Wayne County Historical Society, 1983), pp. 22, 25-26; idem, *A Profile of Service: Protection Engine Company No. 3, 1853-1916* (Honesdale: Protection Engine Co. No. 3, 1986), pp. 40-43; and Ham, "The Old Cannon," August 25—December 1, 1904.

13. Ham, "The Old Cannon," January 12, 1905. W. H. Ham gives the same instrumentation—indeed, the same roster of names—for the band of 1862 in "The Bands of Honesdale," May 12, 1881.

14. The quotation is taken from an unsigned article in the *Wayne County Herald* of August 4, 1898, an article suggesting that lights be installed in the portico of the courthouse so band concerts could be given after dark.

15. Ham, "The Bands of Honesdale," May 12, 1881. See also Leslie, *Canal Town*, pp. 23, 50; idem, *Profile of Service*, pp. 47, 54; and Ham, "The Old Cannon," December 29, 1904—May 4, 1905. In the column of June 29, 1905, Ham refers to an appearance of the Silver Cornet band as late as 1871, but this may be in error.

16. Ham, "The Bands of Honesdale," June 9, 1881.

17. Leslie, *Canal Town*, pp. 159, 164, 178; Ham, "The Old Cannon," May 25—July 27, 1905.

18. Ham, "The Bands of Honesdale," June 16, 1881.

19. This celebration will be discussed in detail in Vernon Leslie, *Things Forgotten: Happenings in Wayne County 1876-1888* (Honesdale: Wayne County Historical Society, in press). My source (Ham, "The Old Cannon," July 27, 1905) mentions only the two out-of-town bands. I am grateful to Vernon Leslie for sharing his information with me.

20. Ibid., August 3, 1905.

21. Leslie, *Profile of Service*, pp. 102-16.

22. *Centennial and Illustrated Wayne County*, 2d ed. (Honesdale: The Wayne Independent, 1902; rept. Honesdale: Wayne County Historical Society, 1975), p. 139. The entry, a discussion of the Maple City band, says that when that band was formed, in April 1900, the Honesdale band "had been in existence about twenty years."

23. *Wayne Independent*, April 21, 1897.

24. Ibid., May 31, 1899.

25. *Honesdale Citizen*, October 20, 1898.

26. *Wayne County Herald*, July 22, 1897.

27. *Wayne Independent*, July 24, 1897.

28. *Honesdale Citizen*, December 30, 1897.

29. *Illustrated Wayne*, pp. 67-69.

30. *Wayne Independent*, September 17, 1898.

31. Ibid., September 21, 1898.

32. *Honesdale Citizen*, January 5, 1899.

33. *Wayne Independent*, May 31, 1899.

34. *Honesdale Citizen*, June 29, 1899.

35. *Wayne Independent*, July 29, 1899.

36. *Wayne County Herald*, August 3, 1899.

37. *Wayne Independent*, September 30, 1899.

38. *Wayne County Herald*, April 26,1900.

39. *Wayne Independent*, December 3, 1898.

40. *Honesdale Citizen*, January 5, 1899.

41. Ibid., February 2, 1899.

42. *Wayne Independent,* February 8, 1899.

43. *Honesdale Citizen,* February 9, 1899.

44. The name is an unusual one and the town a small one, but still there is some confusion about Edwin Lawyer's identity. The returns from the census of 1900 list two men who might be identified with the cornetist. Edward Lawyer, thirty-three, a shoe cutter, lived in Texas township (the township bordering Honesdale) with his wife and two children, twelve and sixteen. Husband and wife were born in New York State, and both children in Massachusetts. Fred E. Lawyer, thirty-eight, also a shoe cutter, lived in Honesdale borough with his wife and two children, twelve and ten. All four were born in New York State. No Edwin Lawyer appears in the local census return at all, but then, the newspapers spell his name all three ways. I use the dominant spelling, "Edwin," herein.

Further evidence is provided by two news items concerning the birth and death of his little daughter. On February 15, 1899, the *Independent* announced that "The Ideal orchestra and Lawyer's band have a new accompanist. Mr. Lawyer thinks the latest is the best." But on June 21, the same paper reported that "Edna May, youngest daughter of Mr. and Mrs. Edwin Lawyer, of West Street, died of whooping cough on Sunday morning, aged four months and eight days." The phrase "youngest daughter" would make sense for either family, but the West Street address (within the borough) makes me lean slighty toward Fred. On the other hand, Edward's name is closer, and he may have moved to Texas township after Edna died.

In either case, the leader of Lawyer's band was a shoe cutter in his thirties who moved to Honesdale from out of state—unless there is a third Edwin Lawyer who moved out of the area between March 1900, when he played in a concert of the Honesdale Philharmonic (see below), and June 1900, when the census was taken.

45. *Wayne Independent,* December 4, 1897.

46. *Honesdale Citizen,* March 9, 1899.

47. Ibid., March 16, 1899.

48. Ibid., March 23, 1899.

49. *Wayne Independent,* March 22, 1899.

50. Ibid., April 21, 1897; see above, p. 27.

51. The Thirteenth Regiment band was itself no stranger to Honesdale: it appears to be the band in the 1879 photograph discussed by Leslie in *Profile of Service,* pp. 102-16 (see especially p. 107). This would, however, have been before Gill's time.

52. *Wayne Independent,* April 1, 1899.

53. *Honesdale Citizen,* May 11, 1899.

54. The *Citizen* of May 25, 1899 even describes the new uniform as being "of Sousa cut." See also Margaret Hindle Hazen and Robert M. Hazen, *The Music Men: An Illustrated History of the Brass Band in America, 1800-1920* (Washington: Smithsonian Institution Press, 1987), pp. 141-42.

55. *Wayne County Herald,* April 13, 1899.

56. *Wayne Independent,* May 3, 1899.

57. From an insurance map of Honesdale dated July 1897, prepared by the Sanborn-Perris Map Company of New York, in the collection of the Wayne County Historical Society. The presence of this large vacant lot in the midst of a heavily-built-up area right in the middle of town suggests that the abandonment of this basin was fairly recent.

58. *Honesdale Citizen*, August 11, 1898; *Wayne County Herald*, August 11, 1898.

59. *Wayne County Herald*, June 14, 1900.

60. *Wayne Independent*, August 1, 1900.

61. Ibid., May 27, 1899.

62. Ibid., May 3, 1899; also *Honesdale Citizen*, May 4, 1899.

63. *Wayne Independent*, June 14, 1899.

64. Ibid., July 19, 1899.

65. Ibid., July 29, 1899.

66. Ibid., September 23, 1899.

67. *Honesdale Citizen*, February 15, 1900; also *Wayne Independent*, February 14, 1900.

68. *Wayne Independent*, October 25, 1899.

69. Ibid., August 2, 1899.

70. *Wayne County Herald*, May 25, 1899.

71. *Wayne Independent*, October 11, 1899.

72. Ibid., October 18, 1899.

73. *Wayne County Herald*, March 29, 1900.

74. But see n. 44.

75. *Wayne Independent*, May 16, 1900.

76. Ibid., June 2, 1900.

77. Ibid., June 6, 1900.

78. *Illustrated Wayne*, p. 139.

79. *Wayne Independent*, June 11, 1898; *Wayne County Herald*, June 16, 1898.

80. *Wayne Independent*, March 25, 1899.

81. The picture appears in *Illustrated Wayne*, p. 139; a better print, however, is preserved in the collection of the Wayne County Historical Society, and Figure 6 is taken from this print. The distinction is important because *Illustrated Wayne* cut out a half-visible cornetist on the far right.

82. *Wayne County Herald*, June 28, 1900.

83. *Wayne Independent*, August 4, 1900; *Honesdale Citizen*, August 2, 1900.

84. *Wayne Independent*, August 18, 1900.

85. Ibid., July 7, 1900.

86. *Honesdale Citizen*, August 8, 1901.

87. Ibid., October 4, 1900.

88. *Illustrated Wayne*, p. 141.

89. *Wayne Independent*, September 12, 1900.

90. Ibid., August 7, 1901.

91. Ibid., July 24, 1901.

92. *Wayne County Herald*, October 3, 1901.

93. *Wayne Independent*, August 25, 1900.

94. *Wayne County Herald,* October 14, 1987.

95. *Honesdale Citizen,* March 16, 1899.

96. *Wayne Independent,* March 25, 1899.

97. *Wayne County Herald,* March 30, 1899.

98. *Wayne Independent,* November 11, 1899.

99. Ibid., March 17, 1900.

100. *Wayne County Herald,* March 22, 1900.

101. *Wayne Independent,* May 12, 1900.

102. *Honesdale Citizen,* May 13, 1900.

103. *Wayne Independent,* October 17, 1900.

4

Three Bands of Northern Wayne County

Three villages of northern Wayne County—Equinunk, Lake Como, and Pleasant Mount—had bands between 1897 and 1901, and Pleasant Mount had an orchestra as well. Their stories are parallel: they began about the same time, they played in the same sorts of situations, and they often exchanged personnel and concerts.

All three bands are relatively well documented in the Honesdale newspapers. Remember, however, that news from the outlying areas reached the papers via correspondents, and thus the coverage is quite uneven in thoroughness and quality. We probably know much more about the big events than the little ones, and we almost never read anything about the repertory of these bands. But the newspaper columns do give us a vivid, if fragmentary, image of musical life in the rural districts—a part of our musical tradition that is still poorly understood.

THE EQUINUNK BAND

Equinunk—A Charming Spot in the Delaware Valley,
Away from the Noise and Dust of the City.
Equinunk, Wayne county, Pa., nestled among the hills on the Delaware river, at the mouth of Equinunk creek, is a pleasant town 154 miles west of New York City and one mile from Lordville station on the Erie railroad. It derives its name from the creek which is by tradition the Indian name for "trout water." Equi-"Aqua"-water "Nunk" trout. It contains between four and five hundred inhabitants, two churches, six stores, three public houses, two acid factories for making pyroligneous acid

from wood, one excelsior mill, one steam sawmill, one cream-
ery and cooler for bottling milk for city use, one furniture
store, milliner store, with blacksmith, carriage and harness
shops and two physicians.

This article, which appeared in the *Wayne Independent* on June 16,
1897, was evidently taken from some sort of brochure promoting
tourism; it goes on to celebrate the pure water of the place, its freedom from malaria, and other attractions, and then to single out one
hostelry as being especially comfortable. But if we allow for a bit of
self-interested enthusiasm, the paragraph makes for a more or less
accurate description of Equinunk at the turn of the century: a
village of perhaps four hundred inhabitants,[1] living off the nearby
farms and forests. And in the 1890s Equinunk also had a band.

Actually, the history of bands in Equinunk goes back at least as
far as September 1880, when the *Hancock Herald* of Hancock, New
York (about eight miles north on the Erie) announced that Equinunk
had organized a brass band. The following January, the same paper
reported that Charles E. Wright, leader of the Pleasant Mount band,
had gone to Equinunk to instruct the band.[2] Further details about
this ensemble are lacking, and it may not have survived much
longer.

In any case, the idea was revived some years later. At the beginning of 1897, the Equinunk band was a very new organization
indeed—probably not more than a few months old. The first reference to it in the Honesdale press was in the *Citizen* of December 3,
1896; optimism at that time was not high: "'It is good to be af-
flicted,' some one has said. Well, a sad chastening has struck our
once quiet hamlet. An amateur brass band! May the Lord endue us
with patience and resignation. Yet we would add to the litany this
invocation, 'From amateur wind jammers and whackers of drums,
base and ignoble, good Lord deliver us.'"

Three weeks later, the prognosis still sounded dismal: "The
catastrophe of horns, alluded to in our last, is yet heavy on our once
quiet hamlet. From every house here, wherein there is a boy over
14, there comes the agonized wail of a tortured horn. Sorrowing
and tortured parents may not, like Job, cuss the day wherein they
were born, but they tear their hair and rave wildly. As aforesaid, it
is a sad chastening."[3] And on December 30, the *Independent* reported
cautiously that the band had played—apparently its debut—on
Christmas night "and surprised all with the progress they have
made in so short a time."

Within a few months, however, the correspondents to both papers were starting to inflate with enthusiasm. An item in the *Independent* of February 20, 1897, shows the change:

Equinunk supports an organization known as the Equinunk Cornet Band. It was organized last fall with Rev. C. W. Alberti as leader; Eb clarionet, Cain Lord; Eb cornet, T. Currie, Edwin Lord, [? Bb cornet], C. W. Alberti, H. Richards, Earl Lord; altos, Everette Green, Shep Warfield; tenors, Delos Lester, Will Lord; baritone, Austin Lord; Bb bass, Robert Shields; base drum, Blake Gray; snare drum, Charles Bauman; cymbals, Chris. Warfield. The progress and proficiency they have made under the leadership of Mr. Alberti surprises everybody considering the short time they have practiced, which they do in Mr. Lord's store twice a week.[4] Their services are already in demand. They filled the bill at an entertainment given here by Mary A. Woolsey, a graduate from Emerson's College of Oratory, and were invited and went with her to Lookout and Lordville. We are proud of the boys and glad to see them interested in this line. They have a very fine set of instruments and make a fine appearance and are a credit to the town.

About the same time, the *Hancock Herald* printed a similar article about the new band, adding that Austin Lloyd's baritone cost $75, and Robert Shields's bass horn $90.[5] If accurate, these figures are surprising: in the Sears, Roebuck catalogue for 1897, baritones ranged from $10.65 to $16.70, and B-flat basses from $11.45 to $19.10.[6] These new instruments were even toward the upper end of the scale for the more specialized instrument dealers: Lyon and Healy of Chicago, in their catalogue for 1898-99, offered baritones from $35.00 to $121.50,[7] and B-flat basses from $37.50 to $149.75.[8] The choice of such expensive instruments so soon after the band's founding reveals a remarkable faith in the organization's future: if the band folded, a B-flat bass would be all but useless.

By August, the band had built up a considerable momentum, and even the *Citizen's* correspondent had abandoned his disapproval, if not his prose style:

Our band—we write "our band," as it is in our place—a real C. B. [cornet band], which deserves more than a passing word. A year since it was not even in embryo. Aside from the leader (more of him anon), it is made up of the young men and youth of our place. Had one asked the writer a year since if such and such ones were likely to become musicians, our reply would have been an emphatic Never. But there were undeveloped possibilities.

> "Full many a flower is doomed to blush unseen,
> and waste its sweetness—etc."

The band boys became ambitious to be musicians. They said "We will," an important factor, and it is a marvel now to hear them jam music through the small horns, and great horns, and wallop it out of the big drum and little drum, and cymbals. Their leader is the minister here. Somehow he inspired the boys with aspirations to form a band, he being a proficient with the cornet. He has taken the crude material, been training it for about nine months, and we think he is well satisfied with the results. The community is, and is proud of the band. We fancy few preachers are varying their work by training or making a band.[9]

Taken together these early news stories give a great deal of information about the Equinunk band, its members, and its history.

First, the band was formed probably in November 1896, by Charles W. Alberti, the thirty-seven-year-old preacher of the Equinunk M. E. church. Reverend Alberti was apparently an expert cornetist as well as the spiritual leader of the community; as we shall see, his name looms large in the history of the ensemble.

Second, the story from the *Independent* tells both who was in the band and what instruments they played. Unfortunately, however, the list seems to be garbled: as printed, it would give the band five soprano cornets in E-flat, and no B-flat cornets at all, which seems most improbable. I have made the emendation in brackets on the hypothesis that Alberti held the first chair of the B-flat cornet section and thus is the first name in that section. If I am correct, then, the band had a fairly standard, although perhaps still a bit top-heavy, instrumentation: E-flat clarinet, two E-flat cornets, three B-flat cornets, two alto horns, two tenor horns, baritone, B-flat bass, and percussion. This instrumentation will be considered in more detail in chapter 7, and the personnel in chapter 6.

Third, the *Citizen*, as well as the earlier items, makes it clear that most of the band was made up of beginners—that Alberti's task was not only to organize the band and conduct it, but also to provide elementary musical instruction. Conceivably a few of the musicians may have learned their craft in the old Equinunk band of 1880-81; in 1897, Cain Lord was forty-five, Charles Bauman thirty-five, and

John Curry thirty-two. But the vast majority were in their teens and twenties, too young to have learned a decade and a half before.[10] If all of this is correct, then, the performance on Christmas night must have been mostly by people who had played their instruments for not much more than a month—which may serve to explain the tactfully vague coverage in the *Independent* on December 30.

And finally, we learn that they practiced, at least at the beginning, twice a week in the basement of Cain Lord's clothing store, across the street from the church. This seems to be the standard frequency of rehearsals for these bands: both Lawyer's band and the Beach Lake band (p. 117) also met twice a week.

Sometime during the Equinunk band's first couple of years, an anonymous photographer, probably an itinerant professional, took their picture (Fig. 9); a copy of this photograph is still in the possession of the sister of two of the band members. Unfortunately it is undated and impossible to date precisely. The members are wearing uniforms, which suggests that the photo is from after September 1897, when the band was reported to be raising money "to purchase dress suits."[11] On the other hand, a relatively early date is suggested by the youth of the two boys in the front (the brothers of the picture's owner); Shep and Charles Warfield were born in 1886 and 1884, which would make them ten and twelve at the time the band was founded in 1896—older, indeed, than they look in the picture.[12] On balance, it is probably safest and most plausible to assign the photograph tentatively to the earliest date consonant with the uniforms, which would probably be the summer of 1898. The musicans are shown with instruments, and their names have been handwritten, in order, on the back of the picture.

If the original roster of 1897 is correct, if the photograph really shows the entire band and is from the summer of 1898, if the names on the back are right, and if I am correctly interpreting some of the more ambiguous-looking instruments in the picture, then the band went through some remarkable changes of personnel and instrumentation in its first year-and-a-half.

1. Five of the original fifteen players had dropped out: Cain Lord on E-flat clarinet, Edward and Will Lord on E-flat cornet, H. Richards on B-flat cornet, and Robert Shields on B-flat bass—and the first four of these are all to be found around Equinunk in the returns of the 1900 census, so apparently they didn't move away.

2. Three of the original players had changed instruments:

9. The Equinunk band, probably in the summer of 1898. The reverse of the picture lists the members' names as follows: front row, Shep Warfield, Charles Warfield; second row, Blake Grey, Horace Green, Delos Lester, Earl Lord, Rev. Alberti, Edgar Holbert, Jake Blaes; third row, Charles Bowman, Jay Lester, Everett Green, Austin Lloyd, Leon Holbert, John Curry (collection of Hazel Peake).

drummer Charles Bauman and E-flat cornetist John Curry both changed to E-flat bass—which suggests that the band may simply not have been able to afford E-flat basses at first, and then switched players onto them when the instruments had been bought.

3. And the five departing musicians had been replaced with Jay Lester on trombone (whether valve or slide is not visible in the picture), Leon Holbert and Horace Green on tenor, Edgar Holbert on B-flat cornet, and Jacob Blaes, snare drum.

The result of these changes is an instrumentation of one B-flat clarinet, three cornets (all, apparently, B-flat), two altos, two tenors, trombone, baritone, two E-flat basses, and three percussion.

Even more conspicuous than the instruments, perhaps, are the uniforms, which are of a fancy and by this time slightly antiquated style, with horizontal patterns of braid down the front, braid on the sleeves, and a braid stripe on the trouser legs. The picture's owner remembers the uniforms as being gray, or possibly blue. The caps are relatively simple, reminiscent perhaps of the Civil War, with an insignia unfortunately illegible in the photo. Three players are not wearing all the regulation uniform: Alberti is wearing a suit with a bowler, probably because a a band uniform would be considered improper to a man in his clerical position, and the two Warfield boys, the youngest members of the band, are wearing dark pants, possibly because the uniform company could not supply uniform pants in such small sizes, or possibly because it was not economical to buy uniform pants for people growing so fast. The bass drum says "Equinunk Concert Band"—the only reference I have found to this name.

In any case, it is clear that the band was performing regularly by the spring of 1897, and that they almost immediately became the darlings of the community. Table 7 shows every performance I have been able to identify for the Equinunk band between 1897 and 1901. And a comparison with the schedules of the Honesdale bands shows the more rural outlook of the Equinunk organization. In the summer, the Equinunk band played more picnics and fewer parades than the Honesdale bands; in the winter, more dinners and fewer dances.

The biggest annual event in Equinunk was the Fourth of July celebration, the highlight of which was traditionally a picnic for the entire town in the yard of William M. Nelson, a retired clergyman,

Table 7.
Performances of the Equinunk Band

Date	Location	Event (Sponsor)
		1897
c. February 1	Equinunk etc.	Entertainments (Mary A. Woolsey)
March 24	M.E. church	Epworth League supper
May 7	Equinunk	Delaware Valley Musical Association meeting
May 29	Equinunk	Memorial Day parade, cemetery exercises
August	South Branch	Sunday School picnic (South Branch Sunday School)
July 3	Equinunk	4th of July parade, exercises
September 4	Tyner's grove	Picnic
September 28-29	Deposit	Street fair and band concert
December 25	M.E. church	Concert & oyster supper (Equinunk band)
		1898
March	Equinunk	Concert in street
April 6	Equinunk	Procession & reception for Rev. Alberti
April 30	Equinunk	Playing in streets?
May 30	Equinunk	Memorial Day parade
June 24	M.E. church	Entertainment (Prof. Sophia's singing school)
July 4	Equinunk	4th of July picnic
July 14	Shohola Glen	Sunday School reunion
July 30	I. K. Hornbeck's house	Flag raising
August 11*	Blace's grove, Springdale	Picnic (South Branch M.E. Society)
August 18	Tyner's grove	Picnic (Equinunk band)
August 27	Upper grove, Lake Como	Picnic (Lake Como band)
November 24	M.E. church	Thanksgiving supper (M.E. church)
December 31	M.E. church	New Year's Eve supper (M.E. Sunday School)
		1899
February 22	M.E. church?	Concert
April 14	Equinunk	Party for Rev. Alberti
July 4	Nelson's grove	4th of July picnic, concert
July	Shohola Glen	Excursion from Lordville
August 24	Nelson's lawn	Picnic and concert (Equinunk band)

Table 7. (Continued)
Performances of the Equinunk Band

Date	Location	Event (Sponsor)
September 6-7	Susquehanna	Band contest
December 18	Lord's hall	Farmer's institute
December 25	M.E. church	Christmas party
		1900
February 22	M. E. church	Martha Washington supper
May 30	Equinunk	Memorial Day parade, cemetery exercises
July 4	Equinunk	4th of July picnic, parade, concert
December 31	M. E. church	New Year's celebration
		1901
February 12	M. E. church	"The Feast of Seven Tables" (M.E. organ fund)
March 1	M. E. church?	Entertainment
April 27	M. E. church	Reception for Rev. G. E. Montrose
July 4	Equinunk	4th of July picnic, parade, entertainment
August 22	Tyner's grove	Picnic (Maccabees & Equinunk band)

*Could be two separate events; see *Honesdale Citizen*, August 18, 1898; *Wayne Independent*, August 20, 1898.
All locations Equinunk except South Branch, Deposit, Shohola Glen, Springdale, Lake Como, and Susquehanna.

businessman, and state senator who lived next door to the Methodist church.[13] The festivities for 1899 were typical.

The Fourth was celebrated here. Not in ancient but in modern form. Young and old America enjoyed the day immensely. The most ample preparations were made by the ladies for a good dinner and supper. The anniversary day and all the exercises were very enjoyable. Mr. Nelson's house, yard, lawn and orchard were thrown open to the public and everyone was made welcome. He had a house full of babies—an unusual thing for him, but seemed to enjoy the situation all the same. The band gave excellent music on the ground and a concert in the evening in front of the church; also took part in the evening entertainment in the church. The entertainment was the best we ever had in the church. The choir gave some excellent patriotic selections. The children were drilled and gave a cantata called "Columbia's Birth Day Party;" Hattie Sherwood Columbia and Austin Lloyd as Brother Jonathan. The presents were fine and kindly received. Then came a recitation by Grace Doyle, "The Little Flower Girls." Music by band and choirs. Recitation by June Southwell on "Love and Marriage Stealing a March on the New Lebanon Quakers." Miss Southwell was warmly encored and gave "The Tables Turned," which brought a round of applause from a packed house. The fireworks followed and were fine. The balloon kicked and refused to go up but did go down and out. Proceeds, $150, to be applied on the church debt. So much for the 4th.[14]

As Table 7 shows, picnics of one sort or another account for almost a third of the known performances of the Equinunk band. In fact, the band often held picnics to raise funds: on September 4, 1897, for example, they invited the Lake Como band to a picnic in Tyner's grove, a mile or so south of town. There are two views, again in contrasting literary styles, of this picnic.

According to notice the Equinunk cornet band gave a concert and dinner in Tyner's grove, Saturday last. The day was favorable and there was a large turnout. The grounds were set in order on Friday by the band. The ladies prepared a sumptuous dinner and the tables were all that could be desired. The Como band and a large delegation of citizens from there came down to enjoy the occasion and assisted in the music and dinner. The bands made a fine appearance and the music was excellent, the proceeds of the tables and stands were $113. The money to be used to purchase dress suits for the band.[15]

The Equinunk Cornet Band held a picnic in Tyner's Grove, on Saturday last. It was, taking it all in all, a large day. The dinner was immense in quantity and quality. Chicken pie, beef a la mode, cake ad lib, including stamakake [stomach ache?] after dinner. Et cetterus were ice cream, the rale genuine thing, made from Jerseys that give milk 80 per cent. cream. With this I 'scold libations of the soft stuff, wherewith to lower the temperature. With all this a big crowd, a crowd kept happy by generous feed at ridiculously low figures. (Just think of a dinner of such dimensions for 25 cents.) With all this, music. The Como Band, S.J. Skellett leader, was there and gave us first class wind jamming. Done finely. The house of Skellett seems to run to music. With the Professor was his three boys, their aggregate weight, we judge, about 150 lbs, one of them yanking music from a trombone, another from a big barritone, the third, a mere might of a boy, whacked the big bass drum in a manner that made the ladies exclaim altogether, "Oh aint he a little daisy, just too cute for anything." The Prof. said he had three more at home, and added, "they can make some noise."

And the Equinunk C. B., didn't they wake the slumbering echoes. Good music too. The two bands united and awoke the memories of '64-5 with "Marching through Georgia," etc.

And everybody was happy.[16]

Formal concerts of the Equinunk band were frequent throughout the winter, but they were seldom covered in much detail by the papers. In general, they seem to have involved not only the band, but also various forms of local talent: "The band concert Wednesday night was a success and the finest musical treat that Equinunk ever had. Rev. C. W. Alberti had been drilling the boys for some time and they were equal to the emergency. The instrumental part of the program was varied by a vocal duet, 'Meet Me by the Running Brook' by C. E. Barnes and Edna Lloyd; Gettie Hornbeck also gave a solo on the organ. The audience was delighted and the band have been asked to repeat it. We join in the request."[17]

A similar lack of detail attends our understanding of the suppers: we often read that the band was there, but seldom find out the musical details. But one unusual supper was worth discussing at some length—a celebration heralding the new century on December 31, 1900.

Public notice was given on Sunday that there would be a social in the church commencing at 9 o'clock Monday evening to watch the old year and century out and the new year and century in. Excellent music was furnished by the Equinunk band and a lunch by the ladies at 10 o'clock with tea and coffee. This over Mrs. Emerson and Mr. Nelson read appropriate selections and a short time before 12 o'clock Rev. Mr. Alberti invited the audience to the front seats and conducted a consecration service, while the old year and century died and the new ones born. The quietness and solemnity of the occasion was very impressive and will not soon be forgotten. Appropriate remarks by the pastor and singing the doxology ended the service. At this point Mr. Nelson rang the church bell with a vim that made its iron tongue shout "Happy New Year!" The greeting was exchanged by all.[18]

Perhaps the most distinctive general aspect of the Equinunk band was its association with the Methodist church in town. Almost all of the band's indoor concerts were held in the sanctuary, and many of its outdoor concerts on church property. Even rehearsals were eventually moved from Mr. Lord's store to the old church building, which had been vacated in the summer of 1896.[19] This close relationship of band and church was quite unusual at the time; bands were traditionally regarded as purely secular organizations, improper for religious purposes. The Honesdale bands, for example, played occasionally at Sunday School picnics, but there is only one recorded instance of a band actually performing in a church.

Why was the Equinunk band different? Part of the reason lies in the structure of the community. The Methodist church was not only the spiritual, but also the cultural center of Equinunk: significantly, the village is represented in *Illustrated Wayne* by just two biographies and an architect's rendering of the new church building.[20] In Honesdale, social life was built around secular institutions like fraternal organizations and fire companies; but in Equinunk these functions were taken over by the church. In the news items I have quoted, even New Year's Eve was celebrated as a kind of quasi-religious holiday. The Methodist church, in short, had a hand in everything in the community, and naturally it was involved with the band as well.

Another part of the relationship lies in the band's history: its founder, instructor, and leader was Charles W. Alberti, the Methodist minister. Alberti was a popular preacher as well as a musician, and he was given full credit for all the accomplishments of the Equinunk band. But there is a problem inherent in having one's band led by a Methodist preacher: his days in town are inevitably numbered by the church's doctrine of itinerancy. Each spring Alberti would go off to conference, and neither he nor the community would know whether he would be reassigned. Conference time, as a result, was a time of special anxiety for the Equinunk band, and Alberti's return each year was a cause for celebration. When he came back in 1898, they gave him a parade: "Rev. C. W. Alberti returned from conference Wednesday, and Thursday evening the people gave him and his wife a reception at the parsonage. They gathered at Mr. Knapp's store and headed by the Equinunk band marched to the parsonage and took po[s]session. The ladies served tea, coffee, and cake. Prof. Bolt, of Walton, was in town, and added much to the enjoyment of the occasion by vocal and instrumental music; this with the band made the visit very musical."[21]

The following year, the band took positive action on their leader's behalf—and evidently with some success:

> If all accounts are true, there are many preachers with sad hearts and churches discouraged and disheartened, within the bounds of the New York and Wyoming Conferences of the Methodist Episcopal church, through the appointments made by Bishop Joyce at the annual conferences recently held. But not so at Equinunk; there the reverse is true; and all the people are delighted by the return of Rev. Chas. W. Alberti as their pastor for the 4th year. Mr. Alberti is a preacher of ability, and also possesses considerable musical talent. Through his leadership a brass band, composed of the young men of the village, has been organized, and they are a credit to the community, to the leader, and to the boys themselves. During the session of the New York conference, the Equinunk band, as a band, forwarded a petition to the church authorities, signed by all the members, some 15 or 16, asking that Mr. Alberti be returned to Equinunk. How far this may have contributed to his return is not known; certainly it was a novel petition before the appointing powers of a church, and could not well be ignored.[22]

Equinunk and the band managed to hold onto Alberti through the 1900 conference as well; but on April 14, 1901, he preached his last sermon,[23] and on April 27, the band played at a reception for the new minister, Reverend George E. Montrose: "The reverend gentleman reached here last Saturday night and in the evening the ladies gave him a reception in the church parlors; served a fine lunch and the Equinunk band furnished excellent music. It was pleasant to minister and people. On Sunday he filled the pulpit very acceptably and as far as we can judge the outlook is good for prosperity."[24]

The loss of Reverend Alberti must have been a blow to the band, but not an immediately fatal one: they continued to play at least throughout the summer, and possibly beyond. A report of the Independence Day celebration of 1901 declared with pride (and some surprise) that the band seemed quite healthy even without its founder: "The entire entertainment in the evening was enjoyable and appreciated by the audience that filled the auditorium and lecture room. We heard it prophesied that after Mr. Alberti went away the bottom would go out of the Equinunk band. Thrown upon their resources and reputation they are doing better than ever. There is plenty of timber felt [left?] and they never did better service."[25]

Reverend Alberti was not the only musical influence working to improve the band; some of the members were instructed in music, at least for awhile, by one "Professor Sophia," a music teacher from Susquehanna who travelled to Equinunk periodically to give lessons and conduct a singing school: "Prof. Sophia was here Monday night, drilling his singing school, which now numbers 30. The school meets in the lecture room of the church and if it is not a success it will not be the fault of the teacher. He spoke in the highest terms of their improvement and what he anticipated. A large number of our band boys are pupils."[26]

In June, the singing school gave a concert to show the public how they were doing. The band had a prominent role in the show:

The event of the week in town was the musical entertaiment by the singing school class, conducted by Prof. Sophia, on Friday night in the church and closed the second term of the school. Miss Sophia presided at the organ with her usual dignity and success. The exercises began with a glee entitled "Merrily On" and consisted of anthems, quartets, choruses, solos, and duets, interspersed with excellent music by the Equinunk band and some excellent remarks by Mr. Sophia and two recitations by June Southwell and closed with a patriotic chorus entitled "Old Glory" which brought down the house. We feel proud of our young people and the proficiency they have attained in musical art and the only way to improve and enjoy what they have secured is to get more. Prof. Sophia is entitled to much credit for his patience and perseverance, for he has spared no pains to bring his place to as high a point as possible. We understand he will continue to visit our town once in two weeks and give lessons in vocal and instrumental music and we can commend him to all who may need his service.[27]

But what, in the end, was the harvest of all these labors? Was the Equinunk band worth listening to? As with the Honesdale band, the answer is obscured by the local pride so obvious in the newspaper accounts. Perhaps the most graphic example of this triumph of loyalty over objectivity is the reporting of a band contest in Susquehanna in early September 1899. On September 14, the *Citizen* reported that "The Equinunk Cornet Band attended the Street Fair at Susquehanna, winning 2d prize in the band contest." And we, the readers of the *Citizen*, are impressed. Unfortunately, however, the Lake Como correspondent to the *Independent* gives the rest of the story: "Four members of the Keystone band, Lake Como, . . . accompanied the Equinunk band to Susquehanna on the 6th and 7th inst. to enter the band prize contest which was a prominent feature of the street fair held there. There were two contestants, the Gibson and the Equinunk bands. The prize of $30 was awarded to the Gibson band, which won by two points. The Equinunk band received $25. Both organizations made an excellent showing."[28] At the only other band contest it entered, in Deposit in September 1897, the Equinunk band took third prize; the number of bands in the competition is not specified.[29]

In short, there is no evidence to indicate that the Equinunk band was what today would be called an expert musical organization, and plenty—not only the band contests but also common sense—to suggest that it was mediocre or poor. But the pride of the people of Equinunk in their band was justified: to put together a band of fifteen grown men, teach them their instruments, and have them ready to play in a few months is a considerable accomplishment—no matter what musical standard is applied to their performance. And to the people of Equinunk, most of whom probably had never heard a better band, and all of whom must have been hungry for entertainment of any kind, the sight and sound of a whole band of local young men, in uniform, must have been inspiring indeed.

THE LAKE COMO BAND

The village of Lake Como, sometimes called simply Como in the newspapers, is about six miles west of Equinunk, in the central part of northern Wayne County. Like Equinunk, it supported itself primarily with agriculture and lumber; and in the summer, the beautiful lake, the peaceful village, and the proximity of town to the O&W also made Lake Como a popular resort for city boarders.

The Lake Como band, also called the Keystone band, is not so well documented in the newspapers as the Equinunk band; as Table 8 shows, only eighteen performances are recorded between 1897 and 1901, surely an incomplete list. But the Lake Como band, despite the fragmentary picture, does offer some features of special interest.

Table 8.
Performances of the Lake Como Band
(Keystone Band)

Date	Location	Event (Sponsor)
		1897
September 4	Tyner's grove, Equinunk	Picnic (Equinunk band)
		1898
August 17	Dillons	Picnic (Lake Como Sunday School)
August 27	Upper Grove	Picnic (Lake Como band)
September 10	A. Jones's house	Flag raising
September 29	Fairgrounds, Honesdale	Wayne County Fair
		1899
April 27	Grange Hall, Winwood	Jefferson's birthday supper (Winwood Grange
May 17	Winwood	Farewell social
July 4	Lake Como	4th of July celebration
August 24	Nelson's lawn, Equinunk	Picnic and concert (Equinunk band)
September 1	M.E. parsonage	Surprise party for Rev. Olver
September 21	M.E. church	Wayne Co. W.C.T.U. Convention
		1900
May 11	M.E. church	Entertainment
May 23	M.E. church	Entertainment
June 2	"The hall"	Concert, ice cream social
July 4	Thompson	4th of July celebration
August 17	A. T. Poole's house	Garden party
		1901
July 4	Lake Como	4th of July celebration
c. December 1	Rock Lake	Oyster supper

All locations presumably Lake Como except Equinunk, Dillons, Honesdale, Winwood, Thompson, and Rock Lake.

Just as the Honesdale bands were dominated by the Gill family of Seelyville, so was the Lake Como band dominated by the Skelletts of Starrucca (a small borough, population 404, about eight miles northwest). The band seems to have been founded sometime early in 1896 by J. D. Skellett and later taken over by his brother S. J. Skellett, both of whom were involved with various other bands as well. The following newspaper article describes a concert that took place on July 30, 1896; although strictly it falls outside the bounds of this study, it provides both specific information about the band and a close look at the interrelationships among several bands of the area.

> July 30th was a great day at Como. The Como, Starrucca and Stevens Point cornet bands [Stevens Point is a village in Susquehanna County near Starrucca] had arranged to hold a meet on the evening of that day and give a concert for the benefit of the Como band. . . .
> In the evening the Grange hall was well filled to patronize the concert. The Starrucca band was not out in force. They divided up, part playing with Como and part with Stevens Point. The latter band is composed of 16 pieces and is led by G. M. Bailey, with S. J. Skellett, leader of the Starrucca band as instructor. The members of the Starrucca band present were C. A. Miles, M. D., Fred Benedict, B. C. Stoddard, A. S. Coon and George Boget. The Keystone band, of Como, is composed of J. D. Skellett, leader, Walter Skellett, Harry Todd, Wayne Lakin, Ernest White, Lewis Robinson, Clay Littell, Will Davall, Tom Farley, William Howell and Arthur Madigan.
> The program consisted of selections by the two bands interspersed with a duet by J. D. Skellett, cornet, Mary Rutledge, organist; song by J. D. Skellett with zither accompaniment was twice encored; trio, J. D. Skellett and A. S. Coon, harmonicas, S. J. Skellett, bones; fife and drum; cornet duet, Messrs. Skellett and Lakin; vocal duet by G. C. Reynolds and daughter Verna. After the concert ice cream and cake were served.
> We were told that the occasion drew the largest crowd to Como that has been there in a long time. Although dinner was served in the hall, 63 ate at P. F. Madigun's. The Steven's Point band started for home about 11 o'clock singing:

> > We've all been over to Como
> > We've all been over to Como
> > We've all been over to Como
> > And drank up all of Patsy's beer.

The Skellette brothers have a talent for music and they have worked some good players in the three bands. "Jack," as he was familiarly called, can play anything from a jaw bone to a piano, but he is perfectly at home with his cornet. One so proficient on that instrument is rarely found in the country. Stephen does not have the time for practice his brother has because he has a farm to manage.[30]

According to this entry, the band in 1896 had eleven members, slightly fewer than the Equinunk band's fifteen. It may have had more in later years; the Starrucca band is never heard from again, and the Lake Como band may have absorbed some of its members—along, apparently, with its leader, Stephen J. Skellett. At any rate, by September of 1897, Stephen and his family were firmly in control, as we saw in a passage already quoted in the discussion of the Equinunk band (pp. 89-90): three of his young sons were playing trombone, baritone, and bass drum.[31] And the *Independent* of September 13, 1899, stated that "Four members of the Keystone band, Lake Como, namely: S. J. Skellett, E [-flat] cornet; Edw. Skellett, tenor trombone; Chas. Skellett, b b [B-flat] bass; Walter Olver, solo alto; accompanied the Equinunk band to Susquehanna on the 6th and 7th inst. to enter the band prize contest. . . ."[32] Note that none of these people appears on the list of 1896, and that three of the four are named Skellett. Perhaps Edward and Charles are Stephen's children. In any case, it is clear that some important personnel changes took place between 1896 and 1899, and that Stephen J. Skellett and his family were the driving force behind the organization.

The history of the Keystone band, as best it can be reconstructed from the newspapers, was for the most part undistinguished. Its activities seem to have been much like those of all the other rural bands: picnics in the summer, entertainments in the winter, and civic occasions as needed. But the band did have one brief moment of glory, although not through any of its musical accomplishments. The tale of "the famous band of Como" begins in, of all places, the poetry column of the *Independent* on August 3, 1898.

Como's Band.

The grand old town of Como lies resting 'neath the hills,
While its waters run on daily, in quiet rippling rills;
And its sights and scenes are glorious—in fact, are simply grand,
But there's one thing does excel all else—it's the music of its band.

It's a fine, quaint village, and its people seldom go
To other towns or cities, because business is too slow;
They love to stay in Como and cultivate the land,
And they never tire listening to the music of its band.

There's Jonathan will vow to you that 'though his hair is gray,
He has lived his life in Como—he couldn't go away,
And when he asks you for a chew, then gives you the glad hand,
He will tell you there is nothing that can equal Como's band.

And Como is so healthy—they never seem to die,
But dry up like the Autumn leaves, then hasten toward the sky,
'Tis said that when some of them before St. Peter stand,
They're shocked to find he never heard of Como or its band.

And Como's lovely maidens go on practice nights to hear
The band boys in their club room, and fill the place with cheer;
'Tis then the boys will play their best, and show that they've got sand,
By the music they will give you, they try "to beat the band."

Now the nights are warm for playing, this I think you will admit,
But the boys don't seem to mind it, not even a little bit;
Each one has got his girl, and by her he's gently fanned,
Oh, I'd like to be a member of the lucky Como band.

                                                    J.H.C.

J.H.C. proves to be J. H. Coghlan, apparently a summer resident
of Lake Como and admittedly not known today as one of the
masters of English verse. Predictably, however, his poem raised
some eyebrows around the county. The very next week, the
Independent's Lake Como correspondent betrayed a certain puzzle-
ment about the poem's meaning: "We think we are safe on behalf of
the 'boys' to return thanks to 'J.H.C.' for his commendable words
for their band, taking the benefit of the doubt as to whether it was
intended as a genuine compliment or as harmless sarcasm."[33] And in
the same issue, on the Honesdale pages, the editors of the paper
tried to smooth things over: "Our highly esteemed Lake Como
correspondent hints that there may be sarcasm in the poet's verses
on the Como band. We cannot think so, because a charming good
nature and a keen appreciation of the art of music ripples along
every line. The vein of humor and wit might be construed into
satire but we think there is an entire absence of good reasons so to
adjudge the effusion."

This fine point of literary criticism was never satisfactorily cleared
up in the newspapers, but whatever its intent, the poem seems to
have been a real boost to the fortunes of the band. On August 24,
the *Independent* reported that "the famous Keystone band" accompanied the Lake Como Sunday school to a picnic at Dillons, and in
September the band was brought to Honesdale so that the whole
county could hear what all the fuss was about: "The famous Lake

Como band of which so much has been written in prose and poetry will furnish music at the [Wayne County] fair. S. J. Skellett, Jr., of Starrucca, is the leader, his brother Jack is one of the cornetists and two of his boys are also members. The Skelletts are all excellent musicians."[34]

The band received good reviews for its performance of the fair,[35] and it was the only one of these bands of northern Wayne ever to play at the county seat. But the fame of the Keystone band seems to have died down shortly thereafter, and the final words of this curious story were written in a new Coghlan poem, "Lake Como," that appeared in the *Independent* on August 16, 1899.

> The "Famous Band of Como" I find is playing still,
> And nightly drawing crowds around its hall that's on the hill;
> And music floats upon the air and fills the vales below,
> While lovely maidens linger near or saunter to and fro.

THE PLEASANT MOUNT BAND (AND ORCHESTRA)

Pleasant Mount is a village about ten miles southwest of Lake Como and about fourteen miles northwest of Honesdale. *Illustrated Wayne* described Pleasant Mount in 1900 as "the highest village in the county, being 2040 feet above sea level. Here are two good hotels, six stores and saw and grist mills. It is three miles from the Erie Railroad at Herrick Center and two miles from the Ontario & Western."[36]

The town had one prominent cultural advantage in the Pleasant Mount Academy, a high school that drew students from all around northern Wayne and Susquehanna counties.[37] The academy served not only to raise the level of Pleasant Mount's culture above that of most villages of comparable size, but also to provide a good auditorium for concerts and plays. It is perhaps the main reason why the town supported both a band and an orchestra.

The Pleasant Mount band probably began as such in the spring of 1897. On May 6, the Pleasant Mount correspondent to the *Citizen* reported that "The brass band movement is still alive and going. A meeting was held last Monday evening to discuss ways and means of perfecting an organization."

This item seems clear enough; but it is confounded by scattered earlier references[38] to a "Belmont band." Belmont is a tiny crossroads a mile west of Pleasant Mount: it seems inconceivable that it could have supported its own band, and even today the names

Belmont and Pleasant Mount are practically, as well as etymo-
logically, synonymous. Moreover, we hear of the Belmont band only
twice more, both times in the Orson columns of the papers (Table
9). From all this it would appear that the Belmont band is simply
another name for the Pleasant Mount band, a name not current in
Pleasant Mount itself. If so, however, the band was performing for
many months before the *Citizen* reported on its inception. But the
Citizen's wording is ambiguous; the term "perfecting an organization" may well refer to the formal organization and development
of a band that already existed in a small and ill-defined form. This
notion is supported, at least negatively, by the matter-of-fact coverage given to Pleasant Mount's Memorial Day exercises of 1897;[39]
there is no suggestion that this performance was the debut of a new
band. Indeed, it is possible that the Pleasant Mount band had existed
more or less continuously since at least 1881, when its leader,
Charles E. Wright, helped to instruct the Equinunk band.

In any case, the band does seem to have been enlarged and
improved during 1897, as the announcement of a fund-raising event
that fall indicates: "The Pleasant Mount cornet band will have a
concert and oyster supper, in the Academy Hall, on Thursday
evening, Nov. 25th. The concert will consist of band and orchestra
music, solos, duets, etc. A free concert ticket will be given with each
supper ticket purchased. The members of the band have purchased
their instruments, and this is their first call for public help, and it
deserves a liberal response. A very pleasant time is anticipated."[40]

The original director of the band was probably E. W. Wright,
described by the *Citizen* of December 2, 1897, as leader of both the
band and the orchestra, and probably a relative of the Charles
Wright who had directed the band sixteen years earlier. E. W.
Wright was a locally prominent and versatile instrumentalist, frequently featured as a soloist on both violin and baritone. How long
he directed the Pleasant Mount band is not clear, but in May 1900,
at any rate, the band was under new leadership: "The band concert
held in the hall last Friday evening, was a very successful affair. The
program consisted of recitations, tableaux, and band and orchestra
music. Those who recited were Ruth Kennedy, Bessie Moase, and
Frank Boyce. E. W. Wright rendered a violin solo, which was
encored. Compliments were heard on all sides for the improved
appearance of the band, which now numbers twenty members.
Arthur Curtis, of Farno, is their leader and instructor, and marked
improvement in the music reflects much credit on Mr. Curtis's

Table 9.
Performances of the Pleasant Mount Band

Date	Location	Event (Sponsor)
		1897
April 7*	R. Men's Hall, Orson	Entertainment (Red Men)
May 29	Pleasant Mt.	Memorial Day parade
July 4	Pleasant Mt.	4th of July celebration
September 2	Bigelow Lake	Picnic (IOOF)
November 25	Academy Hall	Concert & supper (Pleasant Mount band)
		1898
May 30	Pleasant Mt.	Memorial Day parade, cemetery exercises
June 25*	Orson	Concert
September 8	Carpenter's Grove (U'dale?)	Picnic (P. Mt. & Uniondale IOOF)
December 5	Pleasant Mt.	Farmers' Institute
		1899
April 7	Academy Hall	Concert and social (P. Mt. band & orchestra)
April 27	Academy Hall	Concert (P. Mt. band & orchestra)
May 30	Pleasant Mt.	Memorial Day parade, cemetery exercises
June 24	Wheeler block	Entertainment and ice cream social (M.E. Sunday school)
July 22	Farview	IOOF reunion (Moosic Lodge, IOOF)
July 22	Ames store, Waymart	Concert
August 9*	Palmer's grove, Orson	Hines family reunion
August 18	Lake Poyntelle	Picnic (P.Mt. Presbyterian and M. E. Sunday schools)
September 8	Academy Hall	Concert (P. Mt. band)
September 15	Vastbinder School	Festival and social (Vastbinder School)
October 13	Academy Hall	Union concert (P. Mt. and Uniondale bands)
October 27	H. T. Wright's house	Birthday serenade for Anna Wright
December 29	Academy Hall	Performance of play "The Golden Gulch" (P. Mt. band)

Table 9. (Continued)
Performances of the Pleasant Mount Band

Date	Location	Event (Sponsor)
		1900
January 19	Winwood	Performance of play "The Golden Gulch" (P. Mt. band)
February 22	Pleasant Mt.	Parade (IOOF)
May 25	Academy Hall	Concert and social
May 30	Pleasant Mt.	Memorial Day parade, cemetery exercises
July 4	Pleasant Mt.	4th of July floral parade, dinner
August 4	O'Hara, Kennedy houses	Open air concert, serenade
August 29	Poyntelle	Clambake (P. Mt. and L. Como IOOF)
September 1	Kennedy house?	Corn roast (Maude Kennedy)
November 9	Academy hall	Box social (P. Mt. High School)
November 2	Orson	Flagpole raising etc.
		1901
January 21	Academy Hall	Concert, play "Dutch Justice," social (P. Mt. band)
February 15	Winwood	Concert and entertainment
April 19	Whites Valley	Concert and dance
May 17	Academy Hall	Concert and box social (P. Mt. band)
May 27	Catholic church	Fair (Catholic Society)
May 30	Pleasant Mt.	Memorial Day parade, ceremony

*Papers say "Belmont band" or "Belmont cornet band."
All locations presumably Pleasant Mount except Orson, Uniondale, Farview, Waymart, Poyntelle, Winwood, and Whites Valley.

leadership. After the concert ice cream was served and a social time enjoyed."[41]

The Curtis administration was short-lived, however: in October a migration of musicians down from Orson (about seven miles north) gave the band a new instructor: "Prof. Mikrantz, of Orson, has been engaged to instruct the Pleasant Mt. cornet band. He commenced on Monday night last. Messrs. Hines, Mosher, and Patten, of Orson, have also become members. The band has much improved by these additions and will soon give the public a chance to hear them at Academy hall. Particulars at the next writing."[42] Professor Mikrantz, besides directing the band, also acted as trombone soloist.[43]

The newspapers mention a good many engagements for the

Pleasant Mount band; unfortunately, however, they seldom go into much detail. But information about a few typical and atypical performances is available.

Pleasant Mount, like most of the communities around the county, celebrated every Memorial Day with a parade, speeches, and exercises at the cemetery; this was perhaps the most conspicuous outdoor appearance of the band each year. The ceremonies for 1899 are representative.

> Memorial Day exercises were held at this place as follows. At 2 p.m. the procession started from the west end of Main street with B. F. Dix, as color bearer, followed by the band; next came the flower girls; next the citizens of the town, and members of the societies, which were followed by the carriages. The line of march was direct to the village cemetery, where the ceremony took place at the grave of Henry Abbott. Prayer was offered by Rev. J. H. Boyce, after which the G.A.R. ritual was read; dirge by the band. The following comrades decorated the graves of departed soldiers: B. F. Dix, D. E. Wilcox, Davis Gaylord, Nathan Carpenter and J. M. Spencer. After the decorations Rev. J. Pope gave a good talk appropriate to the occasion. Frank Spencer, H. T. Wright, B. F. Dix and George Graham decorated the graves in the Meredith and Mumford burial grounds. Memorial services were held last evening in the Presbyterian church.[44]

Concerts of the Pleasant Mount band were apt to include various forms of entertainment, such as local singers and elocutionists, in addition to the band music. The article that introduced Arthur Curtis as director provides a typical example of such a varied program. And when they played a double bill with the band from Uniondale (about three miles southwest, in Susquehanna County), the visitors apparently brought their own local talent.

> The band concert, announced as the last of the season, was well attended. The Uniondale band rendered several selections and their music was well received. Several numbers on the program failed to materialize. The principal numbers by home talent were violin and baritone solos, by E. W. Wright; Piano duets by Mrs. R. W. Niles and Blanche Kennedy; and a tableau by several young ladies, arranged by Lottie Spencer. Anna N. Spencer also sang a solo. A tambourine and bone performance was applauded by some and criticised by others.
> Besides the music furnished by the Uniondale band, the

following were worthy of special mention: Recitation by Miss
Coleman, vocal solo by Howard Crane, and violin solo by V.
Crandall.

Pleasant Mount band had advertised to serve oysters after
the concert. Well, the oysters were not to blame that the
arrangements were not carried out, but they (the oysters) beg
pardon, and promise to be on hand in proper time and style
next time.[45]

As Table 9 shows, the band played at various picnics and parades
both locally and in the surrounding area. But outdoor concerts as
such seem to have been relatively rare; the one instance described in
the newspapers shows the lack of a bandstand in town most
strikingly: "The band gave an open air concert on Saturday evening.
They played several selections from the roof of Mr. O'Hara's house,
and gave a serenade at W. P. Kennedy's, after which they were
hospitably entertained by Mr. and Mrs. Kennedy."[46]

The Pleasant Mount band seems to have been unusually active in
the wintertime. Pleasant Mount was a sociable community, and the
academy was a good place to meet, and so the band played at
suppers and entertainments all year long. It was also involved,
unusually, with drama; in January of 1900, and again a year later,
the band staged plays in Academy Hall. Apparently they should
have stuck to their instruments: the two plays provoked practically
the only bad reviews I have read in these newspapers:

On Friday evening, Dec. 29th, the drama, "Golden Gulch," was
played in Academy Hall for the benefit of the Mount Pleasant
band. The band members were assisted in the play by Mr. and
Mrs. R. M. Niles, Misses Etta McAvoy and Blanche Kennedy,
and Messers. Fred. Demming, Joe Roebel and Earl Spencer.

The play itself did not meet with general admiration, but
even critics admit that the parts were all unusually well
sustained, and the costumes and disguises among the best ever
staged here.[47]

On Thursday evening the band gave a concert and entertainment in the hall. The selections rendered by the band were
well received. An after piece, entitled "Dutch Justice," was of
the kind that some people like to listen to about five minutes,
not longer. This, with a monologue, was far below the grade of
which the band members are capable of producing. The social
was enjoyed by the large company of young people present.

Coffee and sandwiches were served. The receipts of the evening were $25.[48]

Perhaps the most extraordinary feature of the Pleasant Mount band was its relationship with the Pleasant Mount orchestra. As the Table 10 shows, the papers mentioned this orchestra quite frequently between 1897 and 1901; but they give almost no useful detail about it, so that it cannot be described with any confidence. Only a few observations can be made. First, the band and the orchestra were not simply two names for the same organization; they frequently appeared together as two distinct groups. Second, both band and orchestra were led, at least in 1897, by E. W. Wright, who was probably the first violinist of the orchestra. Third, the orchestra had at least some string players, but evidently not many: in addition to what we know about E. W. Wright, the *Citizen* of May 6, 1897 refers to the wedding of "the second violinist," Russell Mumford. And finally, the orchestra seems to have played only indoors. Beyond these few facts it seems most likely that the Pleasant Mount orchestra was a small and unpretentious one, comprising a handful of string players and a few winds from the band, and that its repertory was generally popular rather than classical.

Table 10.
Performances of the Pleasant Mount Orchestra

Date	Location	Event (Sponsor)
		1897
January 13	IOOF Hall	Entertainment
March 13	Pleasant Mt.	Entertainment
April 10	IOOF Hall	Entertainment (IOOF)
		1898
April 12	Pleasant Mt.	Entertainment (ALU)
		1899
February 4	Pleasant Mt.	Local teachers' institute
March 30	W. Fletcher's house, Herrick Center	Ice cream festival
April 7	Academy Hall	Concert and social (P. Mt. band and orchestra)
April 27	Academy Hall	Concert (P. Mt. band and orchestra)

Table 10. (Continued)
Performances of the Pleasant Mount Orchestra

Date	Location	Event (Sponsor)
May 23	Pleasant Mt.	Entertainment (ALU)
May 26	Academy Hall?	Farewell social (P. Mt. Academy)
July 4	St. Paul's Episcopal ch.	Dinner (St. Paul's Episcopal church)
October 20	IOOF Hall	Installation of officers (IOOF)
December 27	IOOF Hall	Oyster supper (IOOF)
		1900
January 13	Academy Hall	Local teachers' institute
February 22	Academy Hall	Concert (IOOF)
		1901
January 1	Academy Hall	Entertainment and supper (IOOF)
July 4	Academy Hall	4th of July entertainment

All locations presumably Pleasant Mount except Herrick Center.

NOTES

1. Kristen Ammerman, in the Centennial Edition of the *Wayne Independent*, February 4, 1978, p. C35, gives the population of Equinunk in 1911 as 425.

2. *Hancock Herald*, September 1880 and January 1881. These and other items from the *Hancock Herald*, which I have not had a chance to see, are taken from the notes kindly supplied by Wellington Lester of the Equinunk Historical Society.

3. *Honesdale Citizen*, December 24, 1896.

4. The *Hancock Herald*, February 1897, adds that they practiced in the basement of the store.

5. *Hancock Herald*, February 1897. "Lloyd" appears to be the correct spelling of the baritone player's name, not "Lord" as it appears in the document above.

6. Sears, Roebuck, *Catalogue No. 104* (Chicago: Sears, Roebuck, 1897; rept. New York: Chelsea House, 1968), pp. 530-31.

7. Lyon and Healy, *Catalogue of Musical Merchandise* (Chicago: Lyon and Healy, 1898-99), pp. 83, 92, 103, 120. These figures include only "baritones"; "euphoniums," both single—and double—belled, tended to be more expensive, but in the picture of the Equinunk band, Lloyd's instrument looks more like a baritone.

8. Ibid., pp. 84, 94, 105, 121.

9. *Honesdale Citizen*, August 19, 1897.

10. For more on the band members' ages, see Table 15.

11. *Wayne Independent*, September 18, 1897; the passage is quoted in full on page 00 of this volume. We do not know exactly when the uniforms were obtained, only that the band was "arrayed in their natty uniforms" by the following September—see *Independent*, September 7, 1898.

12. For more on the ages of the band members, see Table 15.

13. See *Centennial and Illustrated Wayne County*, 2d ed. (Honesdale: The Wayne Independent, 1902; rept. Honesdale: Wayne County Historical Society, 1975), p. 97.

14. *Wayne Independent*, July 15, 1899.

15. Ibid., September 18, 1897.

16. *Honesdale Citizen*, September 16, 1897.

17. *Wayne Independent*, March 1, 1899.

18. Ibid., January 9, 1901.

19. Ibid., June 28, 1899.

20. *Illustrated Wayne*, pp. 36-37, 97.

21. *Wayne Independent*, April 13, 1898.

22. *Honesdale Citizen*, May 4, 1899.

23. *Wayne Independent*, April 17, 1901.

24. Ibid., May 8, 1901.

25. Ibid., July 12, 1901.

26. Ibid., January 15, 1898.

27. Ibid., June 29, 1898.

28. Ibid., September 13, 1899.

29. Ibid., October 2, 1897; *Honesdale Citizen*, October 14, 1897.

30. *Wayne Independent*, August 5, 1896.

31. *Honesdale Citizen*, September 16, 1897.

32. The rest of this entry is quoted on p. 94.

33. *Wayne Independent*, August 10, 1898.

34. Ibid., September 21, 1898.

35. Ibid., October 1, 1898.

36. *Illustrated Wayne*, p. 107.

37. Ibid., pp. 79-80. Ammerman, in "Centennial Edition," p. C13, says that in 1900 the academy was transferred from a private to a public school.

38. In the *Wayne Independent*'s Equinunk column of September 2, 1896 and its Orson column of April 14, 1897.

39. *Wayne Independent*, June 5, 1897.

40. *Honesdale Citizen*, November 25, 1897.

41. Ibid., May 31, 1900.

42. *Wayne Independent*, October 24, 1900.

43. See ibid., November 1, 1900; *Honesdale Citizen*, November 3, 1900; ibid., July 18, 1901.

44. *Wayne Independent*, June 10, 1899.

45. *Honesdale Citizen*, October 19, 1899.

46. Ibid., August 9, 1900.

47. Ibid., January 11, 1900.

48. Ibid., January 31, 1901.

5

Other Bands and Orchestras

This fifth chapter, intended not to present a unified whole, but simply to pick up some loose pieces, will describe a wide variety of musical organizations. A good deal is known about some, others remain mysterious.

THE HAWLEY BAND(S)

Hawley, about ten miles southeast of Honesdale, was the second-largest town in the county, with a population of 1,925 in 1900. In general, it was quite similar to Honesdale, as can be seen in its description in *Illustrated Wayne:*

> It is nicely situated, is a fine place of residence and is a good location for business and manufacturing. . . . The village is lighted by electricity, has five good hotels, excellent railroad facilities, a number of first class manufactories and many fine residences. . . . Prosperity first came to the village with the surveying for the Delaware & Hudson canal and the impetus given the place was augmented twenty years later when the Pennsylvania Coal Co. constructed a gravity railroad from the Lackawanna valley to bring coal to the canal. The town received another boom in 1865 with the building of the Honesdale branch to Lackawaxen. At the present time the Erie & Wyoming Valley railroad joins the Erie at West Hawley. . . . The principal industries are as follows: Dexter, Lambert & Co.'s silk mill; J. S. O'Connor's glass cutting establishment, one of the largest known; Hawley Glass Works; United States

knitting mill; Wall & Murphy's and Pierson's flouring mills. The place has one weekly newspaper, The Times.[1]

This last point is especially significant because copies of the *Hawley Times* unfortunately do not survive from this period. As a result, information about the bands of Hawley, taken from the out-of-town columns of the Honesdale papers, must be regarded as still incomplete, but a brief description of these bands is both feasible and instructive.

The most fundamental unanswered question is whether Hawley had one band or two between 1897 and 1901. This much is clear: that at the beginning of the period Hawley was the home of the Eddy Cornet band, that the Eddy Cornet band disappeared in 1897 and the Hawley band rose in its place, and that the new band survived at least until 1900. But should we consider these two separate organizations, or merely two incarnations of the same band? I am choosing the latter attitude, but in fact the distinction is probably trivial. Given the small size of the community, the two ensembles may well have had substantially the same personnel.

"The Eddy" was a region in the southeastern end of town, by the lower depot of the E&WV. Whether the Eddy Cornet band was named for this section of town, or for its chief hostelry, the Eddy Hotel, is not clear. In any case, the band played at least seven times in the spring of 1897 before its dissolution (Table 11).

The most noteworthy of these is the first, the serenade for Miss Altemus of the Wayne County Hotel.

A short time since the Eddy cornet band tendered Miss Altemus, proprietor of the Wayne County Hotel, a serenade, but were disappointed upon learning that she was out of town at the time. When she returned, her generous disposition impelled reciprocity, and the boys were invited to dine with her on the evening of Washington's birthday. Special invitations were also extended to the E.&W.V. passenger conductor, John Brink, Richard Teeter and a representative of THE CITIZEN. In response to the summons, the boys appeared with instruments and in uniform. After dispersing some good music as a signal of the hostess's kindness, all repaired to the dining room and relieved in part a table groaning under the weight of an endless variety of luscious viands. The company then resorted to the pleasant reading room and indulged in conversation and a smoker. Late in the evening the musicians presented themselves in a body to Miss Altemus, and through their speaker, extended thanks for her hospitality.[2]

Table 11.
Performances of the Eddy Cornet Band

Date	Location	Event (Sponsor)
	1897	
February 22	Wayne Co. Hotel	Serenade for Miss Altemus
March 17	Hawley	St. Patrick's Day parade
March 18	Eddy Hotel	Serenade for J. Bachon Jr.
April 17	Hawley	Playing in streets
April 19	Star Rink	Benefit ball (Eddy Cornet band)
May 29	Hawley	2 Memorial Day parades
June 24	Maennerchor Hall	Dedication of new annex (Maennerchor)

All locations Hawley.

In April, the band gave a fund-raising dance and advertised, "The music will be furnished by an orchestra of 20 pieces."[3] If this refers to themselves, which is probable, the band was a fairly large one, equivalent to the bands of Honesdale.

The Eddy Cornet band survived through June and then vanished from sight, at least in the Honesdale papers. But the *Citizen* of September 23, 1897, reported that "The Hawley band has been reorganized, with F. W. Schalm as an acquisition." And from then on, the ensemble was always referred to as the Hawley band.

As the Table 12 shows, nearly all of the reported performances of the Hawley band were outdoors. This is, however, probably not an accurate sample; more likely, only the most conspicuous engagements of the band are reported. We know they played indoors at least once, at the debut concert of Lawyer's band in Honesdale on March 17, 1899 (see pp. 43-44). But still, the outdoor performances are better documented, and thus they must be our primary concern.

As in most of the other towns in the county, Memorial Day was the big annual patriotic festival in Hawley. Like Honesdale, Hawley celebrated Memorial Day with a variety of different activities, and the band participated in most of them:

> Perhaps no year since the institution of Memorial day was the event so harmoniously and enthusiastically commemorated as on Wednesday in Hawley. The G.A.R. Post was inclined to be a little discouraged as the day was approaching and there seemed to be no provisions for sufficient floral gifts with which to do the work properly, but when the time arrived flowers came in

Table 12.
Performances of the Hawley Band

Date	Location	Event (Sponsor)
		1897
December 13	Maennerchor Hall	Masquerade ball (Hawley band)
		1898
January 1	Hawley	Playing in streets
February 21	Streets, Star Rink	Street serenade, masquerade ball (Maennerchor)
April 27	E&WV station	Playing for Co. E en route to war
May 12*	Hawley	Escorting Dunmore council, JOUAM, from station to Star Rink
May 19	Honesdale	Parade (Red Men)
May 30	Hawley	Memorial Day parade, cemetery exercises
July 21	Maennerchor Park	Picnic and clambake (Maennerchor)
August 3	Lake Ariel	Excursion: parade, picnic (N.E. Pa. IOOF)
October 13	Honesdale	Parade (Protection Engine Co. #3)
November 2	Star Rink	Republican rally
		1899
February 6	Hawley	Escorting guests of Maennerchor from station to Star Rink
February 7	Hawley	Parade, serenade of businesses (Maennerchor)
March 17	Honesdale	Procession, concert (Lawyer's band)
May 30	Hawley	Memorial Day parade, cemetery exercises
June 26	Hawley	Parade with new fire truck
August 4	Hawley	Street serenade
		1900
May 30	Hawley	Memorial Day parade, cemetery exercises; playing in streets?
July 22	Hawley	Processions, cornerstone laying (St. Philomela's church)
August 1	Lake Ariel	Picnic (IOOF)

*May mean American band of Dunmore, not Hawley band.
All locations Hawley except Honesdale and Lake Ariel.

profusion from unexpected sources. At 8 o'clock Wednesday morning everything was in readiness. Delegations accompanied by the Hawley band visited the Hillside Catholic, East End and Walnut Grove cemeteries and deposited floral tributes and flags upon the graves of the heroes of '61-5. During this time patriotic hands were busy decorating homes and business places with the national colors and people were gathering from far and near toward the center of the village where is located the Post headquarters in Odd Fellows' building. Chief Marshall, M. M. Treadwell, was dextrously moving about forming the procession and a few minutes after ten o'clock the long line was ready to move. The order was as follows: Russell Huff, of Tafton, one of the civil war veterans with large flag, Hawley band, flag, Hawley school children on foot marshaled by Prof. Creasy, flag, society of Ancient Order of Hibernians, flag, Red Men, flag, Junior Order of American Mechanics, flag, Grand Army Post and other soldiers twenty in number, wagon with the village clergymen, little John Ames with his small pony and cart, four large wagons with Sunday School children, followed by ten wagons carrying citizens. The procession, nearly a mile long, moved slowly to the East End cemetery where the veterans surrounded the plot in which lies the remains of James M. Thorpe, after whom the Post was named. The band played a dirge, attention of the comrades was called and a salute given to the dead. Rev. R. D. Minch evoked divine blessing. The oration was by James T. Rodman. Fitting tributes were paid to the memory of Wesley F. Rogers, recently deceased, who was a member of the Post. Officer of the day, James M. Ball, decorated the grave of comrade Thorpe. He was followed by E. A. Marshal, who continued the ceremony and placed additional flowers on the mound in memory of the dead soldiers. Eulogistic remarks were made by Mr. Treadwell to the memory of the dead soldiers of the Spanish-American war and a beautiful wreath was added for them. John Giltner, a member of the band, was called to the center of the plot and played what is known to soldiers as "taps." The band gave more music, the procession formed in reverse order and the line of march was continued up the east side and to their quarters where the cortege disbanded. From 12 until 2 o'clock dinner was served by the post and their ladies in Odd Fellows' dining rooms and the appetites of large numbers made keen by the exercise of participating in the doings of the forenoon were satisfied at a cost of 25 cents each. During the afternoon music was freely dispersed by the band. Supper was served from 5 until 7 o'clock, and at 8 o'clock an entertainment was given for the benefit of the post. Barring the heat and dust the day was extremely pleasant and interesting. There was not the slightest accident to any, the best of order prevailed and but very little drunkenness was visible.[4]

But the specialty of the Hawley band, or at least so it seems from the newspapers, was grand welcomes for visiting dignitaries. For example, in chapter 3, we saw Company E leaving Honesdale on the Erie, bound for the Spanish-American War, on April 27, 1898. As they pulled out of the station, they were serenaded by the Honesdale band; a few minutes later, as they pulled into the station at Hawley, they were greeted by the Hawley band:

> Nearly an hour before the time for the special train with Co. E, of Honesdale, en route to Scranton, Wednesday evening, to arrive here, people began gathering at the depot, and when the train hove in sight an immense crowd was ready to greet the soldier boys, and the Hawl[e]y band played continuously during the 15 minutes the train remained here. There was considerable merriment among the young people as they shook hands and conversed with the soldiers, while many a wife and mother who stood by shed tears of sympathy for the families that had parted for the time with husband and father.
>
> All day the town was aglow with the National colors, evincing a spirit of patriotism and recognizing the sacrifice the Honesdale boys were making.
>
> When the train moved from the station, the air was rent with cheers, intensified by the lively music of the band, while those who could recall events of the late war wended their way homeward with tear dimmed eyes, while from their hearts ascended prayers that the soldier life of Co. E, during the existing troubles, might be confined to camp life on our own shores.[5]

The following year, a more complex operation had to be carried out when the Hawley Maennerchor celebrated its silver anniversary. The singing society had invited guests from all over the area, and when the guests arrived aboard several different trains, the Maennerchor and band had to meet each one and escort the passengers to Maennerchor Hall.

Hawley was cheerfully surrendered on Monday to the German invasion, whose object was to assist the Hawley Maennerchor in commemorating the 25th anniversary of its organization.

Elaborate preparations preceded the reception of out of town guests, Monday afternoon. The village, so far as flags and bunting were concerned, assumed the appearance of a revival of Hawley's patriotism during the Spanish-American war.

Monday afternoon was devoted to receiving the guests. The Maennerchor, headed by the Hawley band, marched to the West Hawley station on the arrival of the trains from Port Jervis, Honesdale and Scranton, each time escorting a good number of guests. . . .

On Tuesday at 10:30 a.m., the grand parade formed in front of Maennerchor hall and marched through the principal streets of the borough, accompanied by the band.[6]

And such treatment was not only accorded to human beings: the red carpet might also be rolled out for an inanimate object, as on June 26, 1899: "The long looked for new hook and ladder fire truck equipped with Babcock extinguishers, buckets, ladders, etc. arrived from Chicago, Saturday, June 24. On the following Monday evening the Hawley band accompanied the fire company to the station where they took possession of the truck and paraded through the principal streets."[7]

The last recorded ceremonial function for the band was the cornerstone laying for St. Philomela's Catholic church on July 22, 1900. The band apparently did not participate in the actual ceremony, but did make two trips to the station:

At 9:30 a large procession was formed in the following order: National colors, Hawley band, coach with Rev. P. C. Winters, C.M.B.A. and A.O.H. societies, each headed by a banner of their order, and a large number of Sunday school children, followed by a long line of members of the congregation. The procession moved down 15th to 18th street and to the E.&W.V. depot, passing under a neatly constructed arch spanning the Middle Creek bridge. Inscribed on the side toward the depot was the word "Welcome," and upon the other side, "Bon Voyage."

At 10:30 the regular train from Scranton arrived with six well filled coaches of visitors, Bishop Hoban and the Forest band (of Scranton). The Bishop took a seat, in the coach with Father Winters, and the procession moved on, passing the open ranks of the children, who had been halted, and who were closed in behind the coach. The cortege now continued on to the site of the new building, where they disbanded.

At 3:30, the two bands, with a large number of people, went to the depot to receive and escort the nine car loads of visitors who came by special train from Scranton, and many who arrived from Honesdale by the regular train.[8]

After August 1, 1900, however, the Hawley band disappeared from the Honesdale papers. Whether this implies a dissolution of the band, or merely a gap in the reporting, is not clear; but perhaps significantly, the Beach Lake band provided the music for Hawley's Memorial Day festivities of 1901.[9]

THE BEACH LAKE BAND

The village of Beach Lake, also spelled "Beech Lake," is described well by *Illustrated Wayne*:

Beech Lake, located in Berlin township, is 1330 feet above sea level, 330 feet higher than Honesdale and 616 feet higher than Narrowsburg. It is nine miles from the former and six miles from the latter place. It is a pretty country village but the chief attraction is the lake. . . . There are several commodious cottages in which summer boarders are generously entertained and as the demand becomes greater there will be more erected. Berlin township, in which Beech Lake is located, is noted for its excellent roads. It is an easy grade from either Honesdale or Narrowsburg [New York] to the lake and views along the road from Indian Orchard are unsurpassed for rural scenery. There are no great elevations in the township. The surface is undulating and the lake is on about the highest point, thus giving a grand view of the surrounding landscape with the hills of the Delaware rising up majestically to the eastward.[10]

The Beach Lake band is only sporadically documented in the newspapers; Table 13 is probably an incomplete list. But the band seems to have predated and survived the five-year period of this study—a distinction it shares with only the Lake Como band and possibly the Pleasant Mount band. We also know nothing about its membership and instrumentation, except that at one point it had thirteen members[11] and that one Oakley Henshaw, of Indian Orchard, joined in 1898.[12]

Table 13.
Performances of the Beach Lake Band

Date	Location	Event (Sponsor)
		1897
March 6	B.L. School	Local teachers' institute
July 3	Beach Lake	Picnic (Epworth League)
July 4	Beach Lake	4th of July picnic
		1898
February 10	M.E. church	Farmers' institute
May 30	Honesdale	Memorial Day parade (with Honesdale JOUAM)
August 25	W. Wood house	Party for Hiram D. Wood
		1899
May 30	Hawley	Memorial Day parade, cemetery exercises
July 4	Beach Lake	4th of July picnic
September 4	Dunedin House	Party (guests of Dunedin House)
December 21	M.E. church	Farmers' institute
		1900
July 4	M.E. parsonage grounds	4th of July picnic
August 16	Tyler Hill	Fair and festival (Ladies' Aid Society)
August 23	Dunedin House	Lawn fete & musicale (M.E. church)
September 29	Milanville	Political rally (Republican party)
October 20	Tyler Hill	Flag raising
November 3	Honesdale	Political rally at courthouse; banquet for JOUAM
		1901
May 25	Band room	Ice cream social (B. L. band, Epworth League)
May 30	Hawley	Memorial Day parade, concert
September 28	Band room	Ice cream social (B. L. band, Epworth League)

*May be another band.
All locations Beach Lake except Honesdale, Hawley, Tyler Hill, and Milanville.

It seems clear, however, that the band was active throughout 1897-1901, and that it performed much more regularly than the newspaper accounts indicate. For instance, the Beach Lake correspondent to the *Independent* once wrote, "Our band meet for practice twice a week, and during the fine weather are in the habit of marching through our streets as they play. During M.E. quarterly meetings they courteously suspend practice."[13]

Beach Lake apparently did not celebrate Memorial Day, and as a result, its band was free to be hired for parades elsewhere. I have already mentioned their appearance in Hawley on Memorial Day 1901, apparently in lieu of the defunct Hawley band (p. 115). The Beach Lake band had played with the Hawley band in Hawley's Memorial Day celebration of 1899 as well;[14] in 1898, the band was in Honesdale for Memorial Day, having been specially engaged by the Junior Order of United American Mechanics (J.O.U.A.M.) in addition to the regular Honesdale band.[15]

The Beach Lake band participated in a variety of other political and patriotic occasions, such as a rally in Milanville, about six miles northeast: "A grand McKinley and Roosevelt rally took place at Milanville last Saturday afternoon and evening, marked by the attendance of many Republicans and their families. . . . 'Old Glory' was hoisted to the top, saluted by the Beach Lake band, with a chorus of cheers from the crowd in attendance. The band is an excellent one, and its members are intelligent and gentlemanly young men. Through the afternoon and evening they gave selections of patriotic and other airs, at the Beach mansion, at the acid factory, and at the meeting."[16]

Typical of rural bands, the Beach Lake band played at the Farmers' Institute held in the M. E. church in Beach Lake on December 21, 1899: "The evening session was opened by a selection by the band. This organization is composed of the superstitious number 13 yet they make good music and stick together. They rendered several selections during the session."[17]

The band also fit easily into the resort atmosphere of Beach Lake in the summer; here, in one instance, they entertained at one of the prominent boardinghouses: "On Monday evening the guests of the Dunedin House at Beech Lake entertained the band and other invited guests at that place. The house and porch were decorated with red and white lanterns. Ice cream and cake were served. A pleasant time was enjoyed by all those present."[18]

One final item, a description of the Beach Lake band's participation in a fair at Tyler Hill (six-and-a-half miles to the northeast), tells much about the social importance of the band not only to its members and its home community, but also to the citizens of the villages that heard it: "The Beach Lake band were there and added much to the pleasure of the evening. They serenaded our obliging postmaster, C. M. Pethick, made a call at our pretty Laurel Lake, and I heard one of them say, 'This was his first visit to Tyler Hill, although he had always been a resident of Beach Lake.' . . . Some of our young men were equally pleased with the Beach Lake young ladies, who accompanied the band. Who can tell what may occur before we have another fair?"[19]

THE GOULDSBORO BAND

The Gouldsboro band is not very copiously documented in our sources, probably for two reasons. First, the village of Gouldsboro, in the very southern tip of Wayne County, is far removed from Honesdale, both physically and socially; news from Gouldsboro was relatively sparse in the Honesdale papers. And second, the band seems to have been formed relatively late, probably sometime in 1900.

The first reference to the Gouldsboro band describes its appearance at a reunion of the Geary family in Gouldsboro on August 15, 1900: "As the twilight slowly disappeared, the Gouldsboro band, marching to drum beat, assembled before the house, and by the light of their blazing torches delighted all with their music. The unselfish kindness of the band boys, who had thus honored the family, was rewarded by an invitation to partake of ice cream and water melon. These were so greatly appreciated that the band again assembled, endeavoring to excel its former efforts."[20]

The item gives no hint as to the age of the band at this time, but it was probably relatively new, for the *Independent* of April 3, 1901, carries a legal notice of its incorporation.

IN RE Incorporation of the "Gouldsboro Cornet Band" of Gouldsboro, Wayne County, Pa.

Notice is hereby given that an application will be made to the Court of Common Pleas of Wayne County, on Monday, April 29, 1901, at 2 o'clock p.m., . . . for the charter of an intended corporation to be called the "Gouldsboro Cornet Band," of Gouldsboro, Pa., the character and object of which is the maintenance of a club or society for the promotion of music, for the studying, practicing and performing of music, for the improvement and social enjoyment of the members, and of the citizens of Lehigh township, in said county of Wayne. Said proposed corporation, for the purpose above stated, to have, possess and enjoy all the rights, benefits, and privileges of the said Act of Assembly and its supplements.

M. E. Simons, Solicitor.[21]

Two other engagements of the band were reported during 1901. On July 4, they appeared at a Sunday School picnic at Lewis Robacker's grove at South Sterling, six miles to the east.[22] And on September 5, the band played at a picnic of the Odd Fellows at Newfoundland, eight miles to the northeast: "The exercises were interspersed by selections by the Gouldsboro band. This organization has been in existence only a short time; it is chartered and the boys make good music. There are 22 pieces in the band, which is a large one for a country town."[23]

After this strong start—and the article is right that twenty-two pieces is a large band for a village of Gouldsboro's size—the band probably survived for some years thereafter. But this is all we know for the years 1897 to 1901.

MYSTERIOUS BANDS OF WAYNE COUNTY

The newspapers mention nine other possible bands within the county's borders between 1897 and 1901—each only once. It is, of course, impossible to tell much about these organizations, but some of them probably really did exist, at least briefly. Some may simply be wrong names for other, more familiar bands, and others are probably just rumors. The nine mystery bands follow, in alphabetical order, with as much evidence as I can muster.

The Carley Brook Band. The Calkins correspondent to the *Citizen* reported on July 4, 1901 that "the Carley Brook band" had played at a wedding on June 19. Carley Brook is not far from Honesdale, and it is doubtful that a band could have played there unnoticed by the Honesdale papers for very long; this is, however, a late reference, and conceivably it was a brand new organization. More likely the reference is to a small dance band and not a cornet band.

The Clinton Band. The Waymart correspondent to the *Citizen* reported on June 3, 1897, that the Clinton band had participated in the Memorial Day parade in Waymart on May 29. This does sound like an authentic cornet band; but Clinton township, just north of Waymart, contains, so far as we know, no town that had a band at this time. Possibly the correspondent is confused, or possibly this is the same as the Farno band.

The Farno Band. Farno was an old name for a crossroads in the western part of the county; it has also been called Clinton Centre. It apparently had an especially industrious correspondent, for its coverage in the newspapers was all out of proportion to its size. The one reference to a Farno band, however, was in the Waymart column of the *Citizen*—a circumstance that itself casts doubt on the accuracy of the entry: "In the evening, the Farno and Mount Pleasant bands, which attended the picnic [of the Odd Fellows at Farview], gave a concert in front of Ames & Co.'s store [in Waymart]."[24]

A clue to the identity of this band may be found in chapter 4: it will be remembered that in May of 1900 one Arthur Curtis, reportedly a resident of Farno, became leader of the Pleasant Mount band. A town the size of Farno cannot have contained very many musicians; if it had a band, presumably Arthur Curtis was involved with it. The appearance of both bands together in July of 1899, and Curtis's leadership of the Pleasant Mount band less than a year later, may be more than a coincidence. Two possibilities seem to present themselves: 1) that the two bands played together at this time and merged shortly thereafter; or 2) that Arthur Curtis and some of his neighbors had a little band in Farno that was associated with the Pleasant Mount band, but detachable from it, even before Curtis became leader of the larger organization.

The Hines Corners Band. The Hines Corners column of the *Independent* of May 18, 1898, announced, "Band boys are requested to meet on Saturday night to reorganize and start out more enthusiastic." The *Citizen* said much the same thing the next day. Hines Corners is not very close to any town with a band, so this probably does not refer to some more familiar organization; but the tone of the announcement suggests that this might be an attempted revitalization of a band that had already been dead for awhile (i.e., since before 1897). Evidently the attempt was a failure.

The Maplewood Band. The *Citizen* of August 12, 1899, announced in its Maplewood column that "The sound of the once famous Maplewood band can be heard almost any evening, and it sounds like old times. The boys are practicing under the leadership of J. H. Sloat, and are getting along nicely." This sounds encouraging, like another case of a band being awakened from dormancy. Unfortunately, however, nothing more is heard about it. Most likely it did not survive long.

The Starrucca Band (or Sherman Band). The Sherman correspondent to the *Independent* reported in the paper of September 11, 1897, that "The band convention which was held in Brundage's grove, last

Friday, was not the success they expected it to be, but we understand they cleared about $35. They intended to have three bands beside their home band but the one from Steven's Point was the only one that appeared on the scene."

This entry is puzzling. I have been unable to locate Brundage's grove, and without this knowledge it is hard to know where this "home band" would have come from. It may well have been from Sherman itself: the *Hancock Herald* reported in August 1893 that the "Sherman wind jammers (no offense, gentlemen) discoursed, I am told, good music" at a picnic in Equinunk.[25] And that such a band existed in Sherman for several years without otherwise being known in the Honesdale papers is quite possible; of all the villages in Wayne County, Sherman, in the very northern tip, is probably the most isolated from the county seat.

Another possibility is that the "home band" may be from Starrucca, which is only a few miles form both Sherman and Stevens Point. (Stevens Point, incidentally, is just over the line in northwestern Susquehanna County.) Starrucca, too, had a band at least some years before: Alfred Mathews's history of Wayne County, published in 1886, refers to "the Starrucca Cornet Band, of eighteen members, organized in 1882, and now under the leadership of Professor S. V. Stockman,"[26] and this band or its successor was still in existence, but apparently weak, as late as July 1896 (pp. 96-97). We have, however, presumed that it dissolved in or before September 1897, when its leader, S. J. Skellett, is first seen in charge of the Lake Como band. Possibly, then, the Starrucca band, with or without Stephen Skellett, really did survive until September 1897 and played at this affair; or perhaps the Lake Como band had a sufficient number of people from the Starrucca area for the Sherman correspondent to refer to it as "the home band."

The Varden Band. The Varden column of the *Citizen* reported on March 3, 1898, that "There are rumors of a band being started here in the near future." But there is no more information; presumably the rumors were just that.

The Waymart Drum Corps. A report of the 7-County Veteran's Reunion at Honesdale, printed in the *Herald* of August 5, 1897, says that "a drum corps from Waymart furnished their share of the patriotic music." This may refer to a group of drummers organized especially for the occasion, or perhaps Waymart did have a drum corps for a time. If there was such an ensemble, it was not very visible in the papers, and at any rate it was not a cornet band.

The White Mills Cornet Band. The White Mills correspondent to the

Independent reported on February 24, 1897, that "The cornet band will hold a ball at the opera house on Saturday night." White Mills is about halfway between Honesdale and Hawley, on the railroad, so that the item could refer to either the Honesdale band or the Eddy Cornet band. But if either one is equally likely, why doesn't the paper tell which? The tone of the announcement, then, seems to imply that the band in question is actually from White Mills, which is quite possible, especially when we consider that the item is from very early in 1897 and may refer to a band on its way out.

VILLAGE ORCHESTRAS

Orchestras are even more problematic than bands because of the ambiguity of terminology. We have already seen the word *orchestra* applied to the Honesdale Philharmonic, an authentic orchestra of twenty to thirty members playing mostly classical music; to the Ideal orchestra, which consisted of two violins, flute, cornet, and piano, and which played popular music for dancing; and to the Pleasant Mount orchestra, whose size, instrumentation, and repertory are unknown. The word is also used occasionally to describe a cornet band. So when one of the rural correspondents mentions "the orchestra," it is hard to know just what he or she is describing. In most cases it is probably correct to presume that these orchestras were small groups containing some strings and that their repertory, like that of the bands, was mostly popular. Orchestras associated with schools, such as the Pleasant Mount orchestra and the White Mills Graded School orchestra (p. 123) may have been exceptions; I suspect, however, that the Rock Lake orchestra was more typical: "After all had finished eating, music was then furnished by the orchestra, consisting of Emma Lestrange, organist; Wm. Leonard, bass violin; F. P. McLaughlin and Thomas Leonard, first violin; G. B. McKenna, prompter. All played well, which made everything more enjoyable."[27]

As a result, weeding through all these village "orchestras" is an uncertain business at best; apart from the Rock Lake orchestra above, none gives any clue to either its size or its instrumentation. Perhaps a more useful distinction, then, is between ensembles that bear people's names (such as the McDivitt orchestra), which are almost certainly small dance bands in more or less private hands, and orchestras that are either named after their town or are called "the orchestra" by the local correspondents: these may well have had the same sort of community involvement that the bands did.

This definition yields eight or nine possible community orchestras around Wayne County; in each case the identity remains quite obscure.

The *Dyberry Orchestra*, presumably from Dyberry township, north of Honesdale, played at two picnics in the late summer of 1900: at Erhardt's grove in Girdland,[28] and at the Grange Hall in Beech Grove.[29]

The *Hawley Orchestra* played at a St. Patrick's Day entertainment in its home town in 1897;[30] at an Odd Fellows' Picnic at Lake Ariel in the summer of 1900;[31] and at a performance of the play "Enoch Arden" at Hawley's Standard Opera House the following March.[32]

The *Hollisterville Orchestra*, from a village in the southwestern part of the county, is documented at two performances, both in 1897 and both in the Odd Fellows Hall at nearby Hamlin: a performance of the play "Bound by an Oath" in January,[33] and a musicale in June.[34]

The *Newfoundland Orchestra*, in the very southern tip of the county, played at a local teachers' institute in January of 1897.[35]

Hawley had, at least in 1897, an organization called the *Orchestra of the German Young People's Society*, probably associated with its strong German musical tradition (recall the great celebration for the Hawley Maennerchor's silver anniversary in 1899). Its only known performance was at a "young people's entertainment" in February of 1897.[36]

The *Rock Lake Orchestra*, from a village in Mount Pleasant Township, between Bethany and Pleasant Mount, played twice at Rock Lake in 1901: a box social in April,[37] and an oyster supper in December.[38]

An ensemble called the *Sterling String Band*, from the southern part of the county, was reported in 1897 to be practicing Wednesday evenings at the village opera house.[39]

The *White Mills Graded School Orchestra*, apparently an educational organization, played at the local teachers' institute in Hawley in early 1897,[40] and at the Hawley High School's commencement the following June.[41]

And finally, the *White Mills Orchestra*, which may be the same as or related to the White Mills Graded School Orchestra, participated in the play *Imogen* at the Florence Theater in White Mills in October 1897;[42] at a party for the White Mills Heptasophs, also at the Florence Theater, the following spring;[43] and at a concert and social at St. Juliana's Catholic church at Rock Lake in September 1901.[44]

OUT-OF-TOWN BANDS PLAYING IN WAYNE COUNTY

Just as the bands of Wayne County occasionally made trips outside the county's borders, so did bands from outside frequently come in. Such trips are really not within the scope of this study and will not be examined in detail. But they should at least be mentioned, for these visits were an important part of the musical environment of the bands discussed. Many of the visiting organizations were from larger cities like Scranton and Wilkes-Barre, and some of them were probably of much higher quality than the local product. These must have had some influence on the musical tastes of the Wayne County audience, and on the general standards of playing within which the local bands performed.

These visiting bands may be divided into five types:

1. out-of-town bands hired by local agencies;
2. village bands paying neighborly visits on nearby communities;
3. bands accompanying out-of-town delegations to local events;
4. bands accompanying excursions to Farview, Lodore, or Lake Ariel; and
5. professional touring bands.

We have already seen examples of the first three, in 1) the performance of the Mozart band, of Carbondale, in Honesdale's Central Park for the Honesdale Red Men (pp. 33-36); 2) the exchange concerts of the Pleasant Mount and Uniondale bands (pp. 103-4); and 3) the participation of the Forest band, of Scranton, in the cornerstone laying at St. Philomela's church in Hawley (p. 115). But the other two categories require a closer look.

Farview, Lodore, and Lake Ariel were popular excursion spots not only for the people of Wayne County, but for those of the coal-mining regions of Lackawanna and Luzerne counties as well. And naturally the excursionists brought their own bands to the picnic grounds. Such events were not as a rule described in detail by the newspapers; presumably they involved mostly out-of-town people and thus were not deemed newsworthy. It is clear, however, that local people did attend these affairs and did listen to the sometimes excellent bands.

A large number of Honesdalers went up to Farview on Thursday afternoon of last week, to enjoy the music of Alexander's band, that was there with a mammoth excursion from Wilkesbarre. Our streets were filled with crowds of sight-seers from this excursion, and the dealers in soda and cream reported a brisk trade during the visit of the strangers. If we had some local attraction in the way of music, suburban gardens or picnic grounds, many more excursionists would run down here from the top of the mountain, during times of these immensely attended crowds to Farview, They are out for a day of pleasure, and the retailers here would reap considerable profit therefrom.[45]

The appearance of professional bands in Wayne County was a much rarer occasion. The era of the great touring bands, such as Sousa's, was just beginning at the turn of the century and had not yet spread to the small towns. What did occur, however, were visits from bands attached to touring minstrel shows. These organizations, although humorous in repertory and intent, were often of high musical quality, and they seem to have made quite an impression.

High Henry's great minstrel troupe came here on time on Tuesday last. The members all live upon their train which was left at the Erie Depot, and consequently nothing was seen of them until they came marching up Main street with a band of forty pieces. The weather was freezing cold, so the beautiful instruments had their overcoats on as well as the performers. Band instruments are very susceptible to the cold weather, and the valves and slides refuse to work unless the thermometer indicates above thirty-two degrees. The music was certainly inspiring and thoroughly waked up our somewhat sleepy town. . . . [long discussion of Hi Henry's automobile, possibly the first one ever seen in Honesdale] . . . There was an out door concert, listened to by a large audience, in front of the Opera House just before the evening performance. It was fortunate that our people had this opportunity to hear the largest and best band ever in our town, for at least two hundred persons were unable to get even standing room inside at the performance. The show itself was largely a concert of first-class singing and instrumental music with a good variety of specialty works to enliven it all. The cornet solo of Hi Henry himself was the gem of the programme. A couple of very clever men, while giving most enjoyable duets busied themselves—one being blindfolded—tearing sheets of paper which then unfolded afterward to the gaze of the audience showed most beautiful work and astonishing figures in lace and what not. The stage setting was the deck of a ship all faithfully carried out even to the showy uniforms of the performers. The Opera House was never so packed before. Every seat was reserved and yet there was a fringe of standing humanity in the rear of the hall that filled every available space. The show was unexceptionable in every respect and was liberally applauded throughout.[46]

In addition to Hi Henry's Minstrel Troupe, two other professional minstrel shows performed in Honesdale: Barlow and Wilson's Greater New York Minstrels and Fields and Hanson's Minstrel Stars and Grand Concert Band.[47]

Between 1897 and 1901, Honesdale was also visited fairly frequently by amateur and professional bands from around northeastern Pennsylvania; the newspapers record performances by Alexander's 9th Regiment Band of Wilkes-Barre; the Archbald band of Archbald, in Lackawanna County; Bauer's band of Scranton; the Forest band, also of Scranton; the Mozart band of Carbondale, and the Ringgold band of Scranton.[48]

Of the three railroad-sponsored resorts, Farview seems to have seen the densest band activity, or at any rate to have the most thorough coverage in the paper: in the five years it was visited by Alexander's 9th Regiment Band; the Archbald band; Bauer's band; the Jermyn Band of Jermyn, Lackawanna County; the Lawrence band of Scranton; the Moosic band of Moosic, also Lackawanna county; and the Mozart band.[49] Lodore was visited by Bauer's band and the Mozart band,[50] and Lake Ariel by Bauer's band and the Moscow band of Lackawanna County.[51]

And even the smallest villages were sometimes serenaded by bands from out of the county—particularly, of course, those villages near the border. Besides the exchanges of Pleasant Mount and Uniondale, we also see the Lawrence band playing in Bethany, the Moosic band playing in Farno, and the Tannersville and Tobyhanna bands, both of neighboring Monroe County, playing at Newfoundland.[52]

NOTES

1. *Centennial and Illustrated Wayne County*, 2d ed. (Honesdale: The Wayne Independent, 1902; rept. Honesdale: Wayne County Historical Society, 1975), p. 102.

2. *Honesdale Citizen*, March 4, 1897.

3. *Wayne Independent*, April 14, 1897.

4. Ibid., June 2, 1900.

5. *Honesdale Citizen*, May 5, 1898.

6. Ibid., February 16, 1899.

7. *Wayne Independent*, July 5, 1899.

8. *Honesdale Citizen*, July 26, 1900.

9. *Wayne Independent*, June 5, 1901.

10. *Illustrated Wayne*, p. 105.

11. *Wayne Independent*, January 3, 1900.

12. *Honesdale Citizen*, June 2, 1898.

13. *Wayne Independent*, July 21, 1897.

14. Ibid., June 3, 1899.

15. Ibid., May 28, 1898.

16. *Honesdale Citizen*, October 4, 1900.

17. *Wayne Independent*, January 3, 1900.

18. Ibid., September 6, 1899.

19. *Honesdale Citizen*, August 30, 1900.

20. Ibid., August 23, 1900.

21. *Wayne Independent*, April 3, 1901; see also *Wayne Independent*, May 1, 1901.

22. Ibid., July 10, 1901.

23. Ibid., September 11, 1901.

24. *Honesdale Citizen*, July 27, 1899.

25. *Hancock (N.Y.) Herald*, August 1893; from notes of Wellington Lester.

26. Alfred Mathews, *History of Wayne, Pike and Monroe Counties, Pennsylvania* (Philadelphia: R. T. Peck, 1886; rept. Honesdale: Citizens for the Preservation of Our Local Heritage, n.d.), p. 721.

27. *Wayne Independent*, April 17, 1901.

28. Ibid., August 18, 1900.

29. Ibid., September 1, 1900.

30. Ibid., March 13, 1897.

31. Ibid., June 13, 1900; August 4, 1900.

32. *Wayne Independent*, March 6, 1900.

33. Ibid., January 9, 1897.

34. *Honesdale Citizen*, June 3, 1897; June 24, 1897.

35. *Wayne Independent*, January 16, 1897.

36. Ibid., February 13, 1897; February 20, 1897.

37. Ibid., April 17, 1901, quoted above.

38. Ibid., December 16, 1901.

39. *Honesdale Citizen*, March 18, 1897.

40. Ibid., January 21, 1897; February 4, 1897; *Wayne Independent*, January 23, 1897; February 3, 1987.

41. Ibid., June 2, 1897; *Honesdale Citizen*, June 3, 1897.

42. *Wayne Independent*, October 27, 1897.

43. Ibid., March 9, 1898.

44. Ibid., September 27, 1901.

45. *Honesdale Citizen*, July 28, 1898.

46. *Wayne County Herald*, February 1, 1900. Hi Henry's minstrel show was

apparently an old favorite with the Honesdale audience. Vernon Leslie, in *A Profile of Service: Protection Engine Company No. 3, 1853-1916* (Honesdale: Protection Engine Co. No. 3, 1986), pp. 86-87, describes a fire in 1875 in which T. T. Rainey of "Hi Henry's Combination," which was stopping in Honesdale on a tour, worked for hours to save merchandise from the flames. He was rewarded with a purse of money by some grateful citizen.

47. First references, *Wayne County Herald*, October 20, 1901; October 7, 1897.

48. First references: *Wayne County Herald*, August 12, 1897; *Wayne Independent*, July 21, 1897; *Honesdale Citizen*, July 29, 1897; *Independent*, March 16, 1898; *Citizen*, June 17, 1897; ibid., August 19, 1897.

49. First references: *Honesdale Citizen*, August 21, 1898; *Wayne Independent*, July 21, 1897; *Citizen*, July 29, 1897; *Independent*, August 13, 1898; ibid., July 26, 1897; ibid., July 26, 1899; ibid., September 6, 1897.

50. First references: *Wayne Independnt*, June 23, 1900 and September 5, 1900.

51. First references, *Honesdale Citizen*, August 19, 1897 and *Wayne Independent*, August 7, 1898.

52. First references: *Wayne Independent*, August 15, 1901; *Honesdale Citizen*, July 15, 1987; ibid., June 28, 1900; ibid., June 16, 1898.

6

Personnel

Who played in these bands? The question can be answered, in several cases, quite specifically: complete rosters survive for the Lake Como band of 1896 (p. 96), the Honesdale and Equinunk bands of 1897 (pp. 27-28, 82), and the Maple City band of 1900 (p. 56).[1] For these purposes, however, the actual names are of no great importance; the personnel of these bands must be explored in more general terms. The question is not who these men were specifically, but what manner of men they were.

In Tables 14 and 15, the rosters of the Maple City band and the original Equinunk band have been supplemented with information from the census of 1900 and various other sources. Such a task is always attended with problems of completeness and identification;[2] but even as they are, the tables, combined with information from the newspapers, allow some generalizations about the people who played in the two bands.

Perhaps the most noticeable difference between the two tables is that the Maple City band is substantially larger—twenty members as compared with the Equinunk band's fifteen. This disparity could be interpreted simply as a reflection of the sizes of the two communities, but then, the largest band in the county came from tiny Gouldsboro. More accurately, the relative strength of the Maple City band should be seen as the result of the circumstances of its founding: remember that it was formed, just a few months before this roster was published, by the merger of two more or less self-sufficient bands. The Equinunk band, in contrast, seems to have been started, also only a few months before the roster, practically

Table 14.
The Maple City Band, 1900

Name	Age	Occupation	Instrument
Robert Armbruster	14	At school	Clarinet
John W. Broad	44	Laster & trimmer, shoe factory	Baritone (Trombone? Alto?)
John Bussa	26	Bottom finisher, shoe factory	Clarinet
Andrew Cowles	29	Foreman glass cutter	Cornet
Jacob Doetsch	28	Book-binder	
Robert M. Dorin	27	Tea salesman	
Michael Fannen		[Glass cutter]	
William Geltner			
David Gill	27	Machinist	Drums?
Charles Guenther	20	Shoe cutter	
Judson Keen	23	Day laborer	Cornet
Anthony Lenz		[Hotel proprietor]	
August Laabs	10*	At School	
Rudolph Laabs	19	Farm laborer	
Charles Marsh	27	Mill labor	
Henry Miller	22	Cutter, shoe factory	
Robert Murray	20	Hardware saleman	Alto
William Quick	20	Laster, shoe factory	
Henry W. Rehbein	43	Janitor	Clarinet
George Schiessler	15	Apprentice machinist	

*May be his father, age 51, a day laborer.
Information in brackets from *Honesdale Directory, 1906-7;* roster from *Illustrated Wayne,* p. 139 (some names augmented and corrected from other sources). Instruments taken from various newspaper accounts.

Table 15.
The Equinunk Band, 1897

Name	Age	Occupation	Instrument
Charles W. Alberti	37	M.E. preacher	B^b cornet
Charles Bauman	35	Day laborer	Snare drum
John Curry	32	Stonecutter	E^b cornet
Blake Gray	20*		Bass drum
Everette Green	17	Day laborer	Alto
Delos Lester	20	Dry goods clerk	Tenor
Austin Lloyd	18	Painter	Baritone
Cain Lord	45	Clothing merchant	E^b clarinet
Earl Lord	25*		E^b cornet
Edward Lord	22	Barber	E^b cornet
William S. Lord	17	Day laborer	Tenor
H. Richards	16	At school	B^b cornet
Robert Shields			B^b bass
Charles Warfield	13	At school	Cymbals
Shepard Warfield	11	At school	Alto

*Age estimated from Figure 9.

Roster and instruments: *Wayne Independent,* February 20, 1897; some names have been augmented and corrected from other sources.

from scratch. In any case, most of the bands around the county had between twelve and twenty members; they ranged from the Gouldsboro band's twenty-two down to the early Lake Como band's eleven. And this seems to have been within the usual range for American amateur bands in general: Margaret Hindle Hazen and Robert M. Hazen, after examining hundreds of photographs of bands of the 1890s, conclude that most consisted of sixteen to eighteen young men.[3]

That these were all young *men* is somehow not surprising until we consider that in its most recent incarnation, in the early 1980s, the Maple City band was more than half women. Indeed, the newspapers never mention a single female name associated with

any of these bands, and Hazen and Hazen point out that although
all-girl bands were not uncommon, at least as a novelty, around the
country, bands with both men and women were much rarer.[4] The
male dominance of the brass bands was, I believe, largely a matter
of tradition and perceived propriety: young Victorian girls were
taught to sing and play the piano, but brass bands, with their
worldly and military associations, were thought somehow un-
feminine and unseemly. By the turn of the century, influential
voices were already pleading for the benefits of brass and woodwind
instruments to the mental and physical health of American girls;[5]
but the town band remained a male province at least until the
school band movement of the 1920s.[6] When the newspapers say
that the boys are planning a band concert, boys is what they mean.

Boys, that is, in gender more than in age. The Maple City band
was made up primarily of young men in their twenties, with a
handful of teenagers and two men in their forties. The Equinunk
band shows considerably more variation in age, possibly the result
of the size of the community: there were simply fewer men in their
twenties to choose from. Still, the description of the band as being
made up of "the young men and youth" of Equinunk (p. 82) is
substantially correct: most of its membership was under twenty-
five.[7]

The range of both tables suggests that despite the preponderance
of younger men, all ages were welcome in these ensembles;[8] the
presence of the older men must have made for a certain continuity
in the tradition over the decades. Both John Broad and Henry
Rehbein, the oldest members of the Maple City band, had been
members of the Honesdale band before it, and quite possibly they
had played in that band throughout its twenty-year history. John
Broad had played under his father, perhaps as early as the late
1860s.[9] It is clear, however, that the bands throughout the county
were perceived as being organizations predominantly of young men;
the poet's account of the entourage of "lovely maidens" that surrounded the Lake Como band is further evidence, no less reliable
for being partially fictitious, that the band members were of courting
age.

In many nineteenth-century American cities, town bands developed along ethnic lines. Immigrants from Germany and Italy, in
particular, were famous for bringing their musical traditions to
America and founding German and Italian bands.[10] Honesdale did
have a substantial German population, and in fact in the years
before the Civil War it had at least one German band and probably

more;[11] but by the end of the century the Germanic musical tradition was embodied more in singing societies like the Maennerchor and Liederkranz than in instrumental music. The roster of the Maple City band contains a number of German names, but they are mixed with Irish and English in roughly the same proportion as in the community at large; nor is there any preponderance of German titles in their concert programs.

The bands were made up almost entirely from the working class—as, indeed, were the communities that supported them. Of the nineteen members of the Maple City band whose occupations can be identified, five worked in shoe factories, two in glass factories, four in local small businesses, and the rest in various industries, on farms, and so forth. The roster of the Equinunk band shows a quarry worker, three day laborers (probably farmhands), four men employed in retail and services, three boys at school, and of course one clergyman. All in all, these represent a fairly typical cross-section of the kinds of work available to young men at the time; Table 2 outlines the occupations in Honesdale and in Manchester and Buckingham townships (the townships that contain Equinunk) in 1900.[12]

The predominance of young working-class men in these bands was occasionally a liability, as reported in the *Independent* of July 26, 1899: "It is regretted that Mr. Lawyer and two of his men were unable to accompany the band [Lawyer's band, to an Odd Fellows' picnic], being unable to obtain leave of absence from the shop. Their places were filled by three members of the Mozarts, of Carbondale."

It is hard to say exactly how far the band members had to travel to attend their rehearsals and performances. Equinunk, for example, sits on the corner of three census districts, Manchester and Buckingham townships in Pennsylvania and the Town of Hancock in New York. All of the names I have found are from these three districts, but that narrows them down only to perhaps a hundred square miles. On the whole, it seems probable that most of the band members lived within a few miles of the village. There are, however, several accounts of musicians in these country bands who lived quite a distance from their rehearsals: Stephen Skellett travelled (with much of his family) from Starrucca to Lake Como, a trip of eight miles; Professor Mikrantz and three of his neighbors from Orson to Pleasant Mount, seven miles; and Arthur Curtis from Farno to Pleasant Mount, about six miles. Their efforts must have been considerable, given the condition of the roads of the time. In Honesdale, where rail travel was more convenient, the bands could more easily draw from a fairly wide radius: the roster of the Maple City band is made up mostly of men from Honesdale and the adjoining townships, but it also includes Judson Keen of Keen's, about four miles away along the D&H, and August and Rudolph Laabs of Palmyra Township, between White Mills and Hawley, at least five miles away along the Erie.

Finally, perhaps the most immediately obvious feature of the Equinunk band's roster is the dominance of one name: more than a quarter of the band is named Lord. This is perhaps not so striking as it seems, as Lord was a common and prominent name in Equinunk—indeed, the village across the river in New York is called Lordville. Even today the Lords tend to think of themselves as basically one family, and it seems quite probable that all five men are related somehow; Cain and Edward Lord were certainly father and son. The presence of several members of the same family in a band is not unexpected and was not uncommon—for example, the Skellett family, two brothers and at least three sons, in the Lake Como band, and Fred and David Gill of various bands in Honesdale. To these can now be added two more sets of brothers: the Warfields of the Equinunk band and the Laabses of the Maple City band.[13] By the time its picture was taken in 1898, the Equinunk band had no less than four pairs of brothers: the Greens, the Holberts, the Lesters, and the Warfields.[14]

The organization of these town bands remains somewhat obscure. D. S. McCosh, in "McCosh's Guide for Amateur Brass Bands," suggests that "It is well to have a *President*, to preside at business meetings; a *Vice-President*, to act in his absence; a *Secretary*, to attend to the correspondence; and a *Treasurer*, to care for all money coming into the band-fund, and to pay all bills as instructed by the members. When it becomes necessary, a *Librarian* should be appointed to care for all books and music belonging to the band."[15] It is difficult, however, to know how closely the bands of Wayne County adhered to such a plan. The newspapers say nothing about this aspect of the bands; evidently the activities of the officers were not thought newsworthy. We know from *Illustrated Wayne* that the Maple City band had a president, a corresponding secretary, a treasurer, and a conductor (p. 56); and it seems probable that the other bands had some more or less similar hierarchy of officers to handle the mundane duties of contracting for performances, managing the band's finances, ensuring that the musicians showed up at the right place and time, and so forth. Hazen and Hazen, at any rate, have pointed out that most bands of the time were organized in this way and that their organization paralleled that of other men's clubs such as lodges and fire companies.[16]

The real leader of the band, spiritually as well as musically, was the conductor. Some of these conductors, particularly in the smaller villages, attained a considerable local celebrity, and as a result, we read quite a lot about them in the papers. The conductor was given full credit for the musical accomplishments of his band, and changes of leadership were often considered, and probably were, turning points in a band's career.

The principal duty of the conductor was to conduct the band in rehearsals and performances. He may have taken this role over from the drum major fairly recently, as suggested by the *Citizen* of June 1, 1899: "Drum majors, full of fuss and feathers, seem to be an ornament of the past, all bands having discarded them." Most, if not all, of the conductors were also instrumentalists, and probably the best players in the band; most likely, then, they merely started the band and then rejoined their sections, instead of standing on the podium with a baton. The conductor was the artistic force behind his band, probably in charge of selecting its repertory as well as shaping and polishing its performance. But what he actually did during rehearsals and concerts is not told in the newspaper articles. The conductor was often called the "instructor," and his duties must also have included a certain amount of coaching in instrumental technique. Brass instruments were not taught in the schools,[17] and as a result, the band members had to learn to play from one another. The problem must have been especially acute in the rural areas, where there was no self-sustaining band tradition; there the conductor's first years, at least, must have been largely occupied with elementary lessons, as we have seen in the story of the Equinunk band.

A third role of the conductor was as instrumental soloist. Then as now, it was a common practice for the band concert to feature a solo by one of its best players, usually on the cornet, baritone, or trombone; and more often than not, this soloist was the conductor. The most prominent of these was Fred Gill, who frequently played trombone solos with Lawyer's band, but most of the other conductors must have been soloists too. It is certainly significant that of the eleven conductors listed for these ensembles, seven played the most common solo instruments: Edwin Lawyer, C. W. Alberti, and both Skellett brothers played the cornet, Fred Gill and Prof. Mikrantz the trombone, and E. W. Wright the baritone. (David Gill played the drums, at least in the Honesdale Philharmonic, and Daniel Storms, John Neuser, and Arthur Curtis are not associated in the papers with any instrument.)

The conductorship of some of these bands may have been a paid position. This is not explicitly stated in the newspapers, but is sometimes suggested by their phrasing. For example, the *Independent*, in its discussion of the new Maple City band, says: "Last year people enjoyed the open air concerts given by Lawyer's band. Those concerts were free to all but the band boys who were obliged to purchase new music frequently and spend time in rehearsals. Now how much are the efforts made by the band appreciated? Last year F. C. Gill was the instructor. He is not here this year and the band must be at the expense of hiring an instructor. Are those concerts appreciated to the extent that people will contribute a purse toward meeting the necessary expense?"[18]

This seems to imply that Gill had donated his services and that because no volunteer was forthcoming, the band would have to raise money to pay someone, evidently a common practice. If so, it must have been a false alarm, for Gill's successor turned out to be his brother and probably came on the same terms. Reverend Alberti also seems to have been unpaid; the Equinunk correspondent to the *Independent* says at one point that "We are proud of our band and Rev. Mr. Alberti has spared no pains to make it a success. If they had hired a professional musician to train them for $500 [it] would not [have] made them what they are today."[19]

The organization of these bands, then, seems to have been relatively simple and efficient. The conductor acted as chief musician, with more or less full control over the musical aspects of the band's performance. The everyday administrative tasks were probably left to other members of the band—at least in the case of the Maple City band, to a hierarchy of nonmusical officers.

One final aspect of personnel is the presence of what might be called sister bands—pairs of bands, particularly out in the country, that would get together occasionally for joint activities.

The best documented of these affiliations was that between the Equinunk and Lake Como bands. For at least three years, 1897 through 1899, the two ensembles had an annual picnic at one village or the other. And to judge from the descriptions that have survived from these picnics (pp. 89-90), they seem to have been great social events involving not only the bands, but large crowds of citizens from both towns as well. The bands would play separately

—and one wonders how much overt or covert competition was involved—and then would apparently unite for a spectacular finish.

This loose association of the Equinunk and Lake Como bands could also include exchanges of personnel. When the Equinunk band went off to the band contest in Susquehanna—the infamous event where it "won" second prize even though only two bands were participating—it augmented its ranks with four members of the Lake Como band, including its leader (pp. 94 and 97). And no doubt these bands would exchange musical ideas, and possibly even actual repertory, when they were together.

The situation in Honesdale was rather different. Throughout this period, Honesdale had a fairly steady stream of musical organizations, amateur and professional, local and visiting, playing in town, and none of its bands can really be said to have had a sister band elsewhere. The community itself, however, has always had special ties with Carbondale, sixteen miles to the west. With a population of about thirteen thousand, Carbondale was the nearest town that equalled Honesdale's size and importance, and its position at the other end of the Gravity Railroad not only made it accessible to the people of Honesdale, but also kept it constantly before their minds: until the canal closed in 1898, Carbondale was very literally the source of a good portion of the town's livelihood. It is not surprising, then, that many institutions in Honesdale shared festivities with their neighbors across the Moosics[20]—bands included. We have already seen the joint performances of the Honesdale band and Carbondale's Mozart band in the Red Men's concert and picnic of August 1897 (pp. 33-36), and earlier in this chapter is an account of Lawyer's band borrowing a few members from the Mozarts when they were shorthanded for a concert (p. 133). This borrowing went both ways: "Columbia Hose Co. No. 5, and the Mozart band, of Carbondale, came over the Gravity on a special Thursday morning, enroute for Port Jervis. . . . The Mozarts were strengthened here by the addition of Henry Rehbein and Fred. Gill, of the Honesdale band. The former plays a clarinet and the latter a slide trombone. Twenty-four persons joined the Carbondalers at this place."[21]

A third special relationship was between the bands of Pleasant Mount and Uniondale. This association is less conspicuous here only because Uniondale is in Susquehanna County and therefore its band has not been discussed in detail. But in fact the bands played together at least twice, in September 1898 and October 1899, in what may have been planned as another series of annual picnics, and may well have had other engagements together, too.

NOTES

1. The names written on the back of the Equinunk band's picture, probably from 1898 (see Fig. 9 and pp. 84-86) amount to a fourth roster, but it is not altogether clear that they represent the entire band.

2. Tables 14 and 15 represent efforts to reconcile the printed rosters of these bands with the information recorded in the returns from the U.S. census of 1900. Blank spaces may indicate men who were missed by the census enumerators, who lived too far out of town to be in the census, who are recorded in the census in a manner such that they couldn't be recognized, or who moved away between the time the roster was published and the time the census was taken. The last possibility is more likely for the Equinunk band, where the roster is three years earlier than the census. In a number of cases I have changed the roster's spelling to the census's on the basis of likely spelling errors (e.g., the change from Lobbs to Laabs), handwriting errors (Chris. Warfield to Chas. Warfield), or both (T. Currie to J. Curry). On the whole, I am fairly confident of all my identifications (with the exception of August Laabs, noted in the table itself), but not my spellings.

3. Margaret Hindle Hazen and Robert M. Hazen, *The Music Men: An Illustrated History of Brass Bands in America, 1800-1920* (Washington: Smithsonian Institution Press, 1987), p. 107.

4. Hazen and Hazen, *The Music Men*, pp. 55-57.

5. See, for example, Sidney Lanier, "The Orchestra of To-Day," *Scribner's Monthly* 18 (1879-80): 897-904; May Lyle Smith, "A New Instrument for Women, Giving Health Combined with Pleasure," *Etude* 9 (1891): 108; Fanny Morris Smith, "Women's Work in Music in America," *Etude* 17 (1899): 150; and Henry T. Finck, "The Musical Outlook for Women," *Etude* 17 (1899): 151.

6. Hazen and Hazen, *The Music Men*, pp. 193-94.

7. Of the five musicians added to the band before their picture was taken (p. 86), Jay Lester was eighteen in 1898, Leon Holbert twenty, Edgar Holbert twenty-one, and Jacob Blaes forty-one. Horace Green's age is not known.

8. See Hazen and Hazen, *The Music Men*, p. 47.

9. William H. Ham, "The Bands of Honesdale," *Wayne County Herald*, June 9, 1881.

10. Hazen and Hazen, *The Music Men*, pp. 52-53.

11. Thomas J. Ham, in "The Old Cannon," *Honesdale Citizen*, September 1, 1904—June 29, 1905, mentions a number of occasions attended by "German bands" between 1851 and 1871. Possibly one or more of these may refer to an incarnation of Broad's band.

12. On the social classes represented in bands throughout the country, see Hazen and Hazen, *The Music Men*, pp.46-47.

13. But see n. 1 above on August Laabs.

14. These relationships were confirmed for me by Hazel Peake, owner of the picture and sister of the two Warfield boys.

15. D. S. McCosh, "McCosh's Guide for Amateaur Brass Bands," in Lyon and Healy, *Band Instruments, Uniforms, Trimmings, &c.* (Chicago: Lyon and Healy, 1881), pp. 3-29, quotation p. 5. The "Guide" was printed in Lyon and Healy catalogues throughout the period.

16. Hazen and Hazen, *The Music Men*, pp. 176-77.

17. Arthur Richard Goerlitz, in "A History of Public Education in Honesdale, Pennsylvania (1810-1960)," Ed.D. thesis, Pennsylvania State University, 1969, pp. 108-20, 279-96, shows that in the Honesdale schools at the turn of the century music was a part of the curriculum in grades 1 through 8, but that instruction was in singing, sightreading, and so forth; no instrument was taught.

18. *Wayne Independent*, May 16, 1900.

19. *Wayne Independent*, August 24, 1898.

20. For example, on the relations between the fire companies of Carbondale and Honesdale, see Vernon Leslie, *A Profile of Service: Protection Engine Company No. 3, 1853-1916* (Honesdale: Protection Engine Company No. 3, 1986), pp. 37-38, 40-41.

21. *Wayne Independent*, September 11, 1897.

7

Instrumentation

As we explore the instrumentation of these town bands, we must take special pains not to fall into an obvious trap. Present-day experience with classical music and professional orchestras naturally leads us to consider instrumentation as a more or less purely musical concern: when, say, Wagner wrote for an orchestra with eight horns, no doubt he wanted to hear them. And it is all too easy to assume the same sort of situation for the bands as well. But a moment's reflection tells us that this was seldom, if ever, the case for amateur bands in rural areas. Sousa may have had the luxury of choosing the instruments he wanted, but Stephen Skellett almost certainly did not.

The instrumentation of each of these bands was based on some sort of ideal, whether a "perfect" sound in the director's mind or a vague public sense of what a brass band was supposed to consist of. But the ability of the band to achieve this ideal was inevitably limited by the instruments and players at hand. In other words, real instrumentation of the bands of Wayne County represented a compromise between the ideal and the practical, and to understand them properly, it is necessary to seperate between the two, first establishing what the ideals must have been, and then examining the kinds of compromises and the reasons behind them.[1]

INSTRUMENTATIONS OF AMERICAN BANDS

Nineteenth-century Americans certainly saw the band as a continuous, uninterrupted, generally consistent tradition, and clearly we should follow their example today. But in fact, American bands were in a constant state of slow change throughout the century, and to put the bands of Wayne County into their proper historical perspective, we must try to understand this process of evolution.

At the very beginning of the American brass-band movement, in the first few decades of the nineteenth century, the valve had not yet been developed, and as a result, most of today's brass instruments did not exist. Bands of that time depended on four families of instruments: 1) woodwinds, especially clarinets, flutes, and piccolos; 2) natural trumpets and horns, more or less like their baroque and classical ancestors; 3) trombones; and 4) keyed bugles and ophicleides—brass instruments with keys like those on the woodwinds. This was precisely the sort of instrumentation W. H. Ham described in his discussion of various bands in Honesdale during the 1840s and 1850s (pp. 23-24). As Ham suggests, it was not entirely satisfactory: many of these instruments in these early bands—particularly the keyed bugles and ophicleides—were spectacular in the hands of a master, but could be very difficult for amateurs to learn and for their audiences to endure.[2]

The person most responsible for the first great change in instrumentation—indeed, arguably the one person most responsible for the rise, the enormous popularity, and the suprising longevity of the brass band in America—was Adolphe Sax, the Parisian instrument manufacturer later to become famous as the father of the saxophone. Although Sax was not the inventor of valves for brass instruments, he was the first to perfect and successfully market an entire matching set of valved brasses, soprano through bass. The development of these "saxhorns" in the late 1840s changed the face of bands forever by making relatively inexpensive and easy-to-play brass instruments available worldwide.

The word *saxhorn*, like almost all the terminology surrounding the brasswinds of this period, is open to a wide range of interpretations. Strictly speaking, it refers only to instruments of Sax's own manufacture, but the term will be used more loosely here, as it was at the time, to describe a whole family of brass instruments with valves and a bore more conical than that of the trumpet or trombone. It is a family descended from Sax's first instruments, the group that includes the tuba, euphonium, and flugelhorn.

Sax's instruments had three or four valves, and their conical bore gave them a fuller, more subdued, less brassy sound than is associated with brass instruments today. They were all fingered alike, a great advance in ease of playing and teaching, and they were made in five sizes, about half an octave apart: soprano in E-flat, contralto in B-flat, tenor in E-flat, bass in B-flat, and contrabass in E-flat.[3] In theory at least, these instruments differed essentially only in size and therefore pitch, and as a result, the tone of the saxhorn ensemble was unusually homogenous.

A number of early developments interrupted the purity of the matched saxhorn ensemble. Most significantly, the soprano and contralto saxhorns were replaced by E-flat and B-flat cornets to give a more brilliant sound to the upper voices of the band. And through a series of subtle modifications Sax's "bass" saxhorn evolved into three instruments suitable for various musical lines: the tenor horn, with a relatively narrow bore for playing inconspicuous back-beat patterns; the B-flat bass, with a wide bore for reinforcing the bass line; and the baritone, in between the other two, for more prominent melodies and solos. The resulting combination—E-flat and B-flat cornets, E-flat altos (sometimes called tenors), B-flat tenors, B-flat baritones, B-flat basses, and E-flat basses—quickly became standard throughout the country. This was the ensemble that really began the amateur brass band movement in earnest, the band that dominated the Western world at mid-century, the music that inspired and entertained the troops of the American Civil War.[4] And as we have seen (pp. 24-25), it was also the instrumentation of Honesdale's Silver Cornet band and Broad's band during the 1860s. For present purposes, I shall call this instrumentation the "cornet band," although that term was used much more generally and less precisely at the time.

Throughout the history of the band movement, the cornet band remained influential, as an ideal, all over the United States. As the century progressed, however, the forces of variety were making themselves felt.

The range of brass instruments available was expanded beyond the cornets and basic saxhorns. Some of these new instruments were just modifications on older designs: the cornets were sometimes joined by a B-flat flugelhorn (actually a survival of the old contralto saxhorn), and the E-flat bass by what the catalogues called a "large E-flat bass," with a wider bore and bigger bell for more carrying power. And by the 1880s, some manufacturers also began marketing a double-B-flat (BB$^\flat$) bass, even lower than the E-flat bass.[5]

A more striking departure was the revival of the trombone, with a more cylindrical bore and a brassier, punchier sound than the saxhorns. Although supplanted by valved instruments in bands earlier in the century, the trombone had remained an integral part of the orchestra, and by the end of the century it was popular in band music as well—both in the old form with the slide and a new valved version. The 1898-99 catalogue of Lyon and Healy, a firm of instrument manufacturers in Chicago, offered valve trombones in alto, tenor, and baritone sizes, and alto and tenor slide trombones as well.[6] And the mellophone, also known by several other names, was similar to an alto horn, but had the circular shape and flaring bell of the French horn, whose sound it was supposed to imitate.[7]

And the woodwinds, which had also been practically banished from the band when the saxhorns became popular, were starting to move back in. Clarinets (more often spelled "clarionets") in B-flat and E-flat were appearing more and more, and the piccolo, in a variety of keys, but most commonly D-flat, was becoming a conspicuous top voice in many bands of the latter part of the century. This practice was not without its problems or its opponents. As early as 1875, G. F. Patton wrote in his *Practical Guide to the Arrangement of Band Music* that

> The Clarinet . . . is not capable of sustaining alone the leading part in a Brass Band, for no wood instrument can impart sufficient vibration to the air to counterballance the powerful sound of a dozen pealing horns. When a Clarinet player tries to make himself heard above every body, as the melody should be, he has to put so much force upon his instrument that it loses its mellow tone, and rises into a sort of piercing "squeal". In a very full Band, as from twenty to fifty men, it is desirable to have both Clarinets and Piccolos for the highest notes, but where these instruments are made to do the work of the E^b Cornet in a small Band, the effect is notably imperfect. . . . The Piccolo Flute is particularly out of place in a small Band, and as it is heard whistling away an octave or two above everything else, the effect is so disconnected and its sound so ill assorted, as to be really ludicrous.[8]

But Patton's suggestions apparently went unheeded; the most common instrumentation in the photographs of the 1880s and 1890s is what was sometimes called the "reed band," with clarinets and piccolos supplementing the cornets, and trombones among the tenors and baritones.[9] Flutes, larger clarinets, saxophones, and double reeds were not unheard of in amateur bands, but they remained unusual until the early twentieth century.

By the period of this study, then, bands were not locked into the pure, uncomplicated saxhorn ensemble or cornet band, but had a wide variety of instruments and instrumental colors at their disposal. But the question remains, Were these new instrumental colors still optional, completely at the discretion of the individual band or player? Or did they gradually become standardized, finding their way into the ideal instrumentation that bands used as a model?

The manufacturers themselves provide an answer. Almost every American instrument catalogue of the time contains a chart of suggested instrumentations for bands of various sizes, typically six to seventeen players. If you were starting a new band, and had nine players lined up, you could consult the Lyon and Healy catalogue (or even Sears, Roebuck) to find out how many of each instrument to buy. These charts, coming as they do from the dealers, must be regarded with at least a little suspicion; they might be expected to favor the profit motive over purely musical concerns. On the whole, however, the charts are well balanced, sensible, and thoughtful, and their instrumentations seem to be eminently practical. They are, I believe, as good an indication as can be found of the ideal—ideal in the sense of recommended—instruments of the time.

A baker's dozen of these charts are represented in Table 16. The table gives the "Band of 12" (i.e., twelve wind players, with three percussionists to be added) suggested by various catalogues spanning nearly the whole of the brass band tradition.

Perhaps the most noticeable and reassuring aspect of the table, at least for the first nine columns, is its consistency. There are enough small differences in the instrumentations to show that they are not simply plagiarized from one another, but enough basic similarities to suggest that there really was a considerable consensus among these authorities for most of the last half of the nineteenth century. The observation holds, incidentally, for bands of other sizes as well. Curiously, the table shows only cornet bands even though the nineties; despite the prevalence of reed bands in the outside world, the instrumentation was not recognized as part of the ideal.

By the turn of the century, however, the reed band began to be sanctioned even by the authorities. The last several columns clearly show the rise of the clarinets and decline of the E-flat cornet, and the gradual replacement of the tenors by trombones. But other new instruments remained on the outside: although almost all catalogues from the nineties onward offered mellophones and alto trombones, none ever actually recommended them as part of the brass band.

In short, at the turn of the century the American amateur band was in a state of expansion and revision. The old cornet band was by no means dead, but it was gradually being replaced, first in real

Table 16.
Evolution of the Ideal "Band of 12"

	1 1850s	2 1866	3 1875	4 1880	5 1881	6 1888	7 1891	8 1891	9 1897	10 1897	11 1900	12 1902	13 c1919
E^b Clarinet	0	0	0	0	0	0	0	0	0	0	1	0	1
E^b Cornet	2	2	2	2	2	2	2	2	2	2	0	1	0
B^b Clarinet	0	0	0	0	0	0	0	0	0	0	2	0	2
B^b Cornet	2	2	2	2	2	2	2	2	2	2	3	4	2
E^b Alto	2	[3]	3	3	3	3	3	3	3	2	2	2	2
B^b Tenor	2	2	2	2	2	2	2	2	2	2/1	1/1	2	0/2
B^b Baritone	1	1	1	1	1	1	1	1	1	1	1	1	1
B^b Bass	1	0	0	0	1	1	1	0	1	1	0	1	1
E^b Bass	1/1	1/1	1/1	1/1	1	0/1	1	1/1	1	0/1	1	1	0/1

Bass drum, small drum, and cymbals to be added.
[ ] = number corrected from a misprinted 2.
/ = small E^b bass/large E^b bass *or* tenor/trombone

Sources:

1. S. T. Gordon Co., music publishers; see Bufkin 1973, p. 169.
2. *Root & Cady's Illustrated Catalogue* (Chicago, 1866), p. 56.
3. Patton, *Practical Guide to the Arrangement of Band Music* (New York, 1875), p. 42.
4. J. Howard Foote's *Catalogue of Band Instruments* (New York, 1880), p. 6.
5. Lyon and Healy, *Band Instruments, Uniforms, Trimmings & c.* (Chicago, 1881), p. 38.
6. C. Bruno and Son, *Illustrated Catalogue* (New York, 1888), p. 18.
7. *Lyon & Healy's New and Enlarged Cataloque* (Chicago, 1891), p. 8.
8. H. C. Barnes (Co.), *Musical Marchandise* (Boston, 1891), p. 158.
9. Sears, Roebuck, *Catalogue No. 104* (Chicago, 1897), p. 530.
10. A. E. Benary catalogue (New York, 1897), p. 277.
11. S. R. Leland and Son, *Illustrated Catalogue and Price List* (Worcester, Mass., 1900), p. 3.
12. Sears, Roebuck, *Catalogue No. 111* (Chicago, 1902), p. 210.
13. Rudolph Wurlitzer Co., *All Musical Instruments and Supplies* (Cincinnati, c.1919), p. 8.

bands and later in the ideals themselves, by a more mixed instrumentation of brasses and high woodwinds. This shift toward a greater variety of instrumentation had many causes; but surely the most potent was the example set by the large professional bands. Patrick Gilmore, the most famous American bandsman before Sousa, adopted a mixed brass-and-woodwind instrumentation, like the concert band of today, just after the Civil War: his band in 1878 comprised thirty-five woodwinds, twenty-seven brasses, and four percussion.[10] And Sousa's own band, formed in 1892, also had an enormous range of woodwinds, from piccolo to contrabassoon.[11]

Until the school band movement of the 1920s put instruments in the hands of millions of students everywhere, such instrumentations required far more musicians and resources than were available in most small towns; but their impact was felt just the same. It is easy to imagine that clarinets and piccolos became a kind of status symbol, a sign that a band was following the big guys. Indeed, perhaps that is what the *Citizen* meant when it said that the newly formed Lawyer's band promised to be "an up to-date band."

The notion that the reed band represents a compromise between the old cornet band and the professional bands is given further credence by the 1888 catalogue of C. Bruno and Son, instrument dealers of New York.[12] The catalogue suggests instrumentations for standard all-brass bands of six to seventeen players (Table 16, column 5); then it shows three "reed bands," for sixteen, eighteen, and twenty performers, with cornets, saxhorns (trombones optional), E-flat and B-flat clarinets, and piccolos; and finally, at the bottom of the page, it says, "To larger Reed Bands add Flutes, Oboes, Bassoons, French Horns, Saxophones, BB^b basses"—in other words, if you have enough people, you should get as close to the professionals as possible.

Perhaps it is not too simplistic, then, to see the history of American band instrumentations, at least after the introduction of the saxhorns, as a gradual shift away from an ideal of simplicity and purity toward one of complexity and variety. The change from keyed bugles to saxhorn ensemble to cornet band to reed band to mixed wind ensemble were made at various times in various places, but always by practical musicians first and commentators later. The instrumentations of the bands of Wayne County must be seen as a part of this slow, continuous process of evolution.

FOUR INSTRUMENTATIONS IN WAYNE COUNTY

Concerning the instrumentations of the bands of Wayne County between 1897 and 1901, we have four pieces of information: the roster of the Equinunk band published in the *Wayne Independent* on February 20, 1897 (p. 82), and photographs of the Equinunk band probably in the summer of 1898 (Fig. 9), of Lawyer's band in 1899 (Fig. 4), and of the Maple City band in 1900 (Fig. 6). All four have at least minor problems, and none should be taken uncritically: the roster seems to contain a misprint, which I have corrected as sensibly as I could; the picture of the Maple City band shows only sixteen-and-a-half members of a band of perhaps twenty-one; and

both pictures of the bands of Honesdale contain at least one person
without any instrument. Moreover, in interpreting photographs of
this time, in which instruments are often partially hidden, it is often
difficult to distinguish between E-flat and B-flat cornets, between
alto and tenor valve trombones, between slide and valve trombones,
and among alto horns, tenor horns, baritones, and B-flat basses. But
with these caveats in mind I believe the sources are still useful in
gaining information about the instruments the bands were using.

As best they can be deciphered and recognized, the instruments
in the four bands are listed in Table 17, along with an "ideal" instrumentation of each size. The Sears and Roebuck catalogue for
1897 was chosen as the ideal because it is fairly typical of the
instrumentations being suggested at the time, and because it was so
widely disseminated in rural areas and was surely familiar to these
people. And a comparison of the real bands with each other and
with the ideal will allow a number of generalizations.

Table 17.
Instruments of Wayne County Bands

Instrument	Sears	Equinunk 1897	1898	Sears	Lawyer's	Sears	Maple City
Piccolo	0	0	0	0	1	0	1
E♭ Clarinet	0	1	0	0	0	0	1
E♭ Cornet	2	2	0	2	0	2	0
B♭ Clarinet	0	0	1	0	1	0	1
B♭ Cornet	2	3	3	3	4	2	3
E♭ Alto	3	2	2	3	3	3	2*
B♭ Tenor	2	2	2	2	0	2	1
B♭ Trombone	0	0	1	0	3	0	1
B♭ Baritone	1	1	1	1	1	1	2
B♭ Bass	1	1	0	1	0	1	0
E♭ Bass	1	0	2	2	1	2	1
Snare drum	[1]	1	1	[1]	1	[1]	1
Cymbals	[1]	1	1	[1]	1	[1]	1
Bass drum	[1]	1	1	[1]	1	[1]	1
TOTAL	[15]	15	15	[17]	17	[16]	16

[ ] = Percussion not specified in catalogue.
* = One upright alto, one mellophone.

Lawyer's and Maple City columns include only players photographed with
instruments.

Sears = Sears, Roebuck, *Catalogue no. 104* (Chicago, 1897), p. 530.

Of the Pennsylvania bands, the original Equinunk band is by far
the most conservative: all its brass instruments are the cornets and
saxhorns of the traditional cornet band, and it has only one woodwind. This may reflect a certain conservatism in the community,
but more likely I believe we should see it in a light of the band's
history. This was Equinunk's first band, its first entry into a
distinguished and prestigious tradition; it should be no surprise,
then, if the village hewed as close to that tradition as possible.
Moreover, a band being started from scratch has an unusual degree
of freedom in choosing its instruments: Reverend Alberti didn't
have to worry about how many cornetists and baritone players
were in the community, and he could afford simply to order more or
less the instruments he wanted to have—possibly with the aid of
one of these suggested-instrumentation charts. And perhaps significantly, the one clarinetist in the band, Cain Lord, is also the oldest
member, which suggests that he may have been playing his instrument before the band was founded; this might explain why he is the
one rebel in the otherwise pure cornet band.

In contrast, the two bands of Honesdale were relatively well-
supplied not only with piccolos and clarinets, but also with non-
standard brass: the Maple City band had a valve trombone and a
mellophone, and Lawyer's band had no less than three trombones.
This profusion of trombones may have been due in part to the influence of the band's director, himself an accomplished trombonist
and thus probably an inspiration to some of the players. But in
general, the more varied instrumentation of the Honesdale bands
probably reflects the more cosmopolitan character of the community
and the longer history of the bands themselves: Honesdale had had
cornet bands for several generations by this time, and it was ready
for something a little different and more modern.

Compared with the ideal, most of the bands, and particularly the
Equinunk band of 1897, are top-heavy—skewed toward the cornets
and away from the tubas. The main reason for this is probably
financial: smaller instruments were less expensive and thus more
easily obtained by farm laborers and shoe lasters. One might also
suspect an opposite bias in the ideals themselves, for the charts
were published by people making a profit for the sale of the
instruments. It seems probable, moreover, that the cornet was a
more popular instrument just because it was more conspicuous and
spectacular: the same sort of thing occurs today in junior-high
bands, which are almost always long on trumpeters and short on
euphonium players. And it may have been that, given the demanding

nature of the cornet parts, and the amount of time available for practice, it was a musically wise choice to reinforce the top lines.

The shift in instrumentation experienced by the Equinunk band between February 1897 and the summer of the following year tended, in fact, to make it a more modern and better-balanced ensemble. It still maintained the basic cornet-band configuration (the E-flat clarinet was replaced by a B-flat clarinet), but added a trombone; and the profusion of E-flat cornets disappeared in favor of E-flat basses, possibly as the result of the band's improved financial position.

Finally, we must bear in mind that the instrumentation of these bands must have been continually changing. This is perhaps most obvious in the case of the Equinunk band; after its first year and a half, only seven of its charter members were still playing their original instruments. But the same process must have been going on, even if less dramatically, in all of these bands as men moved in and out of town and as new instruments were bought and old ones broke down. Because all these valved brasses are fingered alike, it is relatively easy to switch from one instrument to another. Such doubling, particularly on the inner voices, may have been a common practice: John Broad, for example, played a baritone solo in one concert of the Maple City band, but played trombone and alto horn in performances of the Honesdale Philharmonic.[13] And three members of the Equinunk band switched instruments between the roster of 1897 and the photograph of 1898. So these four sample instrumentations should be seen not as snapshots, but as stills from a movie; and given that, all three are within reasonable reach of the ideal. They are fairly well balanced, with nothing essential left out, and I have no doubt that they worked.

The task of the small-town bandmaster was to balance the possibilities against the practical restrictions. Then as now, everyone had at least a vague idea of what instruments consituted a band, and professional advice on the specifics was not hard to find. On the other hand, the whole tradition was in a state of change, poised between the pure brass band of the nineteenth century and the mixed wind ensemble of the twentieth—so that the citizens and the authorities did not always agree. And above all this were the pragmatic considerations of putting a band together in a place where musicians were always in short supply and where one had only limited control over what instruments they would take up. The Equinunk band is a particularly good example: Reverend Alberti was starting his band from scratch, he was apparently the only brass player in town, and he was also the spiritual leader of the whole community. He was, one would think, in a position of supreme power to ask for and get what he wanted; yet whether from financial reasons or from the desire of his members for personal glory, what he got—at least at first—was a band rather heavy on the cornets and light on the tubas.

NOTES

1. In this chapter I am especially indebted to a long series of discussions with, and demonstrations by, Robert E. Sheldon of the Smithsonian Institution. Margaret Hindle Hazen and Robert M. Hazen, in *The Music Men: An Illustrated History of Brass Bands in American, 1800-1920* (Washington: Smithsonian Institution Press, 1987), pp. 90-111, provide an excellent comprehensive introduction to the evolution of American band instrumentation.

2. For a contemporary discussion of these early instruments, and the saxhorns that succeeded them, see Allen Dodworth, *Dodworth's Brass Band School* (New York: H. B. Dodworth, 1853).

3. I have simplified Sax's original terminology slightly; for a fuller treatment, and more information on the history and technology of saxhorns, see Wally Horwood, *Adolphe Sax, 1814-1894: His Life and Legacy* (Bramley, U.K.: Bramley Books, 1979), pp. 27-34, 49-69, 135-43; Malou Haine, *Adolphe Sax (1814-1894): sa vie, son oeuvre, ses instruments de musique* (Brussels: Éditions de l'Université de Bruxelles, 1980), pp. 64-72 et passim; and Clifford Bevan, *The Tuba Family* (New York: Charles Scribner's Sons, 1978), pp. 101-20.

4. On the bands of the Civil War, see especially William A. Bufkin, "Union Bands of the Civil War: Instrumentation and Score Analysis," Ph.D. diss., Louisiana State University, 1973; Kenneth E. Olson, *Music and Musket: Bands and Bandmen of the American Civil War* (Westport, Conn.: Greenwood Press, 1981); and Robert Garofalo and Mark Elrod, *A Pictorial History of Civil War Era Musical Instruments and Military Bands* (Charleston, W.V.: Pictorial Histories Publishing, 1985).

5. See, for example, Lyon and Healy, *Catalogue of Musical Merchandise* (Chicago: Lyon and Healy, 1898-99), p. 108.

6. Lyon and Healy, *Catalogue,* pp. 87, 96, 109-110, 123, 135-136.

7. Ibid., p. 101; in this catalogue the instrument is known as the "Concert Alto."

8. G. F. Patton, *A Practical Guide to the Arrangement of Band Music* (New York: John F. Stratton, 1875), p. 42.

9. For example, see the photographs throughout Hazen and Hazen, *The Music Men.*

10. H. W. Schawartz, *Bands of America* (Garden City, N.Y.: Doubleday, 1957), pp. 106-7.

11. See, for example, the photograph of Sousa's band in 1900 as printed, inexplicably, in the "Brass Band" article of *The New Grove Dictionary of Music and Musicians*, vol. 3, ed. Stanley Sadie (London: Macmillan, 1980), p. 211; and Hazen and Hazen, *The Music Men*, p. 104.

12. C. Bruno and Son, *Illustrated Catalogue* (New York: Bruno, 1888), p. 18.

13. *Wayne Independent*, August 18, 1900; March 25, 1899; and November 17, 1900. John Broad was, however, perhaps an exceptional case with excetional training—recall that his father was the leader of one of Honesdale's longest-lived bands.

8

Repertory

The *Independent* of August 7, 1901 reported that a young man from Honesdale had recently attended a performance of the Maple City band "with his large graphaphone and captured a catchy march entitled 'Crack O' the Whip' played by the band" (p. 64). It is a tantalizing item; what a wealth of information such a recording, however primitive, would yield. But there is no trace of it, and after three devastating floods, innumerable fires, and eight decades of neglect, the odds against an obsolete and fragile wax cylinder seem impossible. Until an old recording comes to light, the music of these bands is lost forever.

We do, however, have an idea of the *kind* of music they played, and at least some of it has survived in printed form. And from examining this repertory we can tell much about the tastes of the bands, their expertise, and the musical tradition within which they were playing.

Nearly all the information comes from concert programs printed in the papers by the three bands of Honesdale: two programs from the Honesdale band (pp. 35,40), seven from Lawyer's band (pp. 50, 52), and two from the Maple City band (pp. 58-60). The programs, plus a few isolated references, yield a total of sixty-three titles shown in Table 18.

This is a fairly substantial repertory, but not necessarily typical, as it represents only the Honesdale bands and only the concert situation. It is probably safe to suppose that music for picnics was essentially the same as that for concerts, and that the pieces used for parades and dances were also available for use in concerts. But we would probably not be justified in extending gereralizations

Table 18.
Partial Concert Repertory of the Honesdale Bands

Title	Genre	Composer/ Arranger	Copyright Date	Band
Azure Lake	fantasia			Honesdale
The Banner of the Sea	song	?/Sousa*		Lawyer's
The Blue and the Gray	march	?/J. W. Chattaway	1900	Maple City
Cardinal	overture	Losey	1897	Honesdale
Champion	march	Rockwell	1896	Lawyer's
The Citizen Soldier	march	Tayron		Maple City
The Club	galop	L. P. Laurendeau		Lawyer's
Colonel Roosevelt's March	march	O. R. Farrar	1898	Honesdale
Comique	schottische	Miller		Lawyer's
Consolatrix	overture	H. Ditzel		Honesdale
Crack o'the Whip March	march		1901	Maple City
The Crackerjack	overture? march & 2-step?	Nick Brown/ Mackie-Beyer	1906**	Lawyer's Maple City
Dance of the "Do-funnies"	cakewalk	Barclay Walker	1898	Lawyer's
Danny Murphy's Daughter	waltz	Engle		Lawyer's
The Dominion March	march? overture?	W. Beebe	1898**	Honesdale
Echoes from the Circus	galop	Clement		Honesdale
Euphonious	baritone solo	Miller	1887**	Maple City
The Hamtown Minstrels		L. P. Laurendeau	1895	Honesdale
Hands Across the Sea	march	John Philip Sousa	1899	Honesdale
Heap Big Injun War Dance	war dance	George Southwell	1898	Lawyer's
In Old Madrid	selection	H. Trotère/ L. P. Laurendeau	1898	Lawyer's
Inaugural	waltz	Blanche K. Grambs		Honesdale
Intermezzo Sinfonico (from *Cavalleria Rusticana*)		Pietro Mascagni		Lawyer's
Irish Artist	selection	Vernon	1895	Maple City

Table 18. (Continued)
Partial Concert Repertory of the Honesdale Bands

Title	Genre	Composer/ Arranger	Copyright Date	Band
The James Park	march	Miller		Lawyer's
Jasper Jenkins de Cake Walk Coon	character- istic march & two-step	Henry P. Vogel/ R. Recker	1899	Lawyer's
Just One Girl	waltz	Lyn Udall/ W. H. Mackie	1898	Lawyer's
King's Champion	march	Baker	1897	Honesdale
Lehigh Valley	march	E. F. Scholl	1897	Lawyer's
Levi Jackson	cakewalk	Albert Winkler		Maple City
Little Beauty	overture	Benjamin B. Dale	1897	Lawyer's
Love's Old Sweet Song	trombone or cornet solo	James L. Molloy/ L. P. Laurendeau	1898	Lawyer's
Loving Heartz Gavotte	gavotte	Theodore Moses- Tobani	1887	Lawyer's
Lyric	overture	Christoph Bach		Honesdale
Marfy and Lize	cakewalk	Miller		Lawyer's
Masked Battery Q.S.	march & quickstep	W. Buckley	1893	Lawyer's
Minerva Waltzes		H. C. Miller	1898	Maple City
The Nation's Pride	march	W. H. Scouton	1898	Maple City
Notre Cher Alsace	selection			Honesdale
The Old Church Organ	serenade	W. Paris Chambers	1907**	Lawyer's, Maple City
Olympia	overture	Miller		Maple City
Peaceful Slumbers	serenade	Miller		Maple City
Popular Swing	two-step	Miller		Maple City
Princeton Cadets	march	W. Durand	1896	Lawyer's
Romance	trombone solo	Bennett		Lawyer's
Salute to Trenton March	march	Albert Winkler	1898	Lawyer's

Table 18. (Continued)
Partial Concert Repertory of the Honesdale Bands

Title	Genre	Composer/ Arranger	Copyright Date	Band
Shot and Shell	march and two-step	Yule	1896	Honesdale
Silver Jubilee March	march	Albert Winkler		Lawyer's
Solo for Baritone	serenade	Losey		Honesdale
Song and Dance		Voelker		Honesdale
Le Souvenir	overture			Honesdale
The Star-Spangled Banner	patriotic song	W. S. Smith		Honesdale
Sweet Dreams				Maple City
Teddy's Terrors	march	Warner Crosby	1898	Lawyer's
Tenting Tonight	patriotic song			Honesdale
True to the Flag	march	Franz von Blon/ L. P. Laurendeau	1898	Lawyer's
Two Step	two-step	Bone		Honesdale
Union Forever	march	W. H. Scouton	1899	Maple City
Valley Forge	march	J. H. Wadsworth	1899	Lawyer's
Volante Galop	galop	A. Catozzi	1901**	Lawyer's
Waiting for You, Sweetheart	selection? overture?	M. D. Selmser/ Benjamin B. Dale	1897	Lawyer's
Yankee Harp	overture	Miller		Lawyer's
Yankee Hash	medley	Miller		Lawyer's

*Probably a mistake by the newspaper.
**Version copyrighted is probably not the arrangement played by the band.

Information in the newspaper programs has been corrected and augmented, when possible, from the U.S. copyright records.

from these programs to the bands in the smaller villages. The problem of the rural bands will be discussed later, after the music heard at the county seat.

SOURCES

As the "Copyright date" column of Table 18 shows, only about half of the pieces are listed among the copyright records of the United States. Some of the others may have been printed in "band books"— sets of published partbooks containing a dozen or more pieces.[1] Ordinarily, the compositions in these books were not copyrighted separately and therefore are extremely difficult to find. Still other titles may simply have been so garbled in the newspapers that they are not recognizable in the copyright records; and some pieces, such as the national anthem, existed in so many arrangements that we cannot know which the bands used. Despite all these considerations, however, the possibility still exists that some of the repertory was written or arranged locally.

In the early years of the band movement, very little music for bands was published; band directors would write their own arrangements, and the musicians would copy them into their blank partbooks. As the nineteenth century progressed and the tradition grew, however, published music became more accessible. But home-made arrangements remained a necessary and economical expedient for many bands, and the amateur arranger had published bandbooks available to guide his efforts. And the band that had its own arranger—or better yet its own composer—gained in prestige.[2]

Unfortunately, the actual partbooks of the Wayne County bands do not survive. But in the archives of the Smithsonian Institution are a set of six solo B-flat cornet books, dating apparently from the 1880s to the early 1900s, that belonged to George M. Noll of the Montrose band.[3] Montrose, about fifty miles west of Honesdale, is the county seat of neighboring Susquehanna County; its population in 1890 was 1,735. It was a town much like Honesdale, and as a result, the books provide a fascinating insight into the practices of the surrounding area. Of the eighty-two folios of music bound into the six books (many other pages are loose), only twenty-one are printed parts; the other sixty-one are in manuscript. In other words, a considerable majority either was locally produced or was copied by hand from music owned by someone else.

More than fifty compositions in the Montrose partbooks are attributed, as composer or arranger, to one Jacob Guth, a local bandleader and the first instructor of the ensemble.[4] Some of these are settings of familiar tunes and may be simply reworkings of old arrangements—for example, Guth's "Potpouri" contains two sections that seem to be taken directly from Allen Dodworth's arrangements published in 1853.[5] But most of Guth's contributions have the look of original compositions, and some of them are fairly ambitious. It seems, then, that this band was content to rely largely on the labors of its own local composer.[6]

Did such a situation exist in Honesdale too? On the whole, it seems hard to believe; if any hometown composer had dominated these bands so prominently, no doubt he should have achieved a considerable fame in the newspapers. Among the repertory, however, are seven pieces attributed to a "Miller" that cannot be identified in the copyright records. And a number of pieces of evidence suggest, at least tenuously, some sort of local or regional connection. First, the roster of the Honesdale band in 1897 (p. 28) included a Henry Miller, and twenty Miller families are listed in the Honesdale directory for 1906-07.[7] Second, the Montrose partbooks have two pieces, handwritten on both sides of the same folio, attributed to "Miller" and "Miller of Lock Haven" (a small town in north central Pennsylvania), and another folio has the cryptic marginal inscription "Mar 23rd 1886 / Locums [?] school house / 1st of Prof. Millers."[8] And finally, the one Miller piece I have been able to find in the copyright records, "Minerva Waltzes" by H. C. Miller, is listed there as having been played by the H. C. Parker band of Parkersburg, Pennsylvania. There is no Parkersburg on any map I have consulted, but it may be a very small village or a misspelling of Parkersville or Parkesburg, two small towns in Chester County, in the southeastern part of the state. It is at least conceivable that some of these Millers are the same person—perhaps an itinerant band director who held positions in various towns around the state and whose music reached Honesdale after being passed from band to band in manuscript form. Possibly he even lived in Honesdale for awhile before 1897 and left his music behind when he departed. But of course the name is a common one, and all of these clues may amount to nothing.

At least two numbers performed by the Honesdale bands were indeed local products, at least in some sense. I have not been able to locate either of these pieces, but here is what the newspapers say:

The Honesdale Band has procured, through the courtesy of the composer, advanced manuscript copies of the new waltz, "Inaugural," by Blanche Kesler Grambs, of Seattle, Washington, formerly a Honesdale girl. This, her latest composition, is dedicated to and performed by Wagner's 1st Reg't Band, Washington National Guard, and is already on the repertoire of Victor Herbert's 22d Reg't band, New York; also Sousa's band, and promises to add new laurels to the musical reputation of the fair songstress and composer.[9]

The public will be invited to a concert to-morrow—Friday— evening, from the pagoda by Lawyer's band. Homer Greene's "The Banner of the Sea," will be rendered. The music was arranged by Sousa.[10]

Homer Greene was an eminent Honesdale lawyer and poet, and "The Banner of the Sea" one of his best-known poems.[11] Contrary to the *Citizen's* item, however, it does not appear in the standard catalogue of Sousa's works, [12] and there may be more salesmanship than fact in the attribution to the great bandmaster.

The printed sources used by these bands show no striking pattern of choice. Of the twenty-one pieces whose publishers I have been able to identify with some certainty, at least six were printed by two of the largest band publishers of the time, Carl Fischer of New York and the John Church Company of Cincinnati. Four others were published by a less eminent house, Benj. B. Dale of Philadelphia. And the remaining eleven pieces came from eleven different publishers.[13] Clearly, then, the bands shopped around rather than simply relying on one or two publishers' catalogues.

It is equally clear, however, that in choosing their repertory from the publishers, the bands of Honesdale were surprisingly up-to-date. Of the twenty-nine pieces whose dates seem secure, only two were copyrighted before 1895. Indeed, the bands frequently performed music that was only a few months old. Lawyer's band, for example, played "Heap Big Injun" on May 5, 1899, and perhaps even earlier, although it had been copyrighted only on November 7 of the previous year.

GENRES

In the programs of the time, the genre of a piece was often given equal billing with its title and composer. The typical form was something like this:

March—Silver Jubilee . . . . Winkler

Quaint as this practice seems today, it was practically universal in the late nineteenth century. No doubt it was adopted primarily as a matter of custom—the same form occurs not only in dance programs, which followed a prearranged sequence of genres (waltz, polka, quadrille, schottische, and so forth), but also in programs of the Honesdale Philharmonic (Fig. 8), in which the titles and composers were certainly of paramount importance. But conventions are not trivial, and perhaps it is not too much to say that this typographical preoccupation with genre reflects an attitude among the musicians and the audience that emphasized form over content. In other words, a piece of music may have been seen more as a generic product than as an individual work of art; to many people, it was more important that the band was playing a march than that it was playing "Silver Jubilee" by Winkler.

Of all the genres in this repertory, the march was by far the most numerous and prominent: all of the programs have at least two, most have three, and many begin and end with marches. Marches are the traditional métier of bands everywhere, and of course a great many of the performances of these ensembles were parades. So it should be no surprise to see marches finding their way into concert programs as well; not only was the audience expecting a couple of foot-stompers, but the band already knew them.

More puzzling, perhaps, is the presence of only one Sousa composition among all these marches. The main reason for this may be problems of instrumentation: most of the Sousa marches were published for the mixed wind ensemble, and they may not have been easy to adapt to the smaller reed band. They are also notoriously demanding and may have been beyond the reach of these small-town musicians. At any rate, the programs do include works by O. R. Farrar and W. H. Scouton, both of whom were well-known march composers of the time, although they are forgotten today.

Among the titles of the marches, two clusters stand out. The only two pieces that seem to be based on historical events, "Colonel Roosevelt's March" and "Teddy's Terrors," both celebrate the exploits of the future president in the Spanish-American War. And more curiously, the four titles that have specific geographic references all evoke the Philadelphia area: "Lehigh Valley," "Princeton Cadets," "Salute to Trenton," and "Valley Forge." Even if we knew nothing apart from the programs, we might be able to guess that these bands were playing at the turn of the century and in Pennsylvania or New Jersey.

Second to the marches in importance was dance music. Indeed, marches and dances are not altogether distinct: publishers frequently labelled pieces as "March and Quickstep" or "March and Two-Step," and the archetypal two-step was Sousa's "Washington

Post." But the repertory of these bands also includes the other popular dance forms of the day: galops, schottisches, gavottes, and of course waltzes. Again, the presence of this music on the concert stage reflects the other activities of the bands: throughout the winter, as we have seen, the bands would hold dances to raise funds, dances at which the bands themselves provided the music. And what the audience danced to in the armory in the winter, they sat and listened to in the park in the summer.

A third category is rather more vaguely defined. When the editor of the *Herald*, describing the Red Men's concert of 1897 (p. 34), says that "The programmes of both bands were mainly made up of 'concert pieces,' and were listened to with the greatest pleasure," he is referring to a sort of music not suited for marching or dancing, but intended expressly for this more formal situation. In the programs these went by a number of names—overture, selection, serenade, fantasia—that are not readily distinguishable in musical terms. Indeed, as Table 18 shows, the genre of a particular piece was frequently changed from one program to the next. These concert pieces were more substantial and ambitious than the marches and dances, and they were intended to make a more or less serious impression; they often included the instrumental solo that was the most glorious moment of the evening. But still they tended to remain within the popular sphere: in contrast to the professional bands, which depended heavily on orchestral transcriptions and operatic excerpts,[14] the bands of Honesdale played only one piece of "classical" music, the selection from *Cavalleria Rusticana*. Even at its heaviest, then, the repertory remained light and accessible and included some of the most popular sentimental songs of the day, such as "In Old Madrid" and "Waiting for You, Sweetheart." A fourth category might be termed novelty numbers—medleys, cakewalks, war dances, and so forth that would inject a note of humor into the proceedings and ensure that everyone had a good time. The predominant ethnic quality of these pieces is certainly in tune with the humor of the time, and the number of cakewalks on the programs serves to underscore the close association of the band tradition and the blackface minstrel tradition. Recall that the annual Firemen's parade often included a "Darktown band" in addition to the regular town band; that the best and most famous professional bands that came through town were part of touring minstrel shows; and indeed, that the first performance of the Maple City band was supposed to be a "home talent minstrel performance."

SCORING

As described in chapter 7, the American band movement by the end of the century admitted a bewildering variety of instrumentations, from all-brass bands of half a dozen players to mixed brass-and-woodwind ensembles of a hundred or more. This flexibility was no doubt a boon to the small-town musician, who had to make do with whatever instruments were available. To music publishers, who had to prepare arrangements that could be used by all these instrumental combinations, it was a real headache.

For example, Lyon and Healy's "Quickstep Journal" series, dating from the 1870s and early 1880s, was advertised as being "Arranged for brass and reed bands": "Piccolo; E flat Clarionet; 1st and 2d B flat Clarionets; 1st and 2d E flat Cornets; 1st, 2d and 3d B flat Cornets; 1st, 2d and 3d E flat Altos; 1st and 2d B flat Tenors; B flat Baritone; B flat Bass; 1st and 2d Tubas; Snare and Bass Drums." If each of these instruments had its own unique part, however, a band of less than twenty instruments could not play the music without the risk of leaving out something important. So the catalogue goes on: "Although all the above parts are published, every piece in this collection can be played complete with one E flat Cornet, two B flat Cornets, two E flat Altos, one B flat Tenor, Baritone and Tuba."[15] In other words, the element of flexibility was built into these arrangements by the provision of profuse doubling, so that if one instrument happened to be missing, its part would likely be covered by another.

A typical composition from the repertory of Lawyer's band can be used to see how this worked. Figure 10 shows the introduction and first strain of the march "Lehigh Valley" by E. F. Scholl, in long score.[16] The instrumentation is essentially the same as that given by Lyon and Healy, except for the addition of trombones and the deletion of the second E-flat cornet. And like the Lyon and Healy series, the march is designed to be usable by much smaller forces.

After a rousing unison introduction, the various instruments separate into essentially four layers:

1. the bottom layer, in which the basic harmonic rhythm is set by the tuba (in the case of Lawyer's band and most others, an E-flat bass), playing a steady pattern of eighth notes on the beat, which is doubled at the octave by the third trombone and B-flat bass and reinforced by the bass drum;
2. a second layer, in which the altos, tenors, and trombones, frequently assisted by the second B-flat cornet, play a

LEHIGH VALLEY
March

10. E. F. Scholl, "Lehigh Valley March," 1897.

E. F. SCHOLL
1897

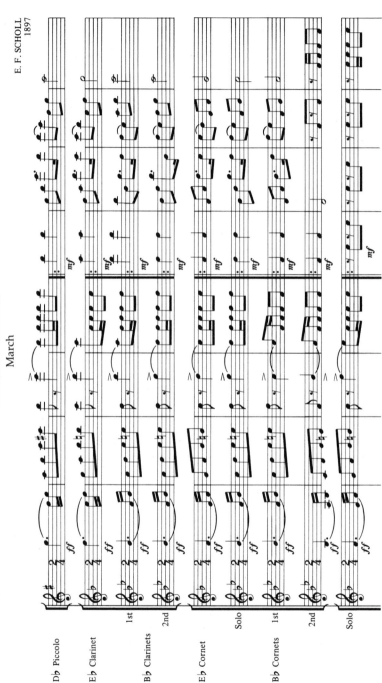

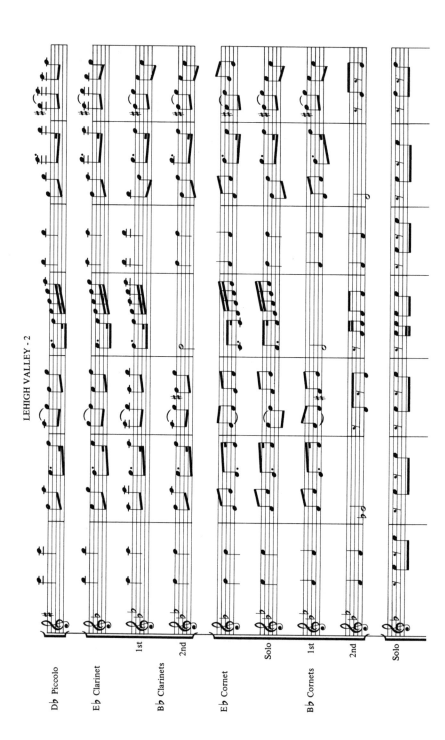

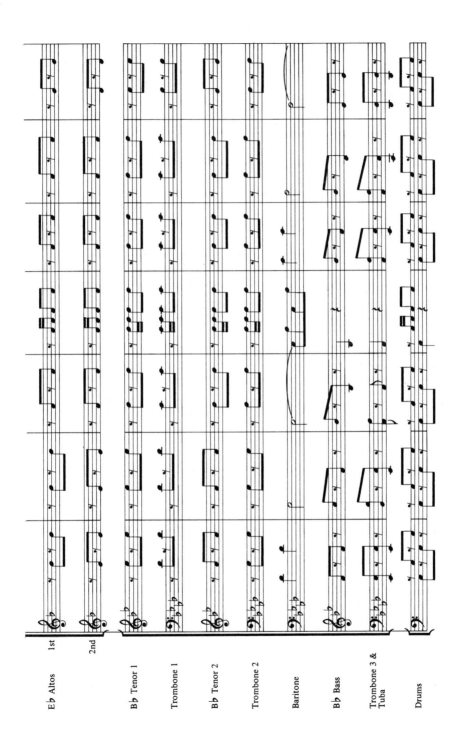

LEHIGH VALLEY - 3

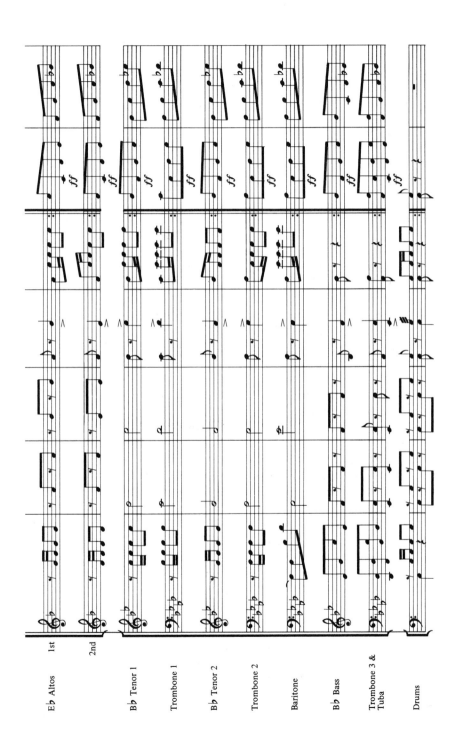

stereotyped off-beat pattern of eighth notes and sixteenth notes (a pattern reinforced by the small drum);

3. the melody, played by the solo B-flat cornet and doubled at the unison by the E-flat cornet, at the octave by the first B-flat clarinet, and two octaves up by the piccolo and E-flat clarinet; this is harmonized in the first B-flat cornet and second B-flat clarinet parts; and

4. the baritone part, which plays another melody in counterpoint to the cornets and winds (in this case, a rather simple counter-melody, though often it was more complex).

For the sake of simplicity I have used the word *doubling* here rather loosely: the first B-flat clarinet part, for example, follows the cornet part more or less note-for-note, but it switches octaves so often that the shape of the melody is distorted and obscured. In the lower voices, however, the doubling is exact and systematic, so that in effect all the parts between the altos and the tuba are printed twice, in treble and bass clefs. The B-flat bass is simply a treble-clef version of the third trombone; the first and second trombone lines are bass-clef versions of the tenors; and the baritone is printed in both clefs just as it usually is today. The result is to allow not only for various instrumentations, but also for players who can read only one clef or the other.

Clearly, then, the music was deliberately scored to be as flexible as possible. But how would this work in practice? To answer the question we might only return to the portrait of Lawyer's band in Figure 4. Fred Gill, passing out this piece of music to those who happened to be standing in this same formation, might decide to distribute the parts as follows (omitting the man with no instrument):

(player)— (part)
EᵇBass— Tuba
Baritone— Baritone
Slide Trombone— Trombone 1
Valve Trombone— Trombone 2
Valve Trombone— Trombone 3
Alto— Solo Alto
Alto— Alto 1
Alto— Alto 2
Piccolo— Piccolo
Bᵇ Clarinet— Bᵇ Clarinet 2
Bᵇ Cornet— Bᵇ Cornet 2
Bᵇ Cornet— Bᵇ Cornet 1

Bb Cornet—Solo Bb Cornet
Bb Cornet—Solo Bb Cornet
Drums & Cymbals—Drums

DIFFICULTY

In his "Guide for Amateur Brass Bands," D. S. McCosh had some very specific advice to the beginning bandmaster about whom to choose for the various instruments: "To decide about the players for different instruments, let the best musicians take the 1st Eb Cornet, 1st Bb Cornet, and Baritone. Next select a large good natured gentleman for the Tuba, and one with some ability for the 2nd Bb Cornet. The 1st and 2nd Altos, and 1st and 2nd Tenors are about equally difficult. For the Bass Drum, have some one who will keep good time, and for the small drum, it is well to have a man who has played before either in a martial [perhaps a fife and drum corps?] or a brass band."[17]

McCosh recognized, as all experienced band directors have, that some parts are traditionally more demanding and conspicuous than others; and his advice, echoed by other contemporary sources,[18] seems generally very sound. Although it is hard to say whether the dimensions and temperament of the tubist would materially affect his ability to play the bass part of any given piece, certainly the cornet and baritone parts do tend to require the greatest skill and musicianship, and the altos and tenors less.

The difficulty of a piece of music is of course not a simple matter to quantify, but perhaps a few more or less subjective comments about "Lehigh Valley" will suffice. First, most of the instrumental parts have a range of only a ninth to an eleventh, and only three brass parts (the solo and first B-flat cornet and the first tenor) go as high as a G above the treble-clef staff. Second, the alto, tenor, and trombone lines, with their rhythmic repetition and smooth voice-leading, are very elementary indeed—in the first part of "Lehigh Valley," for example, the solo alto goes for ten measures without stirring from a C. The tuba, third trombone, and B-flat bass are not much harder; they do have a key signature of four flats, but this was so common in band music of the time that it cannot have caused many problems. The clarinet and piccolo parts, being in fact brass parts rewritten for woodwinds, are well within the elementary technical capabilities of the instruments. And true to McCosh's advice, the cornet and baritone parts make the heaviest demands in flexibility, in range, in technique, and in responsibility.

But even the cornet and baritone lines cannot really be called difficult by any usual standard. At any rate, I have played through all of the parts of several of these pieces myself, and have shown them to a middle-school band director, who confirms that there is nothing in this music beyond the skills of an average junior-high band.

Is this a reasonable estimate for the town band tradition as a whole? I suspect that it is. Junior-high musicians of today are in fact well trained by nineteenth-century standards: they have had several years of fairly intensive lessons, they have more leisure time for practice, and they have heard more music by professional players. They have simply had more opportunities than their great-grand-fathers. Certainly many of the bands around the country, including some amateur bands, played at a remarkably high level; the cornet parts in the Montrose partbooks, for example, are in general more difficult than those in the Honesdale repertory, and some are quite spectacular.[19] But on the whole, it seems clear that these town bands chose music suited to the tastes of the audience and the ability of the players, not music that would impress us much today.

SOME EXTRAPOLATIONS AND CONCLUSIONS

The repertories of the rural bands are much more mysterious. The five years of newspapers have provided only five titles: the Equinunk band is reported once to have played "Pleasant Dreams"; the Lake Como band to have played "The Star-Spangled Banner" and "Hail, Columbia"; both of bands to have combined for a performance of "Marching through Georgia"; and the Beach Lake band to have performed "We'll Rally Round the Flag, Boys."[20] Beyond this we know nothing, but a few cautious extrapolations might not be out of place.

First, the apparent patriotic bias is surely an illusion: the information comes not from the musicians themselves, as with the programs of the Honesdale bands, but from local correspondents, who would naturally report titles only for pieces they recognized.

Second, the country bands played a rather different schedule of performances from their urban cousins, and this may have influenced the music they chose. As we have seen, the Honesdale bands took much of their concert repertory from the music they played at parades and dances, but the rural bands were preparing primarily for picnics, concerts, and serenades. This probably would not have affected the number of marches—marches were so much a part of the tradition that no self-respecting band would have been without them. But it does seem possible that the rural bands may have had more sit-down concert pieces in their programs and fewer waltzes, gavottes, and so forth.

Third, the rural bands, and particularly the Equinunk band, played more often at functions of the church, and thus their repertory may have included more sacred music than that of the Honesdale bands. Sears and Roebuck offered in 1897 a "Sacred Band Journal" containing ten hymns suitable "for Sunday playing, Sunday school picnics, concerts, etc.," and indeed such books were available from many publishers.[21] And it is somehow difficult to imagine Reverend Alberti conducting a band for four years on secular music alone.

Finally, it seems probable, although by no means proven, that the village bands tended to play at a lower level of expertise. At the very least we know that they were often unveiled with alarming haste: the Equinunk band, for example, started rehearsals around late November 1896, and performed on Christmas. At least for the first few years of their existence, then, these bands must have chosen music at a fairly elementary level.

The music of the American amateur brass band tradition remains largely unknown territory. And an enormous territory it was—even by 1881, the Lyon and Healy catalogue listed more than five hundred pieces from which to choose,[22] and this figure was multiplied over and over by the early twentieth century. But even this necessarily quick and tentative look at the repertory of the bands of Wayne County shows how well suited the music was to the occasion.

First and last, band concerts were supposed to be fun; they did not have the aura of cultural self-righteousness that surrounded performances of the Honesdale Philharmonic. And the music wasn't wearing any halos, either. Marches, dances, sentimental songs, crude ethnic humor—it was naive, popular, uncomplicated music for musicians of modest gifts and an audience of simple tastes.

NOTES

1. See, for example, Sears, Roebuck, *Catalogue No. 104* (Chicago: Sears, Roebuck, 1897; rept. New York: Chelsea House, 1968), p. 540

2. See Margaret Hindle Hazen and Robert M.Hazen, *The Music Men: An Illustrated History of Brass Bands in America, 1800-1920* (Washington: Smith-

sonian Institution Press, 1987), pp. 125-27. For a most detailed contemporary portrait of the composer-arranger's duties, See G. F. Patton, *A Practical Guide to the Arrangement of Band Music* (New York: John F. Stratton, 1875), especially pp. 41-174.

3. Smithsonian Institution Archives, Hazen collection of band ephemera.

4. Montrose [Pennsylvania] *Independent Republican*, April 8, 1889.

5. "Potpouri" [*sic*] is found in Book I, ff. 16-16v. The two probable borrowings from Allen Dodworth, *Dodworth's Brass Band School* (New York: H. B. Dodworth, 1853) are "Hail, Columbia!" (pp. 40-42) and "Yankee Doodle" (pp. 34-35).

6. Or to take another, more distant example: Ronald V. Wiecki, in "The Stahl Partbooks: A New Source of Turn-of-the-Century American Band Music," *Journal of Band Research* 23 (Spring 1988): 1-9, shows that of the two hundred pieces represented in the partbooks of the Stahl band of turn-of-the-century Luxemburg, Wisconsin, at least two and possibly eight others are by Alois Stahl, leader of that band. (See especially pp. 3-5.)

7. *Honesdale Directory, 1906-7* (Scranton: Phillipi Directory Co., 1906), pp. 95-96.

8. Montrose partbooks, Book I, folios 32, 32v, 29v.

9. *Honesdale Citizen*, May 6, 1897.

10. Ibid., June 15, 1899.

11. For a short biography of Greene and two more poems, see Alfred Mathews, *History of Wayne, Pike and Monroe Counties, Pennsylvania* (Philadelphia: R. T. Peck, 1886; rept. Honesdale: Citizens for the Preservation of Our Local Heritage, n.d.), pp. 184, 394, 396-97. "The Banner of the Sea" is printed in Homer Greene, *What My Lover Said and Other Poems* (Philadelphia: Macrae-Smith, 1931), pp. 20-21. The poem is printed with this note:

In March, 1899 [only three months before the piece was played by Lawyer's band], the U.S. flagship Trenton while at anchor in the bay of Apia, off the Samoan Islands, was struck and sunk by a terrific hurricane. As the ship was going down the sailors, gathered on her deck, gave three cheers to the American flag flying at the masthead.

The first of its five stanzas is as follows:

By wind and wave the sailor brave has fared
To shores of every sea;
But, never yet have seamen met or dared
Grim death for victory
In braver mood than they who died
On drifting decks, in Apia's tide,
While cheering every sailor's pride,
The Banner of the Free!

Much of Greene's other verse, incidentally, is much better than this.

12. Paul E. Bierley, *John Philip Sousa: A Descriptive Catalogue of His Works* (Columbus: Integrity Press, 1984).

13. The publishers, and pieces published by each, are as follows: Benj. B. Dale (Philadelphia): Little Beauty; Waiting for You, Sweetheart; Valley Forge; Lehigh Valley
Carl Fisher (New York): In Old Madrid; Love's Old Sweet Song; True to the Flag; [also perhaps The Club and The Hamtown Minstrels]
John Church Co. (Cincinnati): The Nation's Pride; Union Forever; Hands Across the Sea.
M. Witmark and Sons (New York): Just One Girl; [also perhaps The Cracker Jack]
J. G. Richards and Co.: Euphonious Quick Step
White, Smith and Co.: Loving Hearts Gavotte
Great North American Music Publishing Co: Masked Battery Q S
Wulschner and Son (Indianapolis): Dance of the "Do-Funnies"
Geo. Southwell (Kansas City): Heap Big Injun War Dance
H. C. Miller (Parkersburg, Pa.): Minerva Waltzes
Henry P. Vogel (Albany): Jasper Jenkins "de Cake Walk Coon"
Howley, Haviland and Co. (New York): The Blue and the Gray
Harry Coleman (Philadelphia): Col. Roosevelt's March
Hamilton S. Gordon (New York): Teddy's Terrors.

14. For example, on the music played by professional band musicians in Washington, D.C., see Katherine K. Preston, "John Prosperi and Friends: A Study of Professional Musicians in Washington, 1877-1900." M.M. thesis, University of Maryland, 1981.

15. Lyon and Healy, *Band Instruments, Uniforms, Trimmings, &c.* (Chicago: Lyon and Healy, 1881), p. 12 of music selection.

16. E. F. Scholl, *Lehigh Valley* (Philadelphia: Benj. B. Dale, 1897).

17. D. S. McCosh, "McCosh's Guide for Amateur Brass Bands," in Lyon and Healy, *Band Instruments*, pp. 3-29, quotation p. 4.

18. See, for example, Dodworth, *Dodworth's Brass Band School*, pp. 11-12, and Patton, *Practical Guide*, p. 176.

19. See, for example, the solo cornet part to Guth's concert polka, "Es ist nicht gut dass der Mensch allein," in the Montrose partbooks, Book II, folios 8v-10.

20. *Honesdale citizen*, September 16, 1897; *Wayne Independent*, September 17, 1897; *Citizen*, September 17, 1899; ibid., October 25, 1900.

21. Sears, Roebuck, *Catalogue No. 104*, p. 540. The J. W. Pepper Co. advertised in 1903 (and probably earlier) a "Gospel Hymns Sacred Band Book" as being "Suitable for Religious Celebrations, Camp Meetings, Sunday School Excursions, Revival Meetings, Etc.," in J. W. *Pepper's Musical Times and Band Journal*, vol. 18 (Philadelphia: Pepper, 1903), p. 10. The Montrose partbooks also have a number of sacred medleys and the like.

22. Lyon and Healy, *Band Instruments*, pp. 12-22 of music section.

9

The Band and the Community

In small places where music is not cultivated in any marked or public
manner, there are many opportunites offered the youth to spend
their leisure time either in trifling amusements or dissipations. The
evening hours are devoted to lounging about saloons and billiard
halls, or standing upon street corners, while the habits that loafing
inculcates are far from improving to the many young men who
inhabit our smaller villages. . . .

Advancement in the arts means an elevation of the mental part of
man, for when a person engages in the cultivation of the beautiful,
either in music, in painting, or in any science, his mind is drawn into
the sphere of the higher influences, and his very nature becomes
impressed by the inspirations that true advancement incites. To have
any organization in a city or town, that has for its aim musical
advancement, has a direct influence upon the culture of the place; for,
whatever improves the people, or gives rational pleasure, is a public
benefit.[1]

It sounds strangely like Professor Harold Hill—as well it might, for
it was written by one of his real-life predecessors. D. S. McCosh's
"Guide for Amateur Brass Bands" was printed in the Lyon and
Healy catalogue for many years, and obviously it was designed to
encourage bands and sell instruments. But what McCosh was advo-
cating, his audience surely was disposed to believe. The band was
not seen merely as a private organization for the enjoyment of its
members, but as an ornament and a blessing to the community at
large. For a band to take the name of its home town was not simply
a convenient custom: the band was always in some sense public
property.

The relationship between the band and the community was of course a complex one; I shall discuss it from six different, but not wholly separate, aspects.[2]

"KEEP THEIR TREASURY UP TO THE NEEDFUL HEIGHT"

We may begin with perhaps the most mundane approach. The bands of Wayne County were all amateur organizations, but even an amateur band could not be run for free. Its expenses had to be met by its members or absorbed somehow by its audience. And the manner and proportion of such public financial support shows much about the place of the band in the community.

Unfortunately, these financial matters are not altogether accessible from local sources: the newspapers do not provide a full fiscal accounting for any of these bands, and none of their ledgers or minute-books has survived. The few bits of available information are difficult to make into a coherent whole; the figures vary widely and may represent primarily exceptional events. But if the newpaper stories are combined with contemporary sources from around the country, some financial aspects of the bands may be at least hypothetically reconstructed.

The most conspicuous, and unavoidable, expense of a band was its instruments. It is not clear to what extent instruments were paid for and owned by the individual players, and to what extent they were bought by the band as a whole. It seems likely that in the larger towns like Honesdale, where musicians were more or less free agents and where instruments had been around town for years, much of the equipment was owned privately. But in the villages, the band tended to spring up as a group, so that the instruments were probably bought all at once, more or less, from one company. In such cases, at least some of the instruments may have been owned collectively and paid for by the band's united efforts: "On Thanksgiving night the members of the Pleasant Mount band will give a supper in academy hall to help defray expenses on some new instruments recently purchased. The public is cordially invited to attend. Two more new instruments were added to the band last week. The boys are doing good work."[3]

McCosh suggests a rather elaborate scheme for balancing the individual and group ownership of instruments, and possibly some version of it was adopted by some Wayne County bands: "Let each member pay a proportion of the amount necessary for the purchase of instruments. If, afterwards, any one wishes to leave the Band, for reasons satisfactory to the other members, let him be paid back a part of the amount invested, which shall be returned to the Band by the new member who enters in his place. If, when first purchasing instruments, the entire cost is advanced by one individual or firm, the instruments should be considered band property until each member has paid his proportion."[4]

The newspapers never say exactly how much money a band is trying to raise, but as an example, if the instrumentation published with the roster of the original Equinunk band in February 1897 is combined with the median or just-below-median prices for instruments in the Sears, Roebuck catalogue of the same year, the total cost would be $135.10; if cheaper instruments were purchased, the figure might well go below $100.[5]

On the other hand, of course, prices could go much higher, and as we have seen, at least two members of the original Equinunk band, Austin Lloyd with his $75 baritone and Robert Shields with his $90 B-flat bass, picked out relatively expensive horns, clearly not from Sears, Roebuck.[6] An item in the *Hancock Herald* from March 1898 further reported that nine of the Equinunk band's instruments at that time were silver-plated and that its three clarinets cost $50 each, which is also relatively high.[7] If these prices are representative, the band's actual instrumentarium may well have been in the $500 range or even higher.

Uniforms were another major expense. Although uniforms were mentioned in the newspapers only when a band was raising money for them or had just acquired them, it seems likely that they were considered more or less mandatory for a properly outfitted band, and that most of the bands had them. We know, at any rate, that the Honesdale band was raising money to buy uniforms early in 1897;[8] that Lawyer's band had eighteen made in April 1899 by Jacob Freeman and Son of Honesdale;[9] that the Equinunk band attended a picnic in 1898 "arrayed in their natty uniforms";[10] and that according to the *Citizen* of September 6, 1900, the Pleasant Mount band at that time presented "a very nobby appearance in their new uniforms."

A contemporary catalog of Henderson and Co., uniform makers of Philadelphia, shows band uniforms—coat, trousers, and hat—ranging in price from $11.70 to $30.15, depending on the elaborateness of design and quality of cloth.[11] The uniforms in the pictures of Lawyer's band and the Maple City band are toward the simpler end of this scale; outfits much like those of Lawyer's could be had for $12.95 to $21.50.[12] These prices, which are listed as "subject to liberal cash discount," are comparable to those of men's mail-order suits in general,[13] and local prices were probably about the same. Uniforms could no doubt be made for even less by volunteer seamstresses, and it seems possible, although unattested, that some of the rural bands adopted this expedient.

Apart from the instruments and uniforms, other expenses must have been relatively minor. As suggested in chapter 6, there is reason to believe that some bands may have paid their instructors, but if so, the amounts are unknown.[14] New music was a constant expense that was frequently mentioned in the papers: "Owing to the storm of Friday evening last the audience at the [Pleasant Mount] band concert was not as large as was expected, although the boys took in $15.55, which will help to defray expenses of new music of which they are in need."[15]

Individual pieces of music (that is, full sets of band parts) generally cost from 50 cents to $1—so the $15.55 raised by the Pleasant Mount band, assuming the figure represents profit, would buy quite a few new arrangements. But it is not certain how many pieces were acquired in a year.

Miscellaneous expenses of the bands, such as hall rentals, transportation costs, advertising, programs, and the like were probably inconsequential. After the Pleasant Mount band's fund-raising dinner on Thanksgiving 1897 (pp. 100), the *Independent* reported, "They took in about $20 and the expenses were $5."[16] The $5 probably included the cost of the dinner itself.

Although we refer to these organizations as "town bands," they did not receive any official support from the municipal governments. It is clear, however, that the bands were regarded as a cultural resource belonging to the community as a whole. This impression was enhanced by the bands' custom of playing their outdoor summer concerts for free, and by their frequent donation of services to help worthy causes; for example, the entertainment in Riverside Park in 1900 to aid the Indian Famine Fund, to which the Maple City band "gave its services gratuitously."[17] And as a result, the newspapers—particularly the *Herald*, whose editor had been a band member—urged their readers again and again to return the favor and support the bands financially whenever they had a chance: "It seems to be generally admitted, and commented upon, that nothing has so much contributed to the healthful enjoyment of our people as these weekly entertainments [of Lawyer's band in Russell Park]. . . . We want constantly to din into the consciousness of our people that bands are expensive affairs, and that the burden of their maintenance should not rest entirely upon the young men who spend hour after hour in laborious practice every week in order to give us pleasure on Friday nights. Keep their treasury up to the needful height."[18]

How was the money raised? The chief source seems to have been entertainments, dances, and dinners through the winter. The band would engage a hall, advertise, charge admission, play, often provide a dinner, and then keep the proceeds. An announcement of a fund-raiser for the Eddy Cornet band is typical: "The members of the Eddy Cornet band will give a ball in the Star rink next Monday night. The music will be furnished by an orchestra of 20 pieces [presumably the band itself?]. Dancing tickets, 50 cents, supper, 50 cents per couple. The generosity of these boys in dispersing good music upon our streets and at public gatherings, should be reciprocated by a liberal public patronage next Monday night, as there is considerable expense attached to the equipping and practicing for such good music, as our citizens have enjoyed from this band recently."[19]

When a band was engaged by an organization to provide music at a parade or picnic or the like, ordinarily a sum of money would be paid. Whether this was a fee set by the band, or a variable donation offered by the hiring organization, is not clear from the papers; the sums are not disclosed consistently enough to reveal a pattern. But the money does seem to have been a firm requirement, as we saw in chapter 3: the Honesdale post of the G.A.R. could not raise $40 to engage the Maple City band to play for Memorial Day in 1900, and so the band went elsewhere.

The newspapers do occasionally mention the amounts of money collected at fund-raising events. But these news items are sparse and inconsistent, and one wonders whether they represent more unusual than typical events. Moreover, it is often impossible to distinguish net and gross in the figures quoted. The funds coming in from these performances varied greatly and were sometimes quite substantial: the Equinunk band once raised $113 at a single picnic, which must have nearly paid for their new uniforms on the spot (p. 89). Figures of $15-$25, however, are more frequent and probably represent a more realistic norm.

The Honesdale Philharmonic was a more expensive operation than the bands, because it performed less often and had to pay its conductor and possibly even some of its out-of-town performers. As a result, its ticket proceeds were supplemented by the sale of associate memberships to culturally minded citizens (p. 66). And such an arrangement was at least considered, and perhaps even implemented, for bands as well.

> Last year F. C. Gill was the instructor [of Lawyer's band]. He is not here this year and the [Maple City] band must be at the expense of hiring an instructor. Are these concerts appreciated to the extent that people will contribute a purse toward meeting the necessary expenses? If this is not done nobody can pass any criticism if there are no open air concerts. Are there not some persons who love music and who are not connected with the band who will take enough interest in this matter to hand around a subscription paper and ascertain how much the concerts are desired?[20]

In general, then, these bands were run as amateur nonprofit organizations for the enjoyment of the players and the entertainment of the community. They did incur expenses, however: constant small expenses for music and the like, and occasional large ones for uniforms or instruments. And to meet these, the bands raised money by performing for a fee or receiving donations. The newspaper accounts do not provide an exact account of how the bands' finances worked, but the suggestion is that they were a matter of constant, although perhaps not really desperate, concern.

> Another band concert to-morrow night in Russell Park by Lawyer's band. Our music lovers must make the most of these pleasant entertainments as chilly evenings are fast coming on. Then, when it is too cold to remain out of doors perhaps our bands may be induced to give free public rehearsals in our town hall. There ought to be some systematic way of procuring a steady supply of money for our bands wherewith to purchase new music. Band tunes quickly become "played out" and we should keep up the exchequer. It is too much to ask the musicians to play for nothing and to furnish their own pieces. Over in Jermyn the people take great interest in their band, and the result is that they have an organization to be proud of.[21]

BANDS AND THE SOCIAL INSTITUTIONS OF THEIR TIME

In small towns of the 1890s, society was highly organized. Practically every gathering of people was engineered somehow by one of the dozens of more or less formal organizations in the community.

The *Honesdale Directory* for 1906-7 lists seven churches, a G.A.R. post, seventeen "Secret Societies," two "Clubs," and thirteen "Miscellaneous Societies and Organizations" (a category ranging from the Brewery Workers' Union to the Women's Christian Temperance Union).[22] These institutions were less numerous in the smaller towns, but they were of great importance to the bands throughout the county.

Within this system the band occupied an unusual place; although it was a social institution in its own right, and quite capable of organizing its own social events, other institutions also employed it to provide music at their affairs. And the relationship of these institutions to the bands depended partly on the character of each institution and partly on that of the community. A church supper was different from the Red Men's picnic, and Honesdale was different from Equinunk.

Community institutions at the turn of the century may be broadly divided into two types: clubs, whose main objective was to have fun, and civic organizations, which at least professed to be devoted to improving the community. The two are not always easy to distinguish, for most organizations contained an element of both—the fire companies, for example, doubtless spent more time around the billiard table than they did fighting fires. But still the distinction is a useful one in examining the interaction of these institutions and the bands.

Among the clubs, the most numerous were the fraternal organizations. These varied greatly in character and intent, and thus in inclination to employ the town bands. In Honesdale, for example, band performances of one sort or another were organized by the Red Men, the Odd Fellows, the Ancient Order of Hibernians, the Knights of Columbus, the Junior Order of United American Mechanics, and the Ladies of the Maccabees; other prestigious orders, such as the Masons and the Royal Arcanum, evidently ignored the bands in favor of dance orchestras. Elsewhere in the county, secret societies sponsoring the bands included the Red Men, Odd Fellows, and J.O.U.A.M. of Hawley, the Red Men and Odd Fellows of Pleasant Mount, and the Maccabees of Equinunk.

Similar in many ways to the fraternal organizations were the Liederkranz and Maennerchor, "singing societies" that thrived among the large German populations of Honesdale and Hawley. In their musical interests these societies were kin to the bands, and thus the bands were featured prominently at their public celebrations.

The activities of the fraternal organizations and singing societies were many and various, but two types of events were likely to involve bands. The more common of these was the excursion, which involved a picnic for the general public, often with a concert or parade as well. Perhaps the most spectacular was the annual band concert and excursion of the Honesdale Red Men, always reported in loving detail by the press (pp. 33-36, 39-41).

Less frequent, but even more gala, were the conventions, where clubs from all around the area could come together for official business and a good time. Sometimes these were annual events, like the Odd Fellows' reunions at Farview, and sometimes they were in honor of some important occasion, like the silver anniversary of the Hawley Maennerchor (pp. 113-14).

Veterans' groups have always tended to straddle the line between the private club and the civic organization. They exist primarily for the fellowship of their members, but they are also charged with maintaining public patriotism, both by organizing patriotic events and by acting as a symbol of past military glory. The great veterans' organization of nineteenth-century America, at least in the northern states, was the Grand Army of the Republic, composed of veterans of the Union army from the Civil War. By the turn of the century the ranks of the G.A.R. were thinning and the men were getting old, but they were still a powerful patriotic force in the community. The most important public activity of the G.A.R. was the Memorial Day celebration. The process followed a similar script from year to year and town to town: the band, the veterans, and various other organizations would march through town in the morning, possibly stopping for speeches along the way, and then would continue to the cemetery, where a ceremony would honor the deceased soldiers and their graves would be decorated. The afternoon would generally be spent in picnics, ball games, and band concerts.

Of the true civic organizations, the one most prominently identified with the bands was Protection Engine Company No. 3 of Honesdale, with its annual firemen's parade in the fall. This affair, too, changed little from one year to the next. The parade included bands, several fire companies, and often the Darktown Fire Brigade, a burlesque fire company in blackface; after the parade, the company would put on an entertainment and ball at the Armory, featuring local talent and small dance orchestras, not cornet bands. The firemen's parade was, in short, possibly Honesdale's best organized and least solemn event of the year.[23]

For the most part, however, civic organizations tended to use bands for excursions and private parties, just as the fraternal organizations and singing societies did. And occasionally they would attach themselves to another larger event, as when the Honesdale Improvement Association sold cake and ice cream at the Red Men's concert in 1897.

One institution with a noticeably small involvement in the bands was the church. Bands frequently played at Sunday School picnics and the like; but very seldom participated in the activities of the church itself. Part of the reason for this may have been that the church already had its own musical organization in the choir, but perhaps even more important, the band tended to be regarded as somehow improper and profane, not suitable for holy purposes. There were, of course, exceptions, especially out in the country, where secular organizations were relatively few and thus the church had a bigger part in the social life of the community. The Equinunk band, for example, was indebted to the local Methodist church for its founder and leader, for its auditorium and practice hall, and for many of its occasions for performance; and parallel, although perhaps less dramatic, situations can be seen with various other country bands as well. But in the larger towns, at least, the churches cannot be considered a potent presence in the life of the bands.

A similar division between town and village may be seen in the participation of bands at institutes—annual local conferences of teachers or farmers wishing to brush up on the latest professional techniques. Agricultural institutes were held, obviously, in rural areas, and the local bands provided entertainment at such institutes in Equinunk, Pleasant Mount, and Beach Lake, and probably elsewhere as well. Teachers' institutes, by contrast, were held in the villages and boroughs alike, and like the churches, they hired bands only in the country. Whenever possible—such as in Honesdale, Hawley, and Pleasant Mount—the teachers would be entertained by an orchestra, which was apparently felt to be more uplifting and educational.

In general, then, these social institutions present a very fragmented picture. Their huge number reflected a variety of philosophies, purposes, and activities, and all of these in turn influenced each institution's involvement with the town bands. Clearly, a group that liked to have picnics was more apt to use a band than, say, a group devoted to Bible study would be. But perhaps the most important point is that the bands met the public not only directly, at their own concerts and entertainments, but also through a wide variety of intermediate agencies, and part of the social coloring of the band came from these other institutions.

THE BAND AS CEREMONY

Throughout the county, holiday parades, mass meetings, and historic occasions were almost always accompanied by the sound of cornets and drums; the ceremonial significance of these town bands was the result principally of three factors.

First, public ceremonies were ordinarily held outdoors—on the streets, in the parks or cemeteries, in front of the courthouse—wherever there was enough room for large numbers of people. For a really important celebration, the ceremonies would usually include a parade. And brass bands were especially well suited to outdoor performances and parades: their instruments were loud enough to be heard at a distance and portable enough to be played on the march. The bands were, in fact, the only musical ensembles of the time that could practically be used in such situations.

Second, bands and brass instruments have always had vaguely military connotations. These bands had descended from the saxhorn ensembles and cornet bands that were so visible and audible during the Civil War, and three decades later they still retained some of their wartime associations. Their uniforms—in the case of Lawyer's band, cut in "the fatigue style of the regular United States Army"[24]—were certainly a relic of this military tradition, as were the marches in their repertory. And at the turn of the century, patriotism was inseparable from militarism, so that patriotic holidays like Memorial Day and the Fourth of July, and of course above all, genuine military occasions like the departure of Company E for the Spanish-American War, were always accompanied by the proper military music.

Third, bands were big, loud, and expensive. If, for example, the Odd Fellows were having an important anniversary celebration, they might hire a band simply, or largely, as a matter of conspicuous consumption and visible pomp. And if, say, the Red Men were having another celebration the next month, they might need to engage the band just to keep up with the Odd Fellows. By the turn of the century, bands had been active at least in Honesdale for several generations, and the tradition of having a band present at every momentous occasion was so firmly entrenched that a big ceremony with no band would have looked puny and incomplete. So institutions kept hiring the bands for their ceremonies, and when the whole town came out for a spontaneous celebration, such as those marking the departure of Company E and the arrival of the first Erie train uptown, the bands might volunteer their services spontaneously.

The town bands, in short, were suited to outdoor ceremonies not only physically, but also symbolically; and ceremonial occasions accounted for a great many of their performances.

THE BAND AS ENTERTAINMENT

To anyone who knows the struggle and the heartbreak of trying to run an amateur band, the profusion and longevity of these bands is astonishing. No matter whether they were good or bad; the fact that they got together and stayed together seems like a miracle. But we must remember that these bands played in an environment much different from our own, an environment in which the band was a much more important source of entertainment than it is today.

To us in the Global Village, it is hard to comprehend the isolation and boredom of nineteenth-century rural America. To us in the Information Age, it is hard to imagine a world without radio or television or stereo, a world in which virtually all the music one heard was live and most of it was made by one's neighbors. But this was the world in which the members of these bands lived, and although the larger towns were not quite so isolated as the villages, the problem was a universal one: in every community of the time, homegrown music was more necessity than luxury. The people of Wayne County were, in a sense, starved for entertainment; if they didn't entertain themselves, no one else was going to entertain them. And it was from this impulse, perhaps more than any other, that the bands sprang up and survived.

The importance of the band as entertainment has been amply documented. In every town that had a band, parades, dances, and concerts were a vital part of the culture, and must be seen not only as musical events, but also as social occasions, a chance for the whole town to come together and get away from the fields or the shoe factories for a few hours.

> The [Lawyer's] band was out in fine feather on Thursday evening last. The weather was pleasant and hundreds of people came out to enjoy the music. Little parties of lads and lasses found convenient places for the chatter upon the board piles in the neighborhood [this was in the early days of Russell Park, before it had been completely cleaned up], but many of the wise ones provided themselves with camp chairs—a happy thought. . . . We trust that the boys will not be allowed to

want for new music, and that these concerts will be kept up so long as the weather remains pleasant.[25]

The bands were not, of course, alone at the task of entertaining the people of Wayne County. They were joined, especially in the larger towns, by a variety of ensembles: orchestras, dance bands, church choirs, singing societies, minstrel troupes, touring operetta companies, and so forth. And even more prevalent was "local talent" —small-scale performances of amateur soloists, small ensembles, and elocutionists, which could be put together quickly and for free. Such local talent was interspersed among the selections of the Pleasant Mount band (pp. 103-5), as it no doubt was among those of all the village bands; it was featured on the agenda of hundreds of club meetings and church dinners; and occasionally it would be gathered together en masse for an entire show. Perhaps the most conspicuous of this last was the entertainment that followed the Honesdale firemen's parade every fall as it did in 1897:

> The armory was packed in the evening to listen to the entertainment preceding the dance. It proved to be unusually good and interesting, and every number was heartily encored. The following was the program:

> Recitation . . . . Homer Greene, Esq.
> Sonata — Op. 7 . . . . Grieg
> Miss Marcia B. Allen.
> Yesterday and To-Day . . . . B. H. Jansen
> Miss Minnie Goesser.
> Ave Maria . . . . Bach-Gounod
> Mrs. C. H. Rockwell, Mrs. L. B. Richtmyer,
> Dr. E. W. Burns, and W. W. Ham.
> Staccato Caprice . . . . Max Vogrich
> Miss Jeannette Freeman.
> Quartette . . . . Selections
> Messrs. Kallighan, Brown, Monaghan, and Carroll.[26]

The need for entertainment was filled by amateur musicians and musical organizations of many kinds and in great numbers. But of all these, the town band was the biggest and most visible. Because it performed outdoors, it had a huge audience; it played frequently and on the happiest occasions; its music had a great popular appeal; and at least in the larger towns, it was part of a long and distinguished tradition. Small wonder, then, that the town band has become a symbol of the artistic self-sufficiency of small-town life, of the ability of these people to amuse themselves. These bands originated and survived because their communities needed them.

THE BAND AND LOCAL PRIDE

Apart from their suitability for outdoor ceremonies, and apart from their efficiency at entertaining their public, these bands had another, less purely musical function. The town band served as a focus of local pride, and part of its energy and individuality was a product of the community spirit of its home town.

The isolation of the rural village forced its inhabitants to draw close together and to develop a powerful sense of community: everything they did, they did with their neighbors. In the larger boroughs, this need for community was perhaps less urgent, but it was supplanted by a sense of local history and local tradition. And as a result, each village and town acquired its own identity—an identity that was cherished by its citizens and supported by and reflected in its band.

In other words, the town band served at least in part as a kind of musical baseball team. Indeed, the parallels are striking. The band was a group of local young men, organized and in uniform, expert at a difficult task; it provided entertainment of a type that the whole town could enjoy; and it could go on the road, visiting other places and showing off the skill and enterprise of the home talent. When, for example, the Beach Lake band marched in the Memorial Day parade in Honesdale, the people of Beach Lake were certainly aware that, in some vague way, their quality of life and the worth of their community were on display.

In one sense, of course, the bands were not quite the same as baseball teams: they were not ordinarily involved in actual competition with other bands. There were exceptions, such as the band contests in Deposit and Susquehanna attended by the Equinunk band, but these were relatively rare and evidently on a small scale. More common were picnics, parades, and other performances attended by more than one band, and although such events were not explicitly competitive and were always conducted in an atmosphere of cordial fellowship and good fun, still one senses an element at least of curious comparison between the bands. For example, when the Equinunk band came to play at a picnic with the Lake Como band in 1898, the *Independent*'s Lake Como correspondent politely gave the highest praise to the visitors, but clearly was also interested in how both bands sounded and concerned that both sounded well.

On Saturday last the band boys gave a delightful picnic in the
upper grove at Lake Como. . . . The boys made admirable
hosts, welcoming in a hearty fashion, fraught with good will
the members composing the Equinunk band, who came,
arrayed in their natty uniforms, accompanied by Rev. Mr.
Alberti, who has been their instructor. They own very fine
instruments and their smooth rendering of some choice selections showed their skill in handling them. The Lake Como
boys have already received their due meed of praise and we are
glad to record that their receipts for the day were $70.[27]

This quasi-competitive attitude intruded itself subtly into news
items from all over the county and throughout our five years. Local
bands were frequently described not only as good, but as somehow
better than the bands of other (unspecified) communities—for instance, the *Independent*'s statement on July 24, 1901 that "Honesdale
has a right to boast that it has one of the best organizations in the
Maple City band that can be found in this section of the country."
And the papers never sound more pleased than when they report on
kind words from strangers—especially strangers from the city.

Many encomiums were bestowed upon Lawyer's band while in
Scranton last week attending the state firemen's convention.
The band accompanied the Forest City firemen and the latter
organization was well pleased with the music rendered. Bands
that were not engaged early in the season obtained large pay
for their service. Lawyer's was among the latter and consequently obtained larger pay for their service than any other
Honesdale band that ever left town. Mr. Lawyer has received
several letters from city people inquiring the name of one of
his popular marches played by the band while in the Electric
City. This is certainly a high compliment and shows that our
boys were noticed.[28]

But local pride had, for our purposes, its dark side, too; it is
difficult if not impossible to get an objective opinion of any of these
bands from the newspapers. Perhaps the most memorable example
of this distortion is the report by an Equinunk correspondent in
1899 that the Equinunk band took second prize in a band contest,
and his omission of the fact that there were only two bands
competing (pp. 93-94). But the more papers I have read, the more
conscious I have become that there are virtually no bad reviews of

any band performance. This reticence is in part a matter of simple courtesy: even today newspapers hesitate to say what they really think of amateur musicians. And in part it may be ascribed to low standards in the audience; most of the citizens of the villages had probably never heard a better band than their own. But perhaps the most potent motivation of all, whether the people realized it consciously or not, was gratitude—gratitude not just for the music and the pomp, but for the band's position as a kind of cultural flagship for the community, a sign to the whole world that the local people had the talent and gumption to put a band together and make it play.

The symbolic importance of the town band to the pride of the community, and the importance of community spirit to the vigor of the band, are evident throughout the newspaper articles of 1897 to 1901. But perhaps nowhere are they better stated than in two stanzas of J. H. Coghlan's poem, "Como's Band":

> There's Jonathan will vow to you that 'though his hair is gray,
> He has lived his life in Como—he couldn't go away,
> And when he asks you for a chew, then gives you the glad hand,
> He will tell you there is nothing that can equal Como's band.
>
> And Como is so healthy—they never seem to die,
> But dry up like the Autumn leaves, then hasten toward the sky,
> 'Tis said that when some of them before St. Peter stand,
> They're shocked to find he never heard of Como or its band.[29]

THE SOCIAL POSITION OF THE TOWN BAND

The world that these bands played in was a complicated place, and the role of the bands within that world was complicated, inconstant, sometimes equivocal. If we are to make some general observation about the social position of the town band, then, we must make some effort, however tentative, to reduce this complexity to simpler terms.

In thinking about the social and intellectual life of Victorian America, I have continually found myself classifying the disparate elements of this society into two general spheres, masculine and feminine—terms I use to refer not so much to real sexes as to traditional (i.e., Victorian) gender roles. The feminine current of thought was characterized by a combination of entertainment and spiritual enrichment; it was institutionalized in religious and semi-religious organizations like the Epworth League and the Women's

Christian Temperance Union, and in more secular groups like the Honesdale Improvement Association and the Musical History Club; it was the spirit that was to be reflected most visibly in the Chautauqua movement of the early twentieth century. The masculine sphere was concerned more with fun for its own sake or in the service of patriotism or community safety; it was institutionalized in fraternal organizations, singing societies, veterans' organizations, fire companies, and so forth.

By distinguishing between these masculine and feminine elements, I mean to imply only a polarity, not necessarily an outright conflict. Both spheres certainly involved many of the same people, and the public events of both were intended for the whole community. Indeed, masculine and feminine institutions frequently worked together; for example, the concert of the Honesdale and Mozart bands in 1897 was sponsored by the Red Men, a masculine organization if ever there was one, but the refreshments were handled, at a considerable profit, by the Honesdale Improvement Association. But what is especially significant is that these two social currents had distinct musical traditions.

The town band was a masculine institution. Not only was its membership all male, but most of its parades and picnics were sponsored by other all-male organizations—lodges, fire companies, the G.A.R. The band provided fun, patriotism, and spectacle, all of which were aims of the masculine institutions generally. And just as significant, bands were seldom sponsored by the feminine institutions. The Wayne County Teachers' Institute, an annual conclave in Honesdale for teachers from all over the county, would seem like a perfect opportunity to show off the Honesdale bands, but in fact no band ever played there—the teachers were entertained by a professional concert company, by local talent, or by the Honesdale Philharmonic. And such was true for church groups, the W.C.T.U., ladies' civic organizations, and the like: they tended to prefer more refined classical music over the brassy vulgarity of the cornet band.

This distinction was less rigidly observed in the smaller villages, I believe for three reasons. First, social life in these rural areas was often controlled by only one or two institutions (as, for example, the Methodist church in Equinunk), and thus these institutions were obliged to take on both masculine and feminine roles. Second, the bands in these communities were less subject to scruples of propriety; they loomed much larger in the public eye and were considered practically a fixture at any large gathering of people. And finally, the rural bands had less competition from other, more genteel musical organizations. This, again, can perhaps be seen most clearly in the teachers' institutes: the Beach Lake band was invited to play at the local institute because it was the only show in town, but in Pleasant Mount, which had both a band and an orchestra, it was invariably the orchestra that performed for the teachers.

Despite the fact that they contained many of the same players and must have been of equivalent quality, local bands and orchestras occupied very different social positions. This difference can be seen not only in the occasions and sponsors for the various performances, but also in the tone of dozens of newspaper articles. In the two items below, referring to Lawyer's band and the Honesdale Philharmonic, note the contrast in attitude: the band is described in jovial, bantering terms, and the orchestra in words of cultural reverence.

> Lawyer's band demonstrated that although a young organization, it is capable of dispensing good music for picnics. It played a number of selections in front of Odd Fellows' hall on their return in the evening, demonstrated [sic] that they had plenty of stamina left.[30]

> Oct. 26, 1898, a fine, music-loving people decided to make a venture in organizing an orchestra, which should be purely amateur. The opportunity of being able to secure such an efficient teacher as Ernst Thiele, of Scranton, gave the new society an impetus which was proven of great service. Rehearsals were held weekly, and the interest of the members grew, as progress was made in the studies undertaken. . . . The prime object of this society is to cultivate a love for a higher grade of orchestra music, there being no social lines, nor distinction drawn—it is strictly cosmopolitan.[31]

The difference in prestige between bands and orchestras tells us much about their function in the society and in the musical world of their time. For the town band and the town orchestra were, in places like northeastern Pennsylvania, the largest and most conspicuous representatives of what H. Wiley Hitchcock has called the vernacular and cultivated traditions in American music: "I mean by the term 'cultivated tradition' a body of music that America had to cultivate consciously, music faintly exotic, to be approached for its edification, its moral, spiritual, or aesthetic values. By 'vernacular tradition' I mean a body of music more plebeian, native, not approached self-consciously but simply grown into as one grows into one's vernacular tongue; music understood and appreciated simply for its utilitarian or entertainment value."[32]

When we reflect on Hitchcock's distinction between cultivated and vernacular music, it is clear that, like the feminine and masculine institutions, the two are opposite, but not really opposed. Indeed, Hitchcock's categories and my own may be thought of as parallel: both represent a duality, although not an outright hostility, between spiritual uplift on the one hand and pure entertainment on the other. All societies have always needed both; and the society of the turn-of-the-century small town developed musical organizations to do both.

NOTES

1. D. S. McCosh, "McCosh's Guide for Amateur Brass Bands," in Lyon and Healy, *Band Instruments, Uniforms, Trimmings, &c.* (Chicago: Lyon and Healy, 1881), pp. 3-29, quotation pp. 3-4.

2. Margaret Hindle Hazen and Robert M. Hazen, in *The Music Men: An Illustrated History of Brass Bands in America, 1800-1920* (Washington: Smithsonian Institution Press, 1987), especially pp. 41-89 and 149-89, examine many of these same issues from a more national standpoint. I shall not attempt to cross-reference all my discussions with theirs, but I do wish to acknowledge my debt to their insights and perspective.

3. *Wayne Independent,* November 17, 1897; see also page 100 of this volume for another announcement of the same event.

4. McCosh, "McCosh's Guide," p. 4. See also G. F. Patton, *A Practical Guide to the Arrangement of Band Music* (New York: John F. Stratton, 1875), p. 177.

5. The roster is printed on page 82 the prices are to be found in Sears, Roebuck & Co., *Catalogue No. 104* (Chicago: Sears, Roebuck, 1897; rept. New York: Chelsea House, 1968), pp. 528-31. Figures used were median prices for each type of instrument; if an even number of models were offered, price given is the lower of the two middle prices. Thus the band would have bought one E-flat clarinet at $6.55, two E-flat cornets at $5.95 each, three B-flat cornets at $7.55 each, two altos at $10.50 each, two tenors at $11.65 each, one baritone at $12.75, one B-flat bass at $14.45, one snare drum at $4.90, one bass drum at $12.35, and one pair of cymbals at $5.25—for a total of $135.10.

6. *Hancock Herald,* February 1897.

7. *Hancock Herald,* March 1898, from notes supplied by Wellington Lester. There is, incidentally, no other evidence that the band ever had three clarinetists: the roster of 1897 lists one, Cain Lord, and the picture, believed to be from the following year, shows a different one, Delos Lester.

8. *Wayne Independent,* April 21, 1897; *Wayne County Herald,* April 22, 1897.

9. *Honesdale Citizen,* April 20, 1899 and May 11, 1899; *Wayne County Herald,* April 20, 1899; see also Figure 4.

10. *Wayne Independent,* September 7, 1898; see also Figure 9.

11. Henderson and Co., *Band Uniforms: Catalogue No. 120* (Philadelphia: Henderson, n.d.), pp. 30-45, 48-50.

12. Ibid., pp. 2-3, 48-49.

13. See, for example, Sears, Roebuck, *Catalogue No. 104,* pp. 168-77.

14. We do know that Lot Crosby received $100 (or possibly $200) for a month's work with Allen Plum's band in the early 1840s, and that about the same time Dr. Hawley Olmstead was paid $5 a night for instructing the embryo Silver Cornet band; it is not, however, safe to extrapolate from these to bands a half century later.

15. *Wayne Independent,* April 12, 1899.

16. Ibid., December 1, 1897.

17. *Wayne County Herald,* June 28, 1900.

18. Ibid., August 24, 1899.

19. *Wayne Independent,* April 14, 1897.

20. Ibid., May 16, 1900.

21. *Wayne County Herald,* August 10, 1899.

22. *Honesdale Directory 1906-7* (Scranton: Phillipi Directory Co., 1906), pp. 28-32. See also Alfred Mathews, *History of Wayne, Pike and Monroe Counties, Pennsylvania* (Philadelphia: R. T. Peck, 1886; rept. Honesdale Citizens for the Preservation of Our Local Heritage, n.d.), pp. 427-431.

23. See also Vernon Leslie, *A Profile of Service: Protection Engine Company No. 3, 1853-1916* (Honesdale: Protection Engine Co. No. 3, 1986), pp. 48-49, 102-16.

24. *Honesdale Citizen,* May 1899.

25. *Wayne County Herald,* June 15, 1899.

26. *Honesdale Citizen,* October 21, 1897.

27. *Wayne Independent,* September 7, 1898.

28. Ibid., October 11, 1899.

29. Ibid., August 3, 1898.

30. Ibid., July 26, 1899.

31. *Honesdale Citizen,* March 16, 1900.

32. H. Wiley Hitchcock, *Music in the United States: A Historical Introduction* (Englewood Cliffs, N.J.: Prentice-Hall, 1974), p. 51.

10

Epilogue

It is unfortunate but inevitable to leave this story in the middle. Over the five years, many bands were born and a few died: at the end of 1901 not only the Maple City band, but also the village bands of Equinunk, Lake Como, Pleasant Mount, Beach Lake, and Gouldsboro were all apparently still playing. And naturally one wonders what happened to them.

I can give only a tentative answer to the question. I have taken a quick look through the *Wayne Independent* for June and July of the next three years, on the hypothesis that Memorial Day and the Fourth of July would be the most likely times to spot a band if one existed. The results are rather sad, but not altogether discouraging.

The Maple City band survived at least through mid-1904, playing a fairly active schedule. Hawley continued to rely on out-of-town bands for its patriotic celebrations; one of these, the Beach Lake band, was reported to be playing evening concerts as late as June 1904. The bands of Equinunk and Pleasant Mount, however, seem to have disappeared after 1901: at a number of occasions where they had always been in the past, they were notably absent. And there is not enough evidence to judge what became of the Lake Como and Gouldsboro bands. On the happier side, two new organizations, the White Mills band and the Union band of Haines, seem to have sprung up.[1]

The town band has never become quite extinct in Honesdale. Whatever may have happened to the original Maple City band, its idea and name were revived by B. Ray Minich in 1949, and the new Maple City band has continued, with some interruptions, ever since. This is the band that I heard as a child, that I played in as a teenager, and that finally I was able to conduct after Mr. Minich's retirement. Today the repertory is the music of our time, the instruments are both brass and woodwind, and the players are both male and female. But I like to think that the spirit of my Maple City band was not so much different from that of David Gill's, and that the town it plays in is not so much different from the Honesdale of 1900. I like to think that the *Honesdale Citizen*'s words of July 6, 1899 are just as apt today—"A spot to wile away an hour at sunset, and with good music to inspire one in the endeavor, who can resist the invitation to be on hand once a week and shake hands with his neighbor?"

NOTES

1. All dates refer to issues of the *Wayne Independent*.
   Honesdale:
   > Memorial Day: Union band of Haines (June 4, 1902)
   > Independence Day: no band listed (July 9, 1902)
   > Red Men's picnic and concert at Russell: Maple City band (July 16, 1902)
   > Memorial Day: Maple City band (June 3, 1903)
   > Memorial Day: Maple City band (June 1, 1904)

   Hawley:
   > Memorial Day: no band listed (June 4, 1902)
   > Independence Day: White Mills band (July 9, 1902)
   > Memorial Day: Beach Lake band (June 3, 1904)

   Beach Lake:
   > Band playing Wednesday and Sunday evenings (June 3, 1904)

   Equinunk:
   > Memorial Day: no band listed (June 4, 1902)
   > Memorial Day: no band listed (June 5, 1903)

   Pleasant Mount:
   > Independence Day: no band listed (July 11, 1902)
   > Unveiling of Meredith Monument: Mozart band, Maple City band (June 10, 1904)

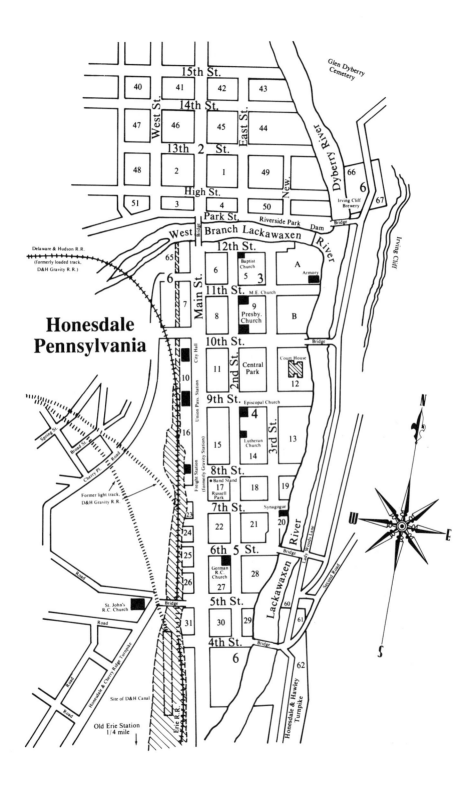

Honesdale
Pennsylvania

Glen Dyberry Cemetery

15th St.
14th St.
13th 2 St.
High St.
Park St.
West Branch Lackawaxen River
12th St.
11th St.
10th St.
9th St.
8th St.
7th St.
6th 5 St.
5th St.
4th St.

West St.
East St.
New
Dyberry River
Irving Cliff
Main St.
2nd St.
3rd St.

Delaware & Hudson R.R.
(formerly loaded track,
D&H Gravity R.R.)

Former light track,
D&H Gravity R.R.

Spring St.
Broad St.
Cherry Pl.
Road

Road

St. John's
R.C. Church
Road

Road
Road

Honesdale & Cherry Ridge Turnpike
Site of D&H Canal
Old Erie Station
1/4 mile

Erie R.R.

Union Pass. Station
Freight Station
(formerly Gravity Station)
City Hall

Riverside Park
Dam
Bridge
Irving Cliff
Brewery

Baptist
Church
Armory
A

M.E. Church
Presby.
Church
B

Central
Park
Court House

Episcopal Church
Lutheran
Church

Band Stand
Russell
Park
Synagogue

German
R.C.
Church

Lackawaxen River
Bridge
Lackawaxen River
Lady Woods Lane
Second Road
Honesdale & Hawley Turnpike

40 41 42 43
47 46 45 44
48 2 1 49
51 3 4 50
65
6
7
8
10
11
16
15
4
14
13
17 18 19
22 21 20
27 28
30 29
66
6
67
6
5 3
9
12
60
61
62
6
31
23
24
25
26

N
S
E
W

Bibliography

A. E. Benary Co. Catalogue. New York: Benary, 1897.

Ammerman, Kristen. Centennial Edition of the *Wayne Independent*, February 4, 1978.

Best, Gerald M. *The Ulster and Delaware*. San Marino, Calif.: Golden West Books, 1972.

Bevan, Clifford. *The Tuba Family*. New York: Charles Scribner's Sons, 1978.

Bierley, Paul E. *John Philip Sousa: A Descriptive Catalogue of His Works*. Columbus: Integrity Press, 1984.

Bufkin, William A. "Union Bands of the Civil War (1861-1865): Instrumentation and Score Analysis." Ph.D. diss., Louisiana State University, 1973.

C. Bruno and Son. *Illustrated Catalogue*. New York: Bruno, 1888.

Centennial and Illustrated Wayne County. Honesdale: The Wayne Independent, 1902; rept. Honesdale: Wayne County Historical Society, 1975.

Dodworth, Allen. *Dodworth's Brass Band School*. New York: H. B. Dodworth, 1853.

Finck, Henry T. "The Musical Outlook for Women." *Etude* 17 (1899): 151.

Fluhr, George J. A. *Shohola Glen*. Shohola, Pa.: Edward S. Jarosz, 1970.

Garofalo, Robert, and Mark Elrod. *A Pictorial History of Civil War Era Musical Instruments and Military Bands*. Charleston, W.V.: Pictorial Histories Publishing Co., 1985.

Goerlitz, Arthur Richard. "A History of Public Education in Honesdale, Pennsylvania (1810-1960)." Ed.D. thesis, The Pennsylvania State University, 1969.

Goodrich, Phineas Grover. *History of Wayne County*. Honesdale, Pa.: Haines and Beardsley, 1880.

Greene, Homer. *What My Lover Said and Other Poems*. Philadelphia: Macrae-Smith, 1931.

Haine, Malou. *Adolphe Sax (1814-1894); sa vie, son oeuvre, ses instruments de musique*. Brussels: Éditions de l'Université de Bruxelles, 1908.

Ham, Thomas J. "The Old Cannon." *Honesdale Citizen*, August 11, 1904-August 3, 1905.

Ham, William H. "The Bands of Honesdale—Personal Recollections of an Old Member." *Wayne County Herald,* May 12-June 16, 1881.

———. "Honesdale Fifty Years Ago." *Wayne County Herald,* February 15, 1900.

The Hancock Herald, Hancock, N.Y.

Hazen, Margaret Hindle, and Robert M. Hazen. *The Music Men: An Illustrated History of Brass Bands in America, 1800-1920.* Washington: Smithsonian Institution Press, 1987.

H. C. Barnes Co. *Musical Merchandise.* Boston: Barnes, 1891.

Henderson and Co., *Band Uniforms: Catalogue No. 120.* Philadelphia: Henderson, n.d. (c. 1900).

Hitchcock. H. Wiley. *Music in the United States: A Historical Introduction.* Englewood Cliffs, N.J.: Prentice-Hall, 1974.

The Honesdale Citizen, Honesdale, Pa.

Honesdale Directory 1906-7. Scranton: Phillipi Directory Co., 1906.

Horwood, Wally. *Adolphe Sax, 1814-1894: His Life and Legacy.* Bramley, U.K.: Bramley Books, 1979.

The Independent Republican, Montrose, Pa.

J. Howard Foote Co. *J. Howard Foote's Catalogue of Band Instruments.* New York: Foote, 1880.

J. W. Pepper Co. *J. W. Pepper's Musical Times and Band Journal,* vol. 18. Philadelphia: Pepper, 1903.

Lanier, Sidney. "The Orchestra of To-Day." *Scribner's Monthly* 18 (1879-80): 897-904.

LeRoy, E. D. *The Delaware and Hudson Canal.* Honesdale, Pa.: Wayne County Historical Society, 1980.

Leslie, Vernon. *Canal Town: Honesdale 1850-1875.* Honesdale, Pa.: Wayne County Historical Society, 1983.

———. *Honesdale and the Stourbridge Lion.* Honesdale, Pa.: Stourbridge Lion Sesquicentennial Committee, 1979.

———. *Honesdale: The Early Years.* Honesdale, Pa.: Honesdale 150 Committee, 1981.

———. *A Profile of Service: Protection Engine Company No. 3, 1853-1916.* Honesdale, Pa.: Protection Engine Co. No. 3, 1986.

———. *Things Forgotten: Happenings in Wayne County 1876-1888.* Honesdale: Wayne County Historical Society, in press.

Lingeman, Richard. *Small Town America.* Boston: Houghton Mifflin, 1980.

Lyon and Healy Co. *Band Instruments, Uniforms, Trimmings, &c.* Chicago: Lyon and Healy, 1881.

———. *Catalogue of Musical Merchandise.* Chicago: Lyon and Healy, 1898-99.

———. *Lyon & Healy's New and Enlarged Catalogue of Band Instruments, Trimmings, etc.* Chicago: Lyon and Healy, 1891.

Mathews, Alfred. *History of Wayne, Pike and Monroe Counties, Pennsylvania.* Philadelphia: R. T. Peck, 1886; rept. Honesdale, Pa.: Citizens for the Preservation of Our Local Heritage, n.d.

McCosh, D. S. "McCosh's Guide for Amateur Brass Bands," in Lyon and Healy Co., *Band Instruments, Uniforms, Trimmings, &c.* pp. 3-29.

Newsom, Jon. "The American Brass Band Movement." *Quarterly Journal of the Library of Congress* 36 (1979): 114-39.

Olson, Kenneth E. *Music and Musket: Bands and Bandsmen of the American Civil War*. Westport, Conn.: Greenwood Press, 1981.

Patton, G. F. *A Practical Guide to the Arrangement of Band Music*. New York: John F. Stratton, 1875.

Preston, Katherine K. "John Prosperi and Friends: A Study of Professional Musicians in Washington, 1877-1900." M.M. Thesis, University of Maryland, 1981.

Root and Cady Co. *Root & Cady's Illustrated Catalogue, and Price List*. Chicago: Root and Cady, 1866.

Rudolph Wurlitzer Co., *All Musical Instruments and Supplies*. Cincinnati: Wurlitzer, c.1919.

Sadie, Stanley, ed. *The New Grove Dictionary of Music and Musicians*. London: Macmillan, 1980.

———. *The New Grove Dictionary of Musical Instruments*. London: Macmillan, 1984.

Sanderson, Dorothy Hurlbut. *The Delaware and Hudson Canalway: Carrying Coals to Rondout*. Ellenville, N.Y.: Roundout Valley Publishing, 1974.

Scholl, E. W. "March: Lehigh Valley," Philadelphia: Benj. B. Dale, 1897.

Schwartz, H. W. *Bands of America*. Garden City, N.Y.: Doubleday, 1957.

Sears, Roebuck. *Catalogue No. 104*. Chicago: Sears, Roebuck, 1897; rept. New York: Chelsea House, 1968.

———. *Catalogue No. 111*. Chicago: Sears, Roebuck, 1902; rept. New York: Bounty Books, 1969.

Shaughnessy, Jim. *Delaware and Hudson*. Berkley, Calif.: Howell-North Books, 1967.

Smith, Fanny Morris. "Women's Work in Music in America." *Etude* 17 (1899): 150.

Smith, May Lyle. *History of the First Presbyterian Society of Honesdale*. Honesdale, Pa.: Herald Press Association, 1906.

S. R. Leland and Son. *Illustrated Catalogue and Price List of the Eclipse Band Instruments, Drums, Supplies, etc*. Worcester, Mass.: Leland, 1900.

A Summer's Vacation in the Highlands of Wayne and Delaware Counties. New York: New York, Ontario and Western Ry., 1901.

Wagner, Lavern John. "Doing-It-Yourself in 1875: George F. Patton on Arranging Band Music." *American Music* 6 (1988): 28-40.

Wakefield, Manville B. *Coal Boats to Tidewater*. Grahamsville, N.Y.: Wakefair Press, 1971.

The Wayne County Herald, Honesdale, Pa.

The Wayne Independent, Honesdale, Pa.

Wiecki, Ronald V. "The Stahl Partbooks: A New Source of Turn-of-the-Century American Band Music." *Journal of Band Research* 23 (Spring 1988): 1-9.

In addition to the above, archives and collections were studied at the Smithsonian Institution, the National Archives, and the Library of Congress in Washington; the Wayne County Historical Society in Honesdale; the Susquehanna County Historical Society in Montrose; and the Equinunk Historical Society in Equinunk.

Index

Books in the Series Music in American Life